CW01499503

Mr. X

CLARISSA WILD

CLARISSA WILD

CONTENTS

MR. X PLAYLIST

"Russian Roulette" by Rihanna

"Illuminated" by Hurts

"Mercy" by Hurts

"We Must Be Killers" by Mikky Ekko

"The Human Stain" by Kamelot

"My Superman" by Santigold

"Burning Desire" by Lana Del Rey

"Cola" by Lana Del Rey

"Right This Second" by Deadmau5

"Crave" by Duology

"One Eight Zero" by Grendel (Life Cried Remix)

"Ich Will" by Rammstein

"Afraid" by The Neighbourhood

"Don't Let Me Go" by Reign

"Quutamo" by Apocalyptica

"Breaking The Habit" by Linkin Park

"She Wants To Move" by N.E.R.D.

DEDICATION

This is for everyone who needs a little evil every now and then. So evil, you realize life isn't so bad after all.

"Punishment is justice for the unjust." - Saint Augustine

PROLOGUE

Jay

THURSDAY, AUGUST 15ᵀᴴ, 2013, 10:30 P.M.

Life is not continuous. Every path we take ends it or prolongs it. Millions upon millions of paths lie in front of us and we choose only one. Each step we take means cutting off a possible path. One by one they all disappear. The choice can't be changed. Accepting the consequences is a must, but impossible for most, including me.

Life is a string of events, each leading to another. One man. One choice. One deadly weapon. It all adds up to this one moment. The gun this man is pointing at my head. The gun that could end my life in a flash.

This man wants to kill me, and I don't know why.

In order to survive I must pass this test. I have to find out what story hides behind his scar. I believe it's my only way out. My life could end any second, but I won't allow it. I'll fight until the very end. Whichever path I choose, I will survive.

***

X

TUESDAY, AUGUST 13ᵀᴴ, 2013. 2:00 A.M.

He was innocent. Or so he said.

The scratch marks on his face tell a completely different story. Not only is he a scumbag, he's a lying scumbag too. Luckily, I know just the thing to do with liars.

Twirling the knife in my hand, I step forward. Sweat drops trickle down his face, making his hair stick to his forehead. He whimpers against the soaked cloth in his mouth, choking on his words. My eye slowly takes him in from top to bottom as I twist the sharp point of the knife softly against my finger, creating a bead of blood. His Adam's apple moves up and down in his throat as he visibly strains his muscles at the sight of my toy.

Yes, toy.

I have many, not all of them equally painful, but some more fun than others. Especially the screwdriver; it's one of my favorites.

But alas, this is a rush job and this Swiss knife is the only thing I have on me.

My victim takes in a deep breath as my eye zooms in on his, the fear settling in his eyes. It's breathtaking. I love that look in their eyes, those begging lips, those sweaty palms, the twitching and jerking muscles as they try to free themselves. It excites me to see them powerless, to know that I can do anything I desire. To know they can see it coming, all the things I will do to them.

The horror that fills their veins as they realize their death will not be quick but painfully agonizing.

A smirk forms on my face as my eye narrows and I savor the moment. Each step I take makes him squirm more, but he and I both know he's not going anywhere. The knot I tied is impervious. Blood stains the fibers of the rope as he twists in his seat, trying to escape his looming fate. It makes me laugh.

Innocent. Right. There's no such thing as innocence. Not in this world.

I lower the knife and draw a line from his hand up his arm. He moans into the cloth, shaking his head, uttering words again.

"Now, you know I won't take it any easier on you if you keep twisting like that," I say.

Putting pressure on the knife, I slide it up his shoulder, drawing blood. He screeches, shaking profusely as I create a few nice lines across his shoulder. Each stroke a little deeper, until his flesh rips and blood pours out. His screams become louder and louder, which only makes me want to continue. I love hearing the sound. Love the squeals of agony as I cut them open.

"Fwop! Fwop! Pwease!" I hear him beg through the cloth.

"You know I can't do that," I mutter.

"I will pway the debt! I swear!"

Pay? He wants to pay?

I raise an eyebrow and lean over him to look him in the eye. "Pay? You think this is about money?"

"I'll give you anywing!"

I laugh. "So you really don't know what this is about? And here I was thinking you were lying."

"Pwease, tell me, I can fix it."

"Nope. Too late for that." I draw another line from his shoulder down to the other hand and smile when I see the stain in his pants. Poor man; pissed his pants. Can't blame him. Actually, I can. It's dripping down the chair and it's soiling my favorite kill spot.

"Sad. Really sad, you know?" I say. "You pissed yourself."

He whimpers again.

Frowning, I flip the knife around and wipe it on his trousers. "Oh, what am I going to do with you?"

"Let me go, pwease, I swear, I won't tell."

"Hmm … you seem to be under the impression this is about something that can be solved." I lean forward and grab his arm right where the wound is. He jerks in the chair from the pain. "Sadly for you, that's not the case." I squint. "It's so unfortunate you can't remember, because that forces me to tell you. See, I don't like it when my victims don't know what they did before I cut their faces. They need to know what they did wrong so they see it coming. There needs to be some kind of morality, you know? Some kind of retribution."

I smirk, and then press my finger into his wound, muddling his flesh.

He squeals and bites his tongue, blood seeping from his mouth.

"Now listen, you fucked-up piece of shit, do you remember that night a few months ago when you went to a children's playground? Remember that little girl with the blue dress? Remember that chloroform in your pocket?"

His eyes widen. Fuck. It's so fucking awesome when they realize why they're here. It's like a little slice of God falling into my hands. It riles me up, gets me started, feeds my soul.

If I had one.

I laugh, shaking my head as I look down at his crotch. Drips draw my attention. This fucktard pissed himself *again*.

So I decide to kick him in the balls.

He makes an *oompf* sound and turns completely red as he gags on the cloth.

He deserves it. If only for making a mess of my property.

No, screw that, for putting his hands on that little girl. Assholes like him don't deserve to exist.

"Yeah, I know all about what you did, which is unfortunate for you. I know everything. That's my job. It's too bad for you her family was rich. Lucky for me I get paid well."

I raise the knife again, right in front of his face, showing him what's in store. He shakes in place, his eyes filling with tears. "Aww … you're gonna cry now? And what about that poor girl? Did you hear her cries too as you sodomized her?" Even though I didn't know her, just the thought of anyone doing that shit to a little girl angers me. I might be a bastard, but I'm not that much of a bastard. Nobody gets to use kids. I know firsthand what it can do to them.

Fury besieges me, and I let it. With fiery passion I raise the knife and jam it right into his other hand.

He screams so loud my ears pop. The noise echoes in this huge hall, but nobody will hear him here except me.

His fingers spasm, but I give him no time to rest. Pulling it right out of him, it takes me two slashes to create my signature mark on his eye.

Scarred for life.

Not that it'll last long.

As my victim screeches and jerks in his chair, desperate to get loose, I step away and admire my artwork before I grab the jerry can and drench him in petrol. I throw the can away and grab a cigarette. Nothing like a cigarette after a good mutilation.

I watch him writhe as I fish the lighter from my pocket and light the cigarette. Not one second after my first drag do I throw the lighter and set him ablaze.

The x that marks his face burns brighter than any of the previous ones I've done.

Such a nice piece of work.

"I am good, but not an angel. I do sin, but I am not the devil." – Marilyn Monroe

CHAPTER 1

Jay

THURSDAY, AUGUST 15TH, 2013. 10:00 P.M.

Show me that money, baby. It's all I live for. All I'd die for.

Okay, maybe not die for, but I'd sure as hell do anything for it.

My body moves along with the music, while I lick my lips like the slut I pretend to be. The man behind me is staring at my ass and I give him every reason to keep on doing just that. Bending over, I wink at him while giving him a real show. His dropping jaw tells me he likes what he sees. Most men do. I know exactly how to give it to them, how to push their buttons, and how to get them to spend more money on me. Of course, that's what it's all about.

They can call me whatever they want; a whore, a slut, a stripper, a bimbo, a bitch. I don't give a crap. Their opinions don't say shit about me and I'm earning all the money I need to maintain myself. I think I'm doing fine for a twenty-three-year-old. I earn more money than any other girl my age. Plus, I love the attention. They're on me like bees on honey, and I love the thrill of it.

The red velvet room and flashing lights put me in a trance as I dance to the sultry music. I sway my hips back and forth, showing the audience my best bits. I'm high as fuck, which only adds to the sensation of not giving a fuck and just enjoying the ride. I honestly don't give a shit, which is exactly what the drugs do for me. Not a care in the world and I can just keep on doing what I'm doing.

I bite my lip and push my chest forward. Hugging the pole, I lick it and drag my tongue up and down. I know they're imagining it's their cock: I can see it in their eyes. All. The. Time. There's a bulge in his pants and it's growing bigger and bigger. If I keep doing this I might even be able to take him back to my hotel room. Two birds with one stone.

Grunting, he pushes himself up from his chair and lunges forward onto the stage, wrapping his hands around my waist. A squeal escapes my mouth, but it's more from surprise than fear. The manager steps out from the back, frowning, pointing his finger at the dude grabbing me.

"Get your hands off her."

"It's okay, Don, I'll take him."

He squints. "You sure about that, Jay? He's been nothing but trouble."

"I can handle it."

The guy puts me down on the floor, twirling me in his arms. "I want you."

"Well, you can have me, babe, as long as you keep paying."

"Oh, I'll pay all right," he groans. Biting his lip, his hands drift down to my ass and squeeze.

I peel away his fingers one by one and wink. "Now, now, let's get to the room first."

"I wanted you minutes ago."

"You can wait another five minutes," I say, and I turn around. "Don, I'll be back in thirty, okay?"

"Make it a quickie."

I raise my thumb and grab ahold of my customer's hand. "C'mon, cowboy."

I walk to the exit and put on one of the long coats hanging on the coat stand for occasions like these where we, the girls, have to go out into the street still wearing our outfits.

"So, what's your name?" I ask.

"Billy."

I squint and give him my cheeky smile. "Darn, Billy!

I guess I'm doing a real cowboy today then."

"You can do me all day if you want," he says with a low voice.

"I bet you'd like that. Hmm … But you know what I offer."

He winks. "Yes, I do, ma'am."

"A suck or a jerk, that's all you're getting, okay?"

"Fine by me."

He smirks and lets me drag him out of the club. My motel room is just a few blocks away, which isn't a coincidence at all. I knew when I started working for Don that there'd be more involved than just dancing naked. Just because it's illegal here in Waco doesn't mean it doesn't happen. And it's not like I'm giving myself to some random dude or something; I'm only going to blow him, nothing else. It's a cheap way to earn an extra buck or two. If I'm lucky, he'll throw in a tip as well. I know how to suck them dry, financially as well as the juices.

I stop a cab on the street and we get inside. Billy tries to fondle me in the car, but I swat away his hand each time he tries. Just because he could touch me in the club doesn't mean he can do it anywhere he wants. I want to see some money first.

When we finally get to The Town House Motel I go to my usual room number seven and make sure nobody saw us before I close the door. The owner knows we do this, but he turns a blind eye to it all. They ignore any weird noises. So long as we pay for the room and clean it before we leave, it's all good. I suppose it's a kind of beneficial agreement he has going with Two Minnies, the club I work for. Whatever it is, I'm cool and I'm definitely not passing up the offer to earn some extra money.

It's the only way to feed my addiction and let all the reins loose.

I lock the door from the inside and tuck the key in between my breasts. Billy is breathing down my neck, his hands on my waist, slowly moving down toward my ass. I frown and turn around, throwing off my coat.

"No touching."

"What?" he says, raising one of his eyebrows.

"First, the payment. It's fifty for a jerk off, hundred for a blowjob."

He laughs and pulls me closer, his hands rough and strong, clamping around my back. Unyielding. Scary.

"No, hun, I want to fuck you," he says, smirking. His hands drift down to my ass and squeeze tight. He leans in and tries to kiss me, but I push back.

"No, I only do blowjobs and hand jobs, that's it. I told you and you agreed. Now pay up or get out."

He grunts, his smile creeping me out to the tenth degree. This isn't good. So totally not good.

I'm normally quite capable of reading customers, so I don't understand why I got so caught off guard with this one. There's something about him that made me think I could do this and trust him, but now … no … this is wrong.

"C'mon, doll." He grinds his cock against my thighs, clenching me close to him, but I shove him away. The look on his face changes from extreme horniness to anger.

"Get. Out." I squint and take out the key again. While I try to unlock the door he storms toward me.

"Fuck you. I paid before, now give me what I want!" He grabs ahold of my arm and jerks it away from the door. The key drops to the floor. I scream as he grabs both my arms and turns me around toward the bed. Kicking backwards, I fight him off, but he's too strong for me. I throw my head back, butting him against the forehead. He growls and takes a step back, which gives me room to escape. I throw my full weight into him, shoving him aside so I can run to the door. Fuck. Fuck. Fuck! I have to get out of here.

I fish the key from the floor and fumble with it, my hands trembling as I try to jam it inside. "C'mon, c'mon, c'mon you piece of shit!"

"You bitch!" he yells, and I hear him stomp toward me. Oh shit.

His hands are around my waist, pulling me back toward the bed, while I scratch and claw at him as fast and hard as I can. His blood is under my fingernails, but he keeps going. He turns us both, twisting my ankle as he throws me onto the bed. He throws himself onto me, pinning both my arms onto the bed while he jerks his pants down.

"Get off me!" I scream, thrashing underneath him.

He lodges his arm against my throat, choking me. "Shut the fuck up, you whore."

He pushes down so hard I can barely breathe. Gagging, I turn my head and bite him as hard as I can. It only makes him more determined to take me against my will. With one hand he rips down my panties. He spreads my legs with his heavy body, and I feel his cock against my thighs. No, no, no, this isn't happening. I won't let him!

I gather all my strength and slam into his balls with my knee. He takes in a sharp breath and staggers, giving me enough time to push his arm away from my throat so I can breathe. I kick him again, and he tumbles to the side, grabbing his balls with both his hands as he rolls around on my bed.

"You fucking bastard!" I make a fist and punch him in the belly.

The sound that comes from his mouth is just a small consolation for what he tried to do to me.

I quickly turn around and jerk open the drawer of the night stand, fishing out the gun I keep for moments like these. One click and it's loaded, ready to fire.

"Get the fuck out!" I say, stumbling off the bed, pointing at the door. With one quick jerk I pull my panties back on, because I don't want that fucking bastard looking at me. The gun is pointed at him, but my hands are shaking. I'm weak. I hate it.

Get over it. This fucking piece of shit deserves to die.

The moment he sees the gun his eyes widen and his

movement stops.

"Get out!" I scream, flicking the gun between him and the door.

He scrambles up from the bed and pulls up his pants, making me painfully aware of the fact that he touched me. That my clothes are ripped, and that he was about to stick his junk into me.

Fuck, this is fucked up.

"I'm not saying it again. Get out or I'll fucking kill you right now!" I yell.

"Okay, okay, I'm going," he says, walking around the bed. I follow his every step, vigilant, because I know pigs like him can't be trusted. He could still change his mind and try to force himself on me again. I've seen it before with another girl at the club. One time this girl was flirting with a customer and I knew she was taking him over the edge with her lap dance. The edge means they aren't able to walk away anymore. The men want more, and they won't stop until they get it. Not all of us are willing to give it, but she was. She wasn't willing to give up her pussy, though. Just like me. We give them pleasure, but the pussy is off limits. Too bad for her she didn't carry a gun around, unlike me. It was the last day I ever saw her.

My anger gets the better of me, because Billy's face while he tried to push inside me is still imprinted on my retinas. So I bend over and take off my high heels, throwing them at the back of his head. "Hurry up, you piece of shit!"

He turns around and rubs his head. "What the fuck? I'm leaving, aren't I?"

"I should kill you for what you did!"

As Billy twists the key in the lock, a knock is audible, and he freezes. I keep the gun pointed at his head, air leaving my lungs in rapid breaths as Billy backs away from the door. The door creaks. I've never heard it creak before.

Suddenly, the door bursts open, a shiny black shoe smashing the lock. I stiffen, chills running down my spine. The leg retreats. A gun appears out of nowhere. A black, velvet-gloved hand holding it. Fingers moving to the trigger.

Bang.

It's not loud, like in the movies. It's a thud, like someone just punched a pillow. The shot is soft, but unmistakably a gunshot.

At first there is nothing. Seconds seem like minutes as I stand here trembling with a gun in my hand, watching everything unfold. Fingers shake and breaths falter. Blood pours from his head. Billy falls to the ground.

My jaw drops because I can't believe my eyes. Billy is dead, but it wasn't me who killed him.

The gun fires again and again, two shots, one right between the eyes and one into the heart. Each one pulling me further away from this world. It all feels like a dream, but I know it's not. I just wish it was so I could force myself to wake from this nightmare.

I want to scream, but I can't. Air is trapped in my throat and it can't escape. I don't even know if I should run. I'm frozen in place as the mysterious killer steps into my room and reveals himself to me. A bald stranger wearing a fitted black suit, a white collar contrasting the colorless ensemble. Lines of ink stick out from underneath, tattooed into his skin on both sides of his throat. However, the most striking of all is the x-shaped scar that marks his right eye. A wound seared into his skin ages ago, leaving ruin and havoc on his face. His eye has been replaced with a metallic fake; an eerie warning of the horrible events that he's involved in. Events that I might get involved in too now.

Who is this man that stepped into my room?

Why is he here?

Can I trust him?

His face turns from Billy to me. An eye as black as night stares back at me, unsettling me to my core. At first both his eyes widen, but then they narrow, as if he's surprised. I shiver, trying to keep the gun steady, but I fail in my attempt to keep it together. The look in his eye reminds me of the stories my nanny used to read to me, stories about the devil.

His steps are fast and big as he comes toward me, indifferent about the gun in my hand.

"Don't come closer! I'll shoot," I warn, but his hand is already locked firmly around my wrist. He jerks it to the side, forcing me to drop the gun. I yelp as his hand moves from my wrist to my neck, choking me. I wrap my fingers around his, desperately trying to claw my way out, but it's no use. He's twice as strong as me, and his will seems unbendable.

Terror fills me as the gun in his hand rises to eyelevel. The cold metal feels like a burn against my skin. He looks me straight in the eye, his coal-black eye filled with chilling determination.

But then he waits.

Seconds pass. Tick. Tock. Tick. Tock. The clock hanging on the wall drives me insane. Death is at my doorstep, but he won't come for me. Instead, I'm left waiting in agonizing fear. I hate this.

"Please, don't do this," I say, my lips trembling.

He doesn't respond; instead his grip on my throat tightens. I try to swallow, but gargle instead. My fingers are still trying to pry him loose, but he won't let go. I'm afraid and yet I can't stop fighting.

Why does he want to kill me? What did I do? Who is he? Why hasn't he killed me yet?

Questions and thoughts rage through my mind. I need to escape. I don't know why. I never cared for my life except now, when it's threatened. My instincts have kicked into full gear.

His eyes narrow and his lips become thin lines as he pushes the gun against my forehead. I stare at him, tears welling up in my eyes. It seems as though he's grinding his teeth, his eye shifting back and forth between my eyes and my lips.

"Please … I don't want to die," I manage to whisper.

His nostrils flare and a long, drawn-out sigh comes from his nose. His eye is on me like that of a hawk, never diverting its attention, but something tells me this isn't normal. This isn't how my life should end. It would be over by now if it was.

He purses his lips, his fingers slowly unraveling from my throat. I cough as the pressure is removed and I'm able to breathe again. My lungs expand rapidly as I soak in the oxygen, inducing a gag reflex. But I have to stay still. His gun is still placed firmly against my head as his hand lowers to his side. Both his eyes have this murderous look in them, like he's possessed.

Or maybe angry. Angry with me? No, that can't be. I don't even know him.

"Don't kill me," I say calmly. I look at him, trying to make him see the innocence in me, even though I know it's barely there. However, even after all the things I've done, I'm not worthy of dying.

His face is unmoving, but lets me know there is something not right. This isn't how it's supposed to go. Something's wrong, because he would've killed me by now if there wasn't. I have to make use of it.

My hand, although trembling, reaches for the gun. Before my fingers can touch it, he opens his mouth.

"Sit." His voice is dark and full of unspoken words. Not dark like liquid chocolate, but dark like death.

His eye briefly darts to the bed next to me as he

sways the gun to the left, just a little, but not enough to make it go away from my forehead. Not enough to keep me from dying if he pulls the trigger.

I shift my feet just enough so that I'm against the bed with my legs, but not enough to make him think I'm trying to escape. I don't want him shooting me for no reason. So I do as he says and gently sit down on the bed, careful not to agitate him.

My heart is racing, practically beating out of my chest as far as I can tell, but I won't show it to him. I need to be calm and watch what he does. I need to see all the tiny details, remember everything that happens, and find a way to escape. This man isn't ordinary; he's a killer. Not a murderer who kills random strangers, but someone who plots and calculates his movements. Someone who's dangerous, because he doesn't care. I can tell by the way he killed Billy without a hint of remorse.

I wonder why he's targeting me.

"Why?"

He doesn't answer. All he does is keep the gun pointed at my face. Although he's a little further away from me than he was before, it still doesn't make me feel like I can handle this. It's unlike anything else I've had to deal with, and I've dealt with some fucked-up shit.

"What do you w—"

"Shut up." His command is short and snappy, as if he's mad at me.

I take in a gulp of air and stare at the carpet, feeling so utterly out of control. My gun is right next to his feet. If I could only grab it, I could fight my way out. If I can shoot him anywhere—in the leg, in the feet, in the balls for all I care, I could distract him long enough to escape.

If only I could reach for the gun without risking him blowing my brains out.

In complete silence I sit on the bed, waiting for my assailant to tell me what he wants. I don't understand why he's here. He killed Billy and then came for me, but why? Why did he kill Billy and not me? What's different about me? What does he want? Is he here for me?

The more I think about it, the more powerless I feel. I used to believe in living until you're sick of it. I danced all night, drank every type of liquor there was, snorted and smoked as much as I could, used myself and let men use me, and did all the things God has forbidden. I thought it didn't matter, because my life was mine and if I was to live it, I'd live it my way.

Now, I'm not so sure about it anymore. My life is on the line and all of a sudden it's become clear that what I've done might be exactly the reason I find myself here in the first place. That my choices and wrongdoings have led to this moment, where a disfigured stranger wants to kill me.

I probably even deserve it.

I snort and swallow away the tears welling up in my

eyes. I'm pathetic. A whining sack of shit. I shouldn't be crying, and I'm trying to keep the tears at bay, but it's hard. As much as I don't want to admit it, because it makes me look weak, and I hate being weak … I don't want to die.

I want to live.

All I've ever wanted is to live and feel alive.

Now, more than ever, I realize that I'm not ready to give up. That I'm not ready to let someone else decide what happens to me. I'll do anything to keep what's mine. My beginning. My middle. My end. I'll fight for it with everything I have.

The mystery man takes another deep breath. His hand moves up and it makes me instantly aware of his movement. He rubs his bare head, avoiding the scars completely, which surprises me, because his head is littered with them. It's something I force myself to remember. It may seem like something unimportant, unnoticeable, but it's not. Every tiny detail is a piece of the puzzle and once they are put together they'll help me put reason to this insanity. To save myself I have to unravel the secrets he hides. In order to escape I have to use all his weak points to my advantage. He's not the type to let his victims run after he's caught them. I can tell by the way he killed Billy; three clean shots. Coldhearted, no mess, precisely as he meant it to be. He's a planner. Someone who knows what he's doing and keeps control at all times. Someone who needs to believe he's in charge. Someone who needs everything to be under his control before he relaxes.

Which is why it surprises me that he has clearly deviated from his plan. His plan was to kill me. He didn't. He still hasn't. That's my way in.

He won't let me go of his own free will. I have to make him believe it first.

I'm still staring at the gun on the floor, the metal that might save my life or end it. The ticking of the clock makes me restless, because I know that every passing second I don't take action I lose the chance to save myself. Only minutes have passed but it feels like a lifetime already.

"Stop. I know what you're doing. It won't work," he says, and then he bends over, still keeping the gun pointed at my face. He picks up the gun on the floor and gets back up into a standing position. He brings it to his mouth and unloads it with his teeth. Then he throws it a few feet away.

Suddenly his own gun moves away from my head in a flash. It's lightning fast. A loud shot. The gun on the floor shatters into a million pieces, bits flung through the room from the explosion. Just when he's distracted, I lunge forward and try to grab his gun. One quick elbow jab and I'm back on the bed.

"I said sit down!" he growls. "Or I'll put a bullet in you, too."

The gun is immediately back in my face. I shriek, covering my face with my arms, protecting myself, even though I know it won't help. I'm terrified.

"Please, let me go. I didn't do anything." It takes a few seconds for him to even let me know he's still in this room, because my eyes are closed. I don't want to look death in the face.

He snorts. "That's laughable."

I lower my hands and look at him. "Please, I'll do anything. Just let me go."

"I doubt there is anything you can do to save yourself. You're already lost."

I don't know what he means by that, but I know there's always a way out. "What do you want? Do you want money? Do you want me?"

"I don't need your money."

"Then what do you want? I can give you anything if you let me go. You can have me if that's what you're after." I open my arms and place them beside me on the bed, flaunting my breasts.

"You think that's what I'm after?" He laughs. It sounds maniacal. "You're pathetic."

His words hurt, but I won't let them get to me. I don't care that I just offered myself to him willingly; I want to live. I'll do anything for it.

I grab myself and wrap my arms around my waist, feeling very exposed all of a sudden. His frown is condescending, but the way he holds the gun is much scarier. He grinds his teeth, almost breathing fire. His fingers are clenched around the metal, as if he's forcing himself to pull the trigger.

But he doesn't. Why? What's stopping him?

"If you're not going to kill me, please … just let me go."

A rumbling laugh comes from deep within his chest. "Who said I won't kill you?"

"Because you would have done it by now if that was the case."

He squints. "Or I'm savoring the moment."

I swallow. The eerie warning behind his message sends shivers down my spine.

"Why did you kill him then?" I ask.

"Business."

"What kind of business? Who kills people like that?"

"My business. Now stop talking."

"No."

He lifts an eyebrow. "Do you think this is a game?"

"No."

"Do you want to die?"

"No."

"Then stop asking questions."

"I'm not just going to sit here with you pointing a gun at my head. If you think I am the type of girl to sit still and be quiet while she waits for her captor to kill her, you're wrong."

He snorts and shakes his head. "Oh, I know what kind of girl you are. You're a whore who'll do anything for money."

Even though I don't know him, his words still reach me. He's right, but nobody has the right to call me that.

"I'm not a whore."

"No?" He steps closer. Sweat rolls down my back as he stops in front of me and leans over. "You just begged me to release you. You offered yourself to a stranger, a killer, as a way out." A devilish smile appears on his face. "As much as I would like to take you up on that offer, I have other things on my mind right now."

"You mean deciding whether or not you're going to kill me?"

"Exactly." The smile on his face is morbidly charming. Only now do I really get a chance to look at him properly. The scar on his face is horrendous, but it's an old one. The skin around his right eye has formed twisted scars in one giant x shape from his cheek to his eyebrow, as if something was seared into his skin. The hair on the back of my neck stands up.

His hand lifts, and I instinctively back away. His fingers curl around my chin as he forces me to look at him. The smell of leather increases my heart rate, and it feels like my skin is on fire where he touches me. His fingers gently move to my cheek, almost as if he's caressing me. His eye stares right into mine, like he's seeing something that's not even there.

I move my head away. "Don't touch me."

A smirk appears on his face. "That's amusing. I must be the only person you say that to."

I want to bite his fingers off after he says that, but I know it'll get me in trouble, so I keep quiet and grind my teeth instead.

Clearing his throat, he steps back again, still pointing the gun at my face. He checks his watch and rubs his temple. It's almost as if he's waiting for something. His expression is dark and he looks frustrated. The watch must have something to do with it, because he can't stop looking at it in between checking if I'm still there. His tongue quickly darts out to wet his lips, and somehow my attention is drawn to it. If I want to escape, I'd better do it before the time he's waiting for runs out.

I slowly get up from the bed in the most sensual way I can, putting the focus on the fact that I'm only wearing panties and a sultry red top from the club. He's completely rigid, but his eye follows my every movement as I step into his shadow. I try to seduce him with my eyes, licking my lips, while I touch his arm and rub my breasts against him. His face is unmoving, not showing even the least bit of interest.

Until that one time he blinks.

There's my chance. I don't need to seduce him to escape. All I needed was a tiny distraction.

I immediately make a run for it, the door within my grasp. Just before I can touch the doorknob, he grabs my arm and jerks me away from my freedom.

"Oh, no you don't," he says, pulling me back by my arms. He has them locked tightly behind my back as he drags me away from the door and throws me onto the bed. A cry escapes my mouth as I land on the mattress, my eyes zooming in on the gun that's pointed at my head again.

"Say bye to your pitiful life, Jay."

"There is only one good – knowledge; and only one evil – ignorance." - Socrates

CHAPTER 2

X

THURSDAY, AUGUST 15TH, 2013. 9:00 P.M.

I check my watch. Only thirty minutes until I have my next job. Another boring clean kill for a secretive client. I hate those types of kills where I don't get to do anything exciting, but at least it pays good money. It's nearby, which is fortunate since it means I have time to come here for a little update as well. I should get ready for the job, though, but this bitch I'm waiting for is late. I sigh.

From the sidelines I watch *her* dance around the pole. It's been some time since I last saw her in the flesh, and I have to say it still stops me in my tracks. She's still as flexible as ever, her long legs elegantly hugging the pole as she hangs from it. Her dark brown hair follows the curves of her shoulders, accentuating her beautiful body. The way she looks at customers with those deadly seductive chocolate eyes of hers … it enthralls them. I know, because I've been in that exact position before. At times like these it's hard to forget why I hate her so much.

I can't wait to get out of here.

The music is loud and annoying, so I'm glad when Hannah finally arrives. "Hey," she says, throwing her long, straight blonde locks back. "Wow, I haven't seen you here in ages! I thought you only wanted to use the phone from now on?"

I give Hannah a nod and then point toward the door in the back. I don't want to stay here and keep talking. Being here makes the bile rise up in my throat. Seeing *her* makes me confused. I don't *do* confused.

"Right … to the back it is," Hannah says as she follows me to the back.

When we're out of sight of the customers and Don I ask, "Did you do as I asked?"

"Yeah, it took me a while to find one and get him interested in the idea, but once I told him about how happy the previous customers were, he was totally in for it."

"Good," I say, grinning. Very good.

"Make sure it's hard and rough."

"He will be, no doubt about it." She holds up her hand, tapping her foot like the unappreciative money-hungry wolf she is. Just another one of those whores.

I lean in and grab her hand, pushing it to the back of the wall, cornering her. Her breathing is ragged and her eyes widen as I pin her against the wall. With my gun against her belly she has nowhere to go. It's hungry for blood, but I don't want to feed it with the blood of the people I might still need to use.

"You should be happy you're still alive," I whisper in her ear.

Hannah shivers, her lips letting out small puffs of air as I retreat again.

"You will report to me tomorrow," I say, and then I pull back the gun and put it back in my holster. "Then you will get your money, and not a day sooner."

"But I got you exactly what you wanted! I've earned—"

"You got me nothing," I hiss, clenching her chin between my index finger and thumb. "I got you your drugs. Your money. Your life. You owe it to me. You owe me everything. I do not owe you." Tears are in her eyes, but I don't give a shit about them. It's pathetic, really. As if crying is going to solve her problem. She got into this mess, and it's her own fault she got involved with me.

I let go of her chin and squint as she hugs the wall to get as much space between us as possible. She rubs her chin and whimpers. "I thought I was doing what you wanted."

"I don't want anything from you other than what I tell you to do. You'll get what I give you. End of story. Now get back to work."

Her blue eyes drift off to the floor, her left hand tentatively scratching the top of her right hand. Such a weakling. "Okay …" She turns around and attempts to walk away, but I grab her hand and stop her in her tracks.

"Do not speak of this to anyone, do you understand?"

"I won't, sir. Never."

With narrowed eyes I watch her face as she speaks the words. I can tell when those bitches are lying. Lucky for her she isn't. This time …

I flash her a brief half-smile. "Good girl."

***

THURSDAY, AUGUST 15TH, 2013. 11:00 P.M.

Watching Jay tie herself to the bed is fucking riling me up. As much as I hate to admit it, that body of hers still manages to get me aroused. So much for having control. I might have her under my thumb, but my cock … it has a mind of its own. My gun isn't the only thing pointing in her direction.

When she's done with her feet, she looks up at me with those pleading eyes that scream fear. It's such a turn-on and at the same time I hate seeing her look at me like that. I hate her looking at me, period. I hate everything about her.

There aren't a lot of people I don't hate, but I hate her especially.

"Bind your left hand to the bedpost." I flick my gun and she takes a short gasp of air the moment I wave it about. It makes me laugh when they act like that, all scared of this puny metal thing. They should be more scared about what I could do to them if I had my tools with me. Alas, it's not always a good day.

I grab the bottle of scotch standing on the cupboard and pour myself a drink while I keep an eye on her, making sure she doesn't do anything stupid like try to escape. Like she could ever escape my grasp. That's a laugh.

I admit, I am an asshole. Do I care? Not in a million years. I do what I do because I love seeing the fear in their eyes before I kill them. I love the thrill of preparing the kill, thinking about all the ways I can make them scream in agony. Of course, their death is not the only thing I enjoy. My profession comes with grand rewards that I'll gladly make use of. Swimming in gold means killing a few people here and there. Not everyone lives like that. You could say I'm pretty lucky. Or just really smart. It's probably a combination of both since I chose this path, but I would never have become this way if it wasn't for ... *her*.

She sobs as the final strap is wrapped around her

wrist. She looks at me, the expression on her face cold and heartless. Closed off from everything around her, as if she's planning to kill me. I love it. It reminds me of myself.

I set my scotch down on the table and pick up my gun. Walking over to her, I point downwards, instructing her to lie down on the bed.

"Please …" she begs.

"Shhh." I put my finger on my lips. "You don't want to spill something you'll regret." I lean forward and inspect the rope around her wrist to see if it's tied up properly. It's a shoddy rope, one I carry around at all times, but not one I'm too fond of. It's sort of an emergency rope, and it saddens me to use it because I don't like it. I would have preferred to use something much nicer on her. Not that she deserves it, but still, I like my works to be beautiful. Like a piece of art.

Her lips part. "Let me—"

I jerk on the rope. A short squeak escapes her mouth. She should watch her mouth. Bad things come from there. "Like I said … shut up."

"But why? Why me? And how do you know my name?" The sudden terror in her eyes captures my attention. A cold rush in their bodies, a staggered breath, hearts that skip beats. I love watching it unfold. Except now.

With her, it's different.

She stops me in my tracks and makes me remember why I hate her so much. Why I am who I am. Why she doesn't remember me.

I hate that part too.

I pull the rope tighter until she can't move her wrist anymore. Her jaw is clenched and her lips look like those of a ravenous dog who's about to bite the head off its victim. Magnificent.

Smiling at her, I walk to where her feet are and do the same, keeping eye contact with her at all times. I want her to see how I love watching her squirm in the bonds that can't be removed by anyone else but me; someone she despises and fears. It's so unfortunate that she has no recollection of how much more I despise her than she can ever despise me.

Which is all the more reason to keep her tied up here. I should make her suffer; she deserves it. Although I never imagined I would go about it like this, it sure beats the hell out of just watching. Now I get to participate.

"Are you comfortable, little bird?" I ask, walking to the other side of the bed.

"Fuck you."

"Now, now, I thought I had already established that is not the purpose of this intrusion."

"Well then what the fuck do you want from me? Are you here to watch me do myself? Are you here to kill me? Are you going to sit there and wait until I confess my darkest secrets to you? Or do you want me to do a little dance for you, huh?" she muses. "Because I sure as hell have no clue why the fuck you are in my room, trying to fucking blow my brains out!"

I laugh and shake my head at her outburst. Grabbing her other hand, I secure it to the bedpost and tie up her last remaining free limb. Strapping it up nicely until she hisses from the pain, I say, "None of that." I wink. "Or maybe all of them."

"Oh, screw you! I don't deserve any of this. What have I ever done to you?"

I frown, gazing down upon her. Her eyes speak the truth. "You don't remember, do you?"

Her eyes widen and her lips part. It takes her a few seconds to answer. "Remember what?"

"Everything."

Grabbing her hair, I force her to lean back and look at me. Gaze at the hideousness that marks my face. Accept the fate that she's been given just as it was given to me.

Time hasn't had any effect on her. She is still a beauty, a seductress, a sinful dancer, a wild girl, and I am still the ugly monster she made me turn into. Nothing has changed. She used to be the only thing on my mind, and now she still is. All I wanted was for her to be mine; now I want her to be dead.

Even after all these years, all this torment, all the hate, all the jealousy stored inside me hasn't vanished. It's only gotten stronger.

But so has my desire to teach her a lesson. To show her what she could have had.

So I hold her hair tight, pulling it back until it pains

her, and then press my lips firmly on top of hers. They are sweet and luscious and all I remember them being.

Until she draws her fangs.

A jolt of pain sears my lips. A metallic taste enters my mouth. I withdraw.

The bitch bit me.

My eyes narrow as I grab her chin. "Bad girl."

She spits in my face.

I wipe it off with my hand and smear it on her lips and cheeks, making sure to clean my hand on her face. "You're a filthy one, you know that? If I wanted your spit I would have shoved my cock in your mouth."

I smile. She has dick-sucking lips, worthy of being face-fucked. For a moment I consider the option.

"Fuck you!" she says, pulling me from my delicious thoughts.

Such a potty mouth. It's annoying.

I take a deep breath and look at her. Her cheeks are red and her chest is rosy. A sign of distress. Or a sign of excitement. I can't say I don't feel it myself. Just that one kiss reminded me how much I miss it, and just how much I envy that she took it all away from me.

I grab the curtain and rip off a piece, twisting it up. Then I stuff it in her mouth and tie it behind her head. Her muffles won't penetrate this material. I stand up and walk back to my seat next to the table. Turning around, I admire my work. Well, sort of. It is partially her work, but it was still instructed by me, thus it is my work.

She grinds her teeth, jerking at the ropes with her wrists as if it will loosen them. Nothing will free her. Nothing can save her. Not now that I have stepped into her life again.

Fuck, I still can't believe it was her in this room. I expected a random girl, and found *her* instead. Fate has a humorous way of messing with people's lives. It's almost pitiful. However, I won't let it interfere. Not this time. I won't let this get the better of me.

The gun is in my hands once again. Her whimpers fill my ears but don't drown out her silent screams. Her eyes shift between the gun and me, whilst my eye is locked on hers. I want her to see me the moment I erase her existence and she fades from this life into the next. I raise the gun to eyelevel and aim for her head. My finger is on the trigger, ready to deliver the final blow. She has to die. This isn't what I wanted, but it must be done. I guess our playtime has come to an end. I knew it had to end sometime, but not that it'd be this quick. Looking at her lying there makes me remember all the things I wish I had forgotten, just like she has.

Clenching my teeth, I take another deep breath and focus on her face. She doesn't remember me. I hate her for it, because she wasn't supposed to forget. It's all her fault.

However, when I look into her eyes, I don't see what I thought I would see. She's not an innocent, but she knows. Her eyes are full of regret. I thought I would see fear, anger, or pain, but instead I see her wishing it'll be over soon. I could end it right now. I could pull the trigger and put an end to all of it. Everything. Even me.

I could, but I can't.

Somehow, this is the only thing I can't do. After all the things she's caused, I don't want it to end like this. I want to make her suffer a bit longer. She doesn't deserve my mercy, but I have to think about this. Do I really want her dead? Or just severely punished?

I still can't believe this was my assignment.

Watching the tears roll down her cheeks, I clear my throat and lower the gun. Her chest rises, air coming out in short gasps as she blinks away the wetness in her eyes.

"You're not going to kill me?" she mutters through the cloth.

"I guess you're gonna have to wait a little longer," I say, walking back to my chair. Slumping down, I grab the glass of scotch and gulp it down all at once. Goddammit. I've become a pussy. I should do something about it, but first I need to decide which choice to make.

I rub my forehead and check my watch. Only six hours left until Antonio's here. Shit. Only six hours to decide what I'm going to do. Six hours to decide her fate. Whatever choice I make, this won't end well. Both our lives have been at stake since the moment I entered this room.

The only question left is: who will surrender first?

"The first step toward success is taken when you refuse to be a captive of the environment in which you first find yourself." – Mark Caine

CHAPTER 3

Jay

THURSDAY, AUGUST 15TH, 2013. 11.30 P.M.

Something's holding him back. I don't know what, I don't know why, but I will find out.

He keeps checking his watch, twisting in his seat as he watches me lie here, getting all drowsy and shit. It's fucking annoying not being able to move whatsoever. He tied me up really well. I guess he doesn't want me running off again, which means a simple distract and run tactic won't work on him anymore. He's too smart. If I want to escape his grasp, I need to listen and worm myself into his favor so that he can't do anything else other than release me. He needs to want it himself, and I'm thinking it's already happening. He didn't kill me. He kissed me.

It must be the kiss.

He knows my name, but I don't know his. He said I don't remember him, but why would I? What does he know that I don't know?

If I'm going to survive this I need to play on his feelings. Play on his heart, if he even has one. There's something he isn't telling me, and it's the only thing that is keeping him from killing me, apparently. I have to do as he tells me; maybe that'll get me freed. That kiss meant something to him. It even meant something to me, although I have no clue why. It feels like I should already know what the kiss means. As if it's tucked deep away in my brain, and it's trying to escape. Something's missing.

Suddenly my vision becomes hazy. The huge headache I've been experiencing the last couple of minutes doesn't help with getting my eyes to focus again. I feel like I'm about to explode. All I can think about is getting my fix. I know what the cause is. Withdrawal.

Crap, why did I have to take my last hit ages ago?

Sweat drops roll down my chest and legs. It's getting so hot, I feel like a volcano erupted right beside me. Goddammit, I hate this feeling. And the worst thing is, I can't do anything about it. My stash is in the bathroom, but I can't get up.

"What's wrong?" he asks.

I stop wriggling. "Nothing." I don't want to tell him, because he could use it against me.

He squints, glaring at me with those dark eyes of his. He's waiting for me to tell him. Maybe I can make use of this.

"I have to pee," I say.

His eyebrow lifts in such a cocky way it makes me want to slap him. "Are you kidding me?"

"No. Do you want me to piss the bed?"

He blinks a few times, silently judging me. Then he sighs and gets up from the chair, grabbing his gun from the table as he walks toward me. One by one he releases my bonds, slowly taking off the rope while keeping his eye solely on me. His gaze haunts me, but at the same time stops me from moving. I think he knows.

The look in his real eye is just so … demanding.

He controls me with it.

His leathery gloves linger on my skin as he releases my feet. His hand moves up all the way along my leg. It's soft and gentle, as if he's appreciating the curves of my body. Somehow it tingles where he touches me. I suck in the air as he passes my breasts.

"Don't."

"Why wouldn't I? I know you like it."

I suck in my lips, feeling betrayed by my own body. I don't want to like whatever he does, but my body reacts to his touch without my consent. Goose bumps appear on the places he touched and my skin feels like it's on fire.

He leans forward and unties my hand. "No matter how much you don't want to admit it, you know there's something between us. Something you feel, but can't remember."

"There's *nothing* between us," I snap. I don't want to give him the impression I'm easy.

His lips curl up into a smile, just like before. Then he gets his gun out. "Up."

"But you didn't untie my other hand."

"You can do that yourself." He flicks the gun as if he's in a hurry.

I work to get my hand free from the rope. It's difficult with one hand, but I manage. There are red burn marks on my wrists and ankles, and they sting. My heart pounds as I move my feet off the bed. I'm afraid that if I make any sudden movement he'll shoot me. If I'm not dead, it'll hurt like a bitch. I'd rather prevent that.

He's at the door, holding the gun steady as I walk toward the bathroom. I know I can't make a move now. Besides, I'm fucking weak with these withdrawal symptoms weighing me down. Can't be weak in the presence of a man holding a gun.

I slowly open the door and go inside. Turning

around, I look at him, waiting for the okay to close the door. Instead, he walks in my direction and promptly stops right in the doorframe.

"Can I pee now?"

"Yes, you can."

"Then I'd like to close the door, please."

"You can pee without the door being closed."

I frown. "I can't do it with you watching."

"Then you won't be peeing at all."

I sigh and clench my fists. His cocky half-smile makes me want to punch him.

"Don't tell me you're afraid of a stranger seeing your pussy. You've been putting it on display with that dance of yours at the club."

"What? No, I haven't. I may be a dancer, a stripper, and occasionally a hooker, but I don't do sex and I don't show my pussy. The pussy is off limits."

He smirks. "We'll see about that."

My jaw drops, and I have to stop myself from punching him in the face. God, my knuckles are itching.

"Are you going to pee, or not?" he says.

I turn around. "Fine." I lower my pants and sit down quickly before he can see anything, although the cheeky look on his face makes me think I'm already too late. Crap.

I turn my head away from him and gaze at the wall instead. I'm not going to feel humiliated because of him. I won't allow it. When I go to grab some paper, I notice he's turned around as well. It surprises me, because I imagined him watching the entire time, being the asshole that he is. Maybe he has a shred of dignity in him after all.

As I grab the roll, I discover the items I use to snort with. Everything fades. My mind goes completely blank, because all I can think of is getting high again. My body craves the addiction, and I need to give in to it.

So I grab the stuff, create a neat line on my leg and snort it up.

The moment he hears it, he steps inside. "You fucking liar." He grasps everything out of my hand and points the gun at me.

"No!" I scream, fighting him for the drugs.

"You're pathetic," he says.

I don't care what he says. I lunge for his gun, but he pulls it out of my reach. I fall down on the ground, my panties still around my ankles.

He laughs. "You want this?" He dangles the packet in front of me. "Too bad, little bird. It's mine now." He flicks the gun and says, "Get up."

I fumble with my panties and pull them back over my ass before I crawl up from the floor. The mirror to my left shows me I'm a complete mess, which is something I'm used to. However, when he says it, it hurts. I don't know why. Maybe it's because he says he knows me. It's as if there was a me before all this that wasn't as fucked up as I am now.

Whatever it is, it doesn't matter. I'm stuck here with this man who is still deciding what he's going to do with me. Whether I'll be killed or not is out of my control, but I know I have an effect on him to some degree. Not that it's of any use right now. I'm already getting high and I couldn't care less what happens to me. So long as I can stay in this trance, even if I die, I'm all good.

***

He pulls on the rope, securing it tightly to the bedpost. My mind has already drifted off into wonderland where everything is cute and magical rainbow ponies drift through the clouds. A ridiculous smile is on my face. Maybe it's because of the funny things I'm thinking about, or maybe it's because he's touching me again.

The rope isn't as tightly wrapped around my ankles and wrists as before. He sits down beside me and cups my face, forcing me to look at him. "You've been bad."

I giggle.

"I know this must seem so funny to you, but you didn't comply. You were supposed to go pee, and that's it. Taking drugs wasn't part of the deal."

"What deal?" I say, snorting.

"That you obey me and in turn I give you what you need."

I burst out into laughter. "I don't need anything

from you."

His grip suddenly tenses and his lips become thin lines again. "Your life. You want it. It's mine. I can take it away any time I want." He releases me again. "And don't you forget that."

"And yet you didn't," I say.

About to get up, he pauses. His eye drifts back to mine, an attempt to see through the veil I hide behind. His hand slips up my leg. My breath falters. He raises an eyebrow. "Just because I haven't yet, doesn't mean I won't." His hand moves up my thigh, stopping right before my pussy. I try to squeeze my legs together, but he jams his other hand in too, forcing my legs apart. "I was thinking of having a little fun time first. I deserve it."

My eyes widen. "You wouldn't."

His lips quirk up into a smile. "Oh, I've already started."

The sharp pain bites my skin before I have time to register what happened.

His hand comes down on my inner thigh, fast and hard. I squeal, but he places his hand on my mouth, preventing the sound from escaping.

"This is your punishment for trying to defy me."

He grabs my thighs again, forcing them apart, and slaps me again. It stings and brings tears to my eyes, but what I hate most is that the blow reverberates in my most sensitive parts. That my skin feels all burned and tingly, and that my body responds to it.

I hate it.

His eyes narrow and he starts rubbing the spot he just hit. Leaning forward, his head hovers right in front of mine. "I think you like this."

"Fuck you!" I thrash around in my bonds, but he steadies me with his forceful hands.

"You can say that, but your body thinks otherwise, Jay." His hand slips up my thigh just a little more until he reaches that one spot I deemed unavailable to everyone except me. I gasp as he presses his thumb down on my panties, right on top of my clit.

"There." He licks his lips. "It doesn't matter if you remember or not. It doesn't matter if I kill you or not. It doesn't matter if you like this or not. Your body wants it. You have no choice but to obey, because I am in control now. I am the only one who can save you."

"Save me? You've done nothing but threaten to kill me!" I buck my hips sideways to escape his fingers, but it's no use.

"Correct. I haven't yet decided what I'm going to do with you."

What? I knew it. He's unsure of his choice, although I have no clue why. His fingers leave my body and I breathe a sigh. I'm not sure if it's from relief or because my body was excited. I don't want to admit it, but it's true. His hands ... they feel so familiar.

Or maybe that's the coke talking.

I close my eyes and take a deep breath, trying to calm myself down. I remind myself that I am bound to this bed, left to his every whim, and that I must do what he asks if I want to survive. I know this man is capable of shooting me down any moment he wants. I have to be careful. I have to give him what he wants in order to escape.

But what does he want?

I hear the gun rattle against the bed, and it makes me painfully aware of the fact that I'm vulnerable and scared. Death haunts my mind, my memories, and soon I'm taken back to my childhood. A short glimpse of something untouchable, something surreal. A woman in a black dress. Her chestnut hair wavy and long, her chocolate-colored eyes filled with fear. A staircase.

I force my eyes open.

My heart beats rapidly, although I have no idea why. I blink a couple of times to reassure myself that I'm still in this room, captive, and that this image I just saw was a figment of my imagination.

The man with the scar is sitting beside me. He's stroking his gun, his face blank as he stares ahead. I guess I'm not the only one thinking about other things. Reality sucks and we are both avoiding it.

I wonder if he has a conscience. If his soul might still be salvageable. If I can save myself before he claims my life. I wonder how far I have to go to get my freedom back.

If I even want to succeed, I should know his name. If only for the sake of knowing the name of the person who wants to kill me. As a memento for the next life. I deserve to know.

"What's your name?" I ask.

His eye darts back to me as if he's pulled from his thoughts. He looks at me like I'm a ghost that's come to haunt him. His hollow, fake eye even stares at me, the expression on his face vapid and emotionless. Then his lips part slowly, separating in a strangely sensual way. "You can call me Mr. X."

"X?"

"Mr."

"Mr. X …" I repeat.

He nods. I frown. I look at his disfigured eye, the fake one, and the gashes and scars that cover it. It's the only reason he would call himself X. Of course. I quickly look away, afraid that if I stare too much he'll punish me for it.

He clears his throat and starts taking off his gloves, finger by finger, like it's some tedious task he rarely undertakes. I watch him do it, since I have nothing else to do anyway. As the black leather is removed, tattoos become visible. The black that stains his skin sends shivers down my spine. Skulls and tribal tattoos. But scariest of all are the letters on his knuckles. In silence I gaze at his fingers, trying to see what it says. However, his hand partially covers the text.

He turns toward me and I try to move away, but can't. He grabs the blanket at the end of the bed and pulls it over my legs. "Thought you might be getting cold," he muses, and then laughs like it's funny as hell.

I don't care. All I can stare at are his knuckles that spell out the words 'GO TO' and on the other hand, 'HELL.'

I swallow away the lump in my throat. When his eye catches me staring at his tattoos, I want to make a run for it. But of course, I'm tied, and can't go anywhere.

"This is a message," he says, pointing at his knuckles.

"A message for who?" I ask.

A devious smile appears on his face. "For whomever I'm going to kill next."

My eyes widen as he says that, and a rush of adrenaline shoots through my body. I was right. He's used to killing people. I know that in this moment I have only one chance to ask this question. To connect the dots that might make it easier for me to understand my situation and find a way out. His scar. It must all be connected.

"Where did you get that?" I ask, looking up at his eye.

His eyes narrow and he growls. It's low and gruff and makes me anxious, because I know he could punish me. I'm willing to risk it. Whatever it costs me, I will find out his secrets and use them against him.

"For death begins with life's first breath and life begins at touch of death." – John Oxenham

CHAPTER 4

X

I raise my hand and look at it. My muscles are cramped, my fingers like blades, because I could cut her right now. If I wanted to. I'm still not sure, but her asking that question gets my blood boiling. She dares ask me that? She dares to look at me like that? Pointing out my one visible flaw is not something most people can afford without losing a few fingers or their eyes in the process.

However, she's different. I know who she is and what she's become. I know what she's done to me, but I remember everything. She doesn't.

I want her to remember. I want to see the look on her face the moment it all comes back. I'm not going to kill her before I can make her see our past, present, and future. I want to see the horror in her eyes as she realizes there's nothing. Only death. It follows us like a parasite, clinging to our bodies, making us diseased until we shrivel up and die.

Life is worthless. Better spend it in all glory than waste it regretting everything. I'm the glory, she is the waste. Blinded by amnesia. How incredibly ironic that she, the girl who was the cause of all my misery, asks me about the scar *she* caused.

I shrug and shake it off, laughing a bit.

"You're not going to tell me?" she asks after a while.

"No."

Just thinking about it brings back the horrific memories I'd rather forget. It has a twisted sense of humor, this brain of mine. No matter how much I try, I can't seem to scrape out the last few inches of my soul. That one bit that keeps nagging, keeps making me furious. Control is an illusion. We have no influence on our history, nor our future. Only our present, which is abysmally small. Realizing this took me a few years. I never let an opportunity to manipulate my present pass.

Like now.

***

Nightmares haunt me. No matter if my eyes are closed or open. Hatred follows me wherever I go. This room ... always this room. The fire is crackling in the distance. Goose bumps scatter on my skin as I watch them walk toward me. I know the pain that will follow. I have to escape it, but I can't. Bound to a chair, I have nowhere to go. My captors are people I know, people I used to trust.

Not anymore.

They talk, but I don't listen. They are evil incarnate and I participated in their every sin. Now they betray me. I can't believe I let them win.

Eternal void surrounds me as they punish me in the most severe way possible. I'm not dead, even though every passing day I feel less alive than before. My face is ruined. My sight is gone.

I can still feel it burn.

FRIDAY, AUGUST 16TH, 2013, 5:00 A.M.

A couple of knocks on the door pull me from my nightmare. I shoot up from the chair and realize I had fallen asleep. Dammit.

Jay is still lying on the bed, tentatively observing me from a distance. She's probably plotting her way out, which doesn't surprise me at all. It's *her*, after all. We were never really that different.

The knocking doesn't stop, so I get up from the

chair and walk to the door with the gun in my hand. I recognize the knocks. It's a familiar rhythm. Frowning, I open the door, but there's nobody there, so I stick out my head.

"Didn't anyone teach you not to look?" Antonio says.

"What the fuck are you doing here?" I say when I spot him leaning against the wall of the building with his hands in his pockets.

"Hello to you too."

I check my watch. "It's way too soon. I was supposed to have until 6 a.m."

He shrugs. "I was early."

"Whatever."

"Have you killed her yet?"

"No."

His eyebrows rise and his eyes narrow. Shit. "Any reason why?"

I smile. "I wanted to have a little 'personal' time with her."

"Personal ..." Antonio cocks his head.

Repeating what I said means he doesn't believe me. And he's right, because I never have personal time with my victims. I couldn't care less about them, and usually want to kill them as fast as possible. However, that's not the case with her. I have to make up something fast, before he becomes suspicious.

"You know. Fun. Ever heard of it?" Of course he knows. We torture people every day.

His lips part, but nothing comes out. He just nods.

"Now, if you'll excuse me, I have a hostage to get back to."

"Stop."

I hear him move away from the wall and step closer to me. This isn't going well. If they even suspect something's up, he'll have to take action, no doubt about it. I'd like to avoid that.

With my back to him, I cease moving.

"You will kill her," he says calmly. Too calm.

"Yes."

"*Now.*"

I take a deep breath and sigh. "Last I recalled, you were not my superior."

"I'm not, but this is just a friendly warning. You know the code."

"Oh, don't worry. I do." I turn around and face him. He runs his fingers through his hair like the impatient dipshit he is. "Be back in thirty. You can help me clean up then." I flash him a smirk, which he gobbles up like no other. His face lights up like a Christmas tree. That bastard always loves the mess I leave. He has a thing for blood.

"I'll see you in a few," Antonio says. I wink and enter the room again, silently closing the door behind me. With my back against the wood, I take a deep breath and grind my teeth. Fuck. I guess I have no choice but to kill her.

Walking to the bed, I try not to pay attention to

her. Try not to notice her fearful eyes and shaking hands as I tear the blanket away from her. I hold up the gun and point it at her.

"Are you going to kill me now?"

"Yes."

She swallows, tears flooding her eyes. I refuse to let it get to me.

"I understand ..." she murmurs. "Please, let me watch the sunrise."

"What?"

"The sunrise. I want to see it one last time."

My mind suddenly stops working. Baffled. That's what I am. This one thing she asks of me peels away the layers of protection I built around myself long ago. The request is one that I didn't expect of her, even though I know her so well. I never imagined she'd still want to watch it come up. Memories long forgotten, but the desire to repeat past experiences still linger. She is still that same person.

Only in a much more fucked-up way.

I shake my head and sigh again. I jerk at the ropes, undoing them quickly, as I don't want to waste any time. I refuse to let this get to me. I have a job to do. This needs to be done, end of story. She needs to die. I will be the one to pull the trigger.

"Time does not exist, only the notion that it does makes us believe we have control over it." – Clarissa Wild

CHAPTER 5

Jay

A cold shiver runs up and down my spine as he unwinds the ropes from my wrists and ankles. His gun is still pointed at my head, his fingers ready to pull the trigger. I know what's coming. The determination in his voice tells me enough. He's finally decided. He'll kill me. There's nothing I can do. I can't escape. I know he'd shoot me in a blink. I can't run, I can't hide. All I can do is hope. Hope is the only thing I have left.

The sun is calling me. Bright orange light shines through the gaps in the curtains, a sight that makes me anxious as well as calm. Knowing that this is where it all ends is frightening, but peaceful. I've never known what it was like to know when you're going to die, but now that I do I find it oddly comforting. To know that I can count down the seconds and wait until he pulls the trigger.

I won't let him get away with it easily, though. I will look him straight in the eye and force him to watch. He should see the evil reflected in my eyes.

"Get your ass up from that bed," he says, flicking his gun.

I push myself up from the bed, my hands sore from the ropes burning my skin. My legs shake as I walk to the window. X perches a chair behind me. His hands are on my shoulders, nudging me down. It's strange to feel his hands on me, strange because they remind me of something ... or someone ... but I have no clue why. He is awfully soft with me, his hand lingering in the nook of my neck. I have no idea why it sticks with me so much, but it does. It feels familiar and secure. Something I haven't felt in a long time.

With his other hand he rips open the curtain, and in a flash I'm blinded by light.

"You're lucky," he says. "I normally never fulfill last wishes, but I'll make an exception for you."

"And why is that?" I ask, staring into the distance. I can't even see the horizon from here, but at least I can see the colors in the sky, and the way the sun paints it like a canvas.

He doesn't answer. Instead, his gun makes a

clicking sound and then I feel the cold metal against the back of my head.

"Can I ask you something?" I say, swallowing away the fear and tears.

"Go ahead, although I can't promise I'll answer."

"I know. I just want to know … Why?"

It takes him a while to answer. "Because you are you."

"That doesn't explain anything."

"You're here because you were meant to be here. The choices you made all led you to this point in time. There is no denying that this is your fault, too."

"Too? So you're admitting this isn't all on me?"

Again, he doesn't answer, which tells me enough.

"You have fifteen minutes," he murmurs.

This time I'm the one who doesn't say a word. Instead, I watch the sun as it rises above the skyline, bathing our world in light. It's almost unbelievable serene, in a morbid way. Still, I'm glad I get to watch this one more time before I'm gone. The sun always meant a lot to me.

"You know, when I was young, I used to watch the sun come up every day."

"Hmm …"

"There was this boy who would come and watch it with me."

X's fingers twitch and for a second I believe he's actually listening to me.

Not that it matters. All I want is to go back to those

days when everything was so much easier and less fucked up. Just thinking about it takes me back to the time I was still oblivious to all the evil in this world.

**

FRIDAY, JUNE 22ND, 2005

People are partying so hard downstairs the entire house is shaking. When I shut the door, the music is suddenly a lot less ear-deafening. I honestly can't believe why the fuck I came to this party in the first place. It's crowded with stupid people.

I check out the room and notice a window in the back. Perfect. I always try to find the most secluded spots in a house, because I love being alone with my thoughts. I love just wandering around and exploring stuff. Besides, this party is so freaking boring, nobody even noticed I was gone. That's obviously not right, since I'm usually the party starter. At least, at parties where they actually play good music and bring out the alcohol, for fuck's sake.

I open the window and make sure there is sufficient space to place my feet before I make the climb. It doesn't take me long to settle on the rooftop and sit my ass down. This house has a perfect view of the skyline, and it's filled with stars. I marvel at the sight of them, appreciating their glow. It almost makes me forget about the horrible music and squabbling of the people downstairs.

It almost makes me forget about my own life.

The world is hell and the stars are the fairytale I cling to.

Sitting here, looking up at the stars reminds me of all those times I used to stare at the sky. During the times my father was away for work and left me with the babysitter who cared more about fucking the sexy boy next door in the master bedroom than she cared about looking after me. Or after the times my father screamed at me for picking my own wardrobe, listening to different music, or otherwise embarrassing him, as he called it. Yup, it happened a lot. When you never get hugged, you forget what it's like to feel loved. When you don't remember what love feels like, you tend to want to escape. Escaping has become a way of life for me. Parties. Drugs. Alcohol. I don't care. Nobody cares, so why should I?

I watch the stars at the times I feel lonely and whenever I need to comfort myself with the thought there is someone looking out for me. Somewhere out there is someone who is looking at the stars right when I am, someone who loves them as much as I do. Someone like my mother. I wish I knew what happened to her.

All I know is that she was there ... and then she wasn't. I was too young to remember any of it, but I know I had a mother before I was six ... somewhere after that she just disappeared.

I sigh, staring at the sky, wondering where she went. I wonder what she's like and if she would have stayed by my side. If she would love me, because my father can't.

I'm startled by the noise coming from the window. A foot comes out and soon a guy steps out onto the rooftop. There goes my silent little retreat.

He turns to look at me, baffling me with his attention-demanding eyes. Not in a bad way, but in a surprising kind of way. He runs his fingers through his tousled black hair as he comes toward me. Somehow, he looks a bit familiar.

"Got room for one more?" he asks.

"Go ahead."

I scoot over a little, giving him room to sit down. He's carrying a couple of beer cans and sets them down beside him. When he spots me looking at them, he says, "Want one?"

I gasp. "Where did you get them?"

"Found them in the fridge when no one was looking." His answer is straightforward, no-lie, I shit you not. A quirky smile appears on his face, and as my jaw drops, he grins.

I like this guy already.

"I'm not the sharing type, but I'll make an exception for you," he says, throwing one of the cans into my hands.

I snort. "And why's that?"

"Oh, I just wanted a quiet place on the roof and

here I find you doing the same thing. Meeting random strangers is a fun way to pass the time."

I shake my head, laughing to myself as I open the can. "Other than going crazy at some random party?"

"I was never really a partygoer."

I take a sip. "Same here." I look at him, and he smiles. I can't stop thinking that I know that smile from somewhere. "Do I know you somehow?" I ask tentatively.

He laughs. "I don't know. You tell me."

I shrug and take another sip. "Forget it."

"So why are you here then?" he asks.

"Oh, no reason. I just like staring at the stars."

"Really? Me too. They remind me that the world is so puny in comparison to what's out there."

"Hmm …" I take another sip and lean back. "You're right. It does put everything in perspective."

"Right." He winks and lifts his can. "To the stars."

We toast and drink some more, silently staring at the sky.

"So why aren't you down there with the rest?" I ask after a while.

"I told you, I'm not a partygoer."

"Yeah, but why are you here then?"

"Oh … some other reason. I prefer to just enjoy the view here."

"Other reason?" I ask.

He raises an eyebrow and cocks his head. "Do you always ask that many questions to random strangers?"

A flush spreads across my cheeks. "Hey, I'm only trying to get to know this random stranger."

He smiles. "No need. You probably won't ever see me again."

I frown.

Suddenly a scream alerts all my senses. I sit up straight as an influx of screams fill the hallways of the house. My eyes widen and I get up immediately. The guy next to me looks confused, but I'm too curious to find out what happened. I put my feet back through the window before I look. "Oh God …" I stammer. The bed in the room is stained red and the pillow is ripped apart, feathers scattered across the room. On the floor is a trail of blood.

My eyes widen. I get the urge to throw up, but manage to keep it down by closing my eyes right away. I turn around, back to the window, and take in a huge gulp of air. It feels like my lungs are constricted. From the corner of my eye I spot people running out of the house, yelling, "There's a dead body!"

When I look to the left, up to the roof, the stranger is gone.

***

FRIDAY, AUGUST 16TH, 2013. 5:30 A.M.

"Are you done?" X asks, putting his gloves back on.

I nod, taking a deep breath. Tears well up in my eyes, because I can't believe this is the end. It's too soon. I regret that I haven't done all the things I wanted to do before I died. Traveling the world, climbing a mountain, doing some charity work, sailing the oceans. I wanted to do it all.

And now it's too late.

I was weak. Years wasted on drugs and sex. Mindless fucking with strangers never got me anywhere. Instead, I ended up here, being a fucking pole dancer, a hooker, someone who lives for the money to waste it all on simple pleasures. What a failure.

I lower my head and contemplate my sins. X places the gun against the back of my head, the cold metal making my heart beat in my throat. It's happening. It's really happening. In a few moments I'll be dead. Will it hurt? Or will it be quick and merciful? Where will I go?

I hear him take in a sharp breath, his hand steadying on my shoulder. "If you move, I will hurt you. If you stay still, this will be quick and painless."

I nod, closing my eyes. A single tear trickles down my cheek. This is it. This is the end. Tick, tock, tick, tock. The clock reminds me that I'm still here, on this very earth. Each passing second is another granted. If I could do it all over, I would, but it wouldn't be the same. I've learned from my mistakes. I would appreciate the short-lived life I received.

And as I hear the rattling of the gun, and feel the

way it shifts on my skull, his fingers tense up, squeezing my shoulder. I say goodbye to the brief life I was given.

But then the gun disappears from the back of my head and the man that was standing behind me is gone.

"Goodness is subjective." – Notes of X

CHAPTER 6

X

Control is an illusion. Even in the direst situations we are incapable of influencing that which cannot be influenced. My conscience is one of those things.

I look at my watch and check the time. Five minutes past the deadline. The choice has been made. A choice that will not go unpunished. However, I will be damned if I do what they ask of me. Killing her wasn't part of the plan, it never was. She was supposed to suffer, but not to the point of annihilation. I wanted her to live with the pain, the regret, the anger, the hurt, but what I found was worse. Someone who had lost all will to live. Someone just like me.

Except, when I burst into her room, she suddenly

regained the strength to fight.

I can't lose that. It's the best thing I've ever seen. That viciousness in her eyes as I took from her what she deemed hers: her freedom. I don't want to lose it. I treasure it. I want to keep it and claim it as my own.

I will take her and make her mine. Her suffering should last longer than just these few years. If they want her dead, they can pry her from my cold hands. I will not let them take what is mine. Her life is mine to give and take. I decide when this game is over.

Opening the door, I peer outside and spot the two black cars in the parking lot. There's one more down the road. Three guys. One is inside, the others are missing. Going from previous experience, one will be waiting in the clerk's room, while the other is perched right beside the building, waiting for me to come out.

I turn back around and close the door. Jay comes up from her seat, her face pale like she's seen a ghost. Her eyes dart from the closed window to the door I'm standing in front, and then to my gun. I know what she's thinking.

"You won't escape. The window is locked."

"Why haven't you killed me?" she asks, her face going slack. She's falling apart. Being on the brink of death has ruined her. I am a monster, because I revel in the sight. I live to see this anguish on her face.

With determination I stride toward her and grab her arm firmly. All of a sudden she recovers her will to fight back and she's trying to jerk herself free. I push the gun into her stomach. "Stop resisting."

"What are you doing? Let go of me!"

I ignore her and move straight for the door, dragging her along with me. If this is going to happen, it'll happen now. I have the upper hand. They're not expecting me to come out yet. The ball is in my court now, and I have made my decision.

Before I open the door, I turn her toward me, forcing her to look me in the eye. "Don't make a sound. Don't move unless I tell you to. You come with me and do as I say, got it?"

She nods rapidly, her breath coming in short bursts. Not convinced.

"Say it!" I push the gun further against her belly. "I won't hesitate to end your life anyway."

"I know. I won't."

"Good girl. You're starting to learn." I open the door and take her with me, my gun against her waist so I can shoot her if she attempts anything crazy. First, I need to find those bastards and kill them. I'm going against everything I was taught, but I have no choice. They're going after what's mine, and I won't allow it. Even if they put me on the job, I'm not finishing it. And I'll be damned if I let them finish it for me. I'll fucking keep her to myself if I want to. Fuck the organization. Fuck the code. I'll kill them all if I have to. I don't give a shit about them or anyone else. I'll get my money elsewhere.

As we walk along the boardwalk, one of the guys

steps around the corner. The sound of my gun going off surprises Jay so much she shrieks.

"Quiet!" I hiss, moving forward.

One dead, two to go.

I can't find Antonio anywhere, and something tells me he got tired of waiting and left it to his buddies to solve this problem. Asshole. I'll deal with him later. First, I need to get out of here.

The one in the car comes next. The burger that was in his hands drops to the floor as I gun him down. Blood pours from his shirt like a wine stain. Jay whimpers in fear. I can't imagine what she must be feeling. No, seriously, I can't. I don't feel anything. Is that wrong? Maybe. Do I care? No. I live for myself, and fuck me, I will live.

I'm having trouble holding on to Jay, because she keeps lingering on those dead bodies, keeps looking back. I jerk on her arm. "Stop wasting my time!" I say, pushing forward. We have to be quick or we'll die. Be fast or get killed, that's the one rule in life.

Her eyes suddenly widen. "Behind y—"

Before she can speak the words, the bullet has already left my gun. I don't even have to look to know where he's at; her eyes say enough. The smack that follows when his body hits the ground makes me smile. I would grin, if it wasn't for the fact that I take no pleasure in randomly killing people without having had the opportunity of playing with them a bit. I like my victims screaming and begging for death before I take it, not silent and easy.

Oh well, I guess that's bound to happen when you defy the orders you were given.

Jay stares at me, her eyes big, her face white, and her lips slightly parted in a way that is rather attractive. I must say, I do like her looking all perplexed. I can't wait to see what she looks like once I get my hands on her. Oh, the punishment she'll endure … I'm already getting a hard-on just thinking about it.

"Who were they?" she asks.

"Business people."

"What kind of business?" she squeals, horrified.

I roll my eye. "Not this again. C'mon." I drag her with me to my black Bentley Onyx, open the door, and shove her inside. I close it and quickly hop in myself. She jams herself against the window, fiddling with the handle to open it again. I put the kiddie lock on and she screams in frustration, banging the window in anger.

"Let me out of here! You can't do this!"

"Oh, but I can, little bird."

"Are you going to keep me prisoner forever?" she yells. "Let me go!"

She fights with the door again, smashing it endlessly, tearing up my car. In anger I point the gun at her head and shout, "Sit still or I'll put a bullet in your head!"

She stops immediately, her eyes widening again as the gun is against her forehead. Her lips purse and she takes a breath. "If you were going to kill me, you would have done it by now. I don't believe you."

I move the gun and shoot the seat beside her. She jolts from being startled.

"Jesus!"

Such a waste of my car, but I had to shut her up.

"Just because I haven't doesn't mean I can't and won't. This gun is loaded and I *will* use it if I have to. You *will* listen to me. Don't take me for a fool. I've killed more men than you have had sex with, and that says a lot. I murdered the first when I was only nine years old. Do *not* think I will hesitate to put a bullet through you. I'm not someone you mess with."

She shakes her head, her cheeks red and her eyes watery. That little speech shut her up nicely.

"Your life is in *my* hands now, and you'll do as I say." I grab her chin. She whimpers. "Do you understand?"

"Yes," she stammers.

"Yes what?"

"Yes, sir."

It sounds good to hear her say that. For years I have waited for her respect. Not that she gives it to me freely, but still, I enjoy it. She needs to know who's in charge and who she owes her life to. I won't let her die without having all of her first. I won't let her leave until I'm satiated. I need my fill of revenge.

And I plan to take all of it soon.

Just before I drive off, I spot Antonio in the

distance, coming back with a Starbucks coffee. When he sees me and my passenger shoot past him in a car, he drops it.

***

FRIDAY, AUGUST 16TH, 2013. 7:30 A.M.

When we arrive at my private hotel room in Austin the first thing she does is gasp and walk to the windows. With her hands on the glass she admires the view, while I drop my bags of equipment on the floor and close the door behind me. I make sure it's locked before I direct my attention back to her. I wonder if I should tie her up again or if she's going to remain quiet and obedient this time. It would be easier. Then again, I do love the sight of a woman tied up. Oh, the things I could do to her …

But first, I need to figure out what I'm going to do with her. What I'm going to do about the job now that I blew it all. We're both in danger. They'll be coming after me in no time. If I know the organization well, they already know about my cop-out. Antonio must have told them—it's his job. I don't blame him; I would do the same if I was in his position. However, I will have to end their relations with Jay quickly. I'm guessing my best option is to pay the organization with money from my own pocket to shut them up about the lost job. And I suppose I'll have to kill the contractor to stop him from pursuing his desire to kill her. Whoever it is that wants her dead.

I clear my throat, and she turns around. Biting her lip, she wraps her arm around her waist and clings to the window as if it is her only protection against me. How foolish. She's caged with a beast. She can't escape me. She never could.

"You will remain here."

"How long?"

"As long as I desire it."

"Why?" Her frown makes me uneasy. Not because I care, but because it shows her intent on fighting me again.

I fiddle with the gun in my pants. Her eyes dart toward it, which is exactly why I did it. I want her to know my intentions. I want to sear them into her mind so that she'll never forget who owns her now.

"I have decided to spare your life for now." I entwine my fingers behind my back and position myself rigidly in front of the door to show her there is no way out.

"And why's that?"

"Because you are mine now."

She snorts. "Preposterous."

"We'll see."

"I have a job I have to get back to," she says, sighing.

I chuckle. "You can forget about that."

She rolls her eyes. "And what would you have me

do? Spend my days wallowing here in your room? Beg you for my freedom? Be your slave?"

I can't help the devious smile from appearing on my face. I dislike the word 'slave,' but I like the idea behind it. And oh … the marvelous ideas that pop into my head when she says that word 'beg' … all the ways I could make her beg. "Perhaps."

She clenches her teeth. "You can't keep me here …"

"Watch me." I lean against the wall, picking up a lighter and a pack of cigarettes. I've been dying for a smoke ever since I found her in that room.

"And then what? Is this supposed to scare me?" she says, her hand fisted like she's trying to resist, even though there is no way out of this.

I smile and put down the lighter. "If you think I am doing all this just to scare you, you're mistaken."

"Then what is the reason, huh? Why are you keeping me prisoner?" She fights the tears in her eyes. I can't help feel a little overcome with the urge to grab her and kiss her to take away all the hurt. However, I can't. The past cannot be erased. What we are is set in stone and nothing can chafe away the rugged surface of our souls. I'd be a liar if I said it doesn't pain me to see her hurt, but I like pain. I live for it. I was reborn in it.

I don't fear it. On the contrary, I survive on it. Pain is a means to an end and her pain is my end. If she stops feeling pain, then so do I, and that would mean the end.

It's too soon.

I need her pain to feel alive. And so, I will continue to make her answer for her sins.

"A man must do what a man must do," I say.

"A man? How can you call yourself a man? You're a monster." The look in her eyes, so in awe of my wickedness, is exhilarating.

I smile. "Thank you."

Her jaw drops, a brow rises, and she snarls. It's amusing to see the mixed emotions scatter on her face. "Are you insane? Why are you thanking me?"

"Because I'd rather be a monster than a man in your eyes. Being a monster beats being a wretched human being. You've freed me of the burden of having to act sane. So yes, you could say that I am insane."

She just stares at me, her mouth open, but in complete silence, like she's at a loss for words.

"Believe me when I say you are better off with me than out there," I say.

"You're mad! You wanted to kill me, and now you say I'll be safe with you?" she scoffs.

"I never said you'll be safe with me. I can get quite dangerous ..." A smile quirks up my face.

She shivers. Clutching her body, she stampedes toward me. "Let me out."

I grab both her arms, squeezing tight as I hold her back and look down at her. "You *don't* want to do that."

"I want anything *but* staying here with you." She

tries to jerk free, but I keep her close, forcing her to listen. She cannot leave me, because I won't allow it, but I'll give her a good reason as well.

"Do you think I am the worst thing that could overcome you?" I lean forward and whisper into her ear. "There is more evil out there than you think."

Her breath comes in short gasps, her tits pushing up against me as her chest rises. Courage is making place for fear again, I can feel it on her skin. It's riveting. She fights me, her arms locking with mine as she attempts to free herself from my grasp, but I twist her in my arms and keep her hands behind her back. Her ass is bumping against my cock, straining it to the limit. God, I love it when she struggles.

I never stopped loving it.

"Do you think I'm the only one who came for you, huh?" I whisper in her ear. "That I'm the only one who wants you dead?"

She shakes her head, and I can feel her heart thrumming through her chest.

"Did you see those men that were following us? Can you guess what they wanted?"

"Me?"

I smirk. "Great deduction. Now, there is a difference between them and me; can you tell me what it is?"

It's quiet for a few seconds. I guess she really hasn't figured it out yet.

"They want your head. I want your body."

She swallows, and it turns me on so much I want to rip off her clothes right now and do her against the door. But I don't. Taking her would be so easy, it would take all the fun out of it. I want her to offer herself to me willingly. I want to see the regret in her eyes afterwards when she realizes she gave her body to the devil.

"But …. I don't understand. I thought you wanted me dead?"

"I did. Now I want more."

She gasps. "Why? What changed?"

"I did."

I push her forward. She stops and looks back, afraid of what's going to happen. I urge her to sit down on my bed, but she seems reluctant. Still on edge. Love it.

"There is a bounty on your head," I say.

"What? Why? What have I done?" she says, shocked. "Well, I know I've been using … drugs … and … well, I'm not exactly a nice girl." She snorts, and then immediately her face becomes serious again. "But those are all small things; that doesn't warrant me being killed. I haven't done anything outrageous, and I don't have loans."

"There are powerful people out there who want your heart on a platter. Don't think you can take this lightly. You cannot go back to the way it was."

She wraps her hand around the bedpost. "And you? You were hired by them?"

I nod.

"So I was right, you *are* an assassin."

"And I could still easily kill you and claim my bounty."

She cocks her head and squints, and it almost looks like she sees something in that statement. As if she's concocting a plan. "Why are you telling me this now?"

"Because I'm tired of having to keep you from escaping. Tying you up is tedious work, albeit very rewarding." I detect a hint of disgust in her eyes, but at the same time she seems unable to retort. It's like her inner demon is telling her to accept everything that's coming for her. Fascinating. I flash her a smile and cup her chin. "I have decided to keep you as my own."

She snorts. "Right. Like I would let you do that. You don't own me."

"Oh, but I do. You see, I hold the gun." I grab the metal in my holster. "It determines whether you live or die. *I* determine whether you live or die. If you go out there"—I point at the door—"you'll get shot within one second. And do you know what the worst part is?" I lean forward, my thumb tracing her plump lip until it parts. "They want you dead, too. You have no chance out there. With me you might. Now choose. Certainty or uncertainty. Which do you pick?" I coax my thumb into her mouth and raise an eyebrow as she tries to close her mouth. "Anger me, and you'll die. So keep those teeth to yourself, little bird. I enjoy handing out pain, I don't like receiving it."

I draw out my finger and wipe her saliva on her cheek. Then I walk about the room.

She gazes at the painting on the red wall across the room. Her eyes seem dull and vacant, like she's still processing the immense experience she had. It was only a day ago when she was still dangling from a pole, and now she is here, with me, as a prisoner forced to do my bidding.

The realization that she's subjected to my will finally hits her and it's marvelous to see.

I clear my throat. "Now, you'll stay here and behave. There's food and beverages in the tiny fridge. You can use the bathroom if you want. You'll find fresh clothes in the closet. Clean yourself up and get rid of that nasty stench that asshole Daryl left."

"Billy ..." she sighs.

"Right." I shrug.

"Anyway, there are locks on all the windows and the door is closed too; I have the key to all of them. There is no phone and no way out. You cannot get away. Scream all you want, nobody cares. I've told the staff I'm having delirious sex with a prostitute. They know I fancy hard play and toys." The look in her eyes changes a couple of times when I say that, from panic to curiosity to sheer embarrassment. "Plus, I bribed them. So don't even think about escaping. It won't work, and I *will* find out if you've misbehaved. Stay here and wait until I get back."

"Where are you going?" she asks as she gets up

from the bed.

"To take care of unfinished business," I say as I walk toward the door. Before I open it, I look over my shoulder and watch her cover up her body as I slide my eyes over her. "You'd better be dressed properly before I come back or I might claim what's mine sooner than you expect."

Then I walk out the door and lock it behind me.

"All cruelty springs from weakness." -
Seneca

CHAPTER 7

Jay

FRIDAY, AUGUST 16TH, 2013. 11:07 A.M.

Coal and crimson. His eyes are the ashen ground after a war, the blood on his hands staining his soul. Memories fade in and out of my head. They mottle my mind. He's always watching me. In the dark he stalks toward me. Ever vigilant. Ever surrounding me. He's always there, molding me into his desired form; a wretched being, capable of destroying everything she loves.

He wants me. An equal. Someone to loathe this world with.

He ruins me. He is my affliction. My drug.

The one who saved me from eternal agony. The one who now burns for my mistakes.

I'm a sinner.

I don't know him, and yet he believes I do. With each passing minute I convert myself to his truth. Memories from a long-forgotten past sweep through my mind, clouding my judgment. Days spent with the devil. A boy with hair dark as a raven and eyes to match. Laughing. Drinking. Dancing.

And more …

Unfortunate events. Discovery and inevitable shame. Pain as punishment. Regret for not choosing right. Anguish for disappointing and abandoning everyone. Betrayal. Letting go of everything.

These eyes … they haunt me. I know them. I've known them all along. And now they've come to claim me and take me back to hell.

***

My eyes burst open, and I'm blinded by the light of the lamp. They hurt, salt burning at the edges. Rubbing them clean, I blink a few times. It's still morning, but I'm surprised to find myself in this hotel room. This bed. I'm not even under the covers, but apparently I fell asleep here. The pillow is wet from my tears. I must have cried myself to sleep. I was so tired. I don't even remember what I did. I don't even know what time it is, or even how I got here. Heck, I've even forgotten about the dream I just had.

As I sit up and stare ahead, I find the same odd framed painting I noticed before. A countryside with a couple of horses and a lady sitting in the middle is depicted is it. The lady is cutting something up, although I can't spot what it is from this far away. However, the red smudges catch my eye. They make me want to get closer and look at it again. I can't remember what it was and why I've looked at this painting before.

Letting go of the pillow, I slip off the bed and let my feet glide onto the soft, warm carpet. It's not a large room, but an expensive one—that I can tell. With huge windows and sophisticated wooden furniture, I can only imagine what it must cost to stay here each night. The chamber smells like sandalwood and ammonia, an odd combination, which makes me a little queasy. The closer I step to the painting, the more curious I get to find out what I saw. I don't know why. I just need to see.

The red turns into little dots and then I find out they are living beings. Humans. Bodies. Chopped-up limbs. A woman cutting them up with a butcher's knife.

A tiny shriek escapes my mouth as I gasp for air. My hand moves to my face as I keep the sounds from escaping. The horror this painting shows isn't what made me frightened. Everything comes back to me in a flash. Billy. His death. The man with the scar holding me captive. The killing spree. Blood. Death.

I'm surrounded by it.

In panic I turn around and gaze at the bed, the window, the doors. Everything is locked, and all of the sudden I feel like I'm going crazy. It's true. It really happened.

My body is shaking vigorously as I hold myself and cling to the wall at the same time. I'm a bird caged by a beast, and there's no way out of this one. He owns me now. What do I do? I feel so powerless.

Feeling the sudden urge to throw up, I run to the bathroom and let it all out. My body is giving up the fight. I've been strong for too long, and now the realization hits me like a brick to the face. I'm a prisoner and I've lost control over my life. How much worse can this get?

Wiping my face and mouth on a piece of paper, I flush the toilet and throw the paper in, then get up on my feet. I could use a drink to get rid of the rankness in my throat. When I turn around, I pause. There's black tape all over the mirror. From left to right, not a single piece of reflection is available. What the fuck?

I step closer and peel away one of the tapes. My brown hair peeks out as I spot myself in the mirror. A frenzy to rid this mirror of its cover overcomes me. I need to see myself. I need to know if I'm hurt. I need to look myself in the eye as I tell myself it's all going to be okay. One by one I tear them down, each one faster than the last, throwing them into the bin as I go.

As the mirror becomes visible I finally get to see myself again. I check my face, my body, my hair, anything I can see, anything that's visible to me. Nothing seems off, nothing's out of place. For a moment I almost thought he might have scarred me like he is scarred himself.

It's a ridiculous idea, because I would've felt it if he had. It's just fear taking over control of my rationality. Luckily, I seem fine. Well, as far as fine goes. I look like shit. I have dark rings around my eyes, spots on my cheeks, and my body is covered in bruises, and I have no makeup to cover it all. Watching myself in the mirror like this really puts a dent in my confidence. With my hands on the sink I look myself in the eye and feel the tears filling my eyes again. Being here in this room scares me, because I'm alone, and nothing feels worse to me than being alone. Not just alone in the physical meaning, but in all its meanings. Because in the back of my mind I know there's nobody who cares that I'm here. Nobody who will think about me and wonder where I am. Nobody who'll even notice I'm gone. No one who'll come looking for me. No one to rescue me.

It's just me. Me and him.

Turning my head, I look at the clock hanging from the wall. It's been a couple of hours since he left, so he'll probably be back soon. I can't afford to look weak when he comes back. It'll be my undoing. So I wipe away the tear that rolls down my cheek and wash my face with some cold water. Feeling sad for myself won't help a bit. I need to take control of my feelings, my surroundings, my situation, and do everything in my power to get out. Even if nobody else cares, I care. I should rescue me. I want myself to survive, get out, and be free again.

And fuck it, when I get out I'm going to buy a condo in Hawaii and live my life in peace. No men. No drugs. No dancing. Maybe just the alcohol. Yeah, I'm going to start a bar right along the beach and spend my days getting tanned under the sun. That's what I'm going to do.

Suddenly there's a knock on the door.

A cold shiver runs through my body as I walk out of the bathroom and stare at the door. There's another knock.

"Housekeeping."

With furrowed brows I step closer. Why is there housekeeping? And why doesn't she just come in?

The lock rattles. A key goes inside. Some more rattling and then the noise stops.

She unlocked it.

A single thought crosses my mind right at that moment.

Should I try to escape?

With trembling fingers I open the door a few inches. I peek into the shadows. A woman with dark hair turns around after fiddling with a tray behind her.

"Ah, excuse me. I'm here to clean the room."

For a moment, escaping crosses my mind. I could push her aside, run her over, and flee. I could. But for some reason X's warning resonates through my head. If I leave, I will die. I don't know if I can trust him; probably not, but what other choice do I have? Those men who were out there when we left my motel were out to kill us both. I'm not sure how many more there are. What if I get gunned down the moment I leave this room? Then it's all been in vain. I don't want to die.

Even if he's a murderer, a monster, I can still only believe him.

I open my mouth, but nothing comes out. I don't know what to say. For some reason the first thing I think of is that I'm still in this hooker outfit, and her eyes confirm that thought. As I look down, my cheeks turn hot.

She smiles and blinks a couple of times. Then she opens the door further, pushing past me, and steps inside, closing it behind her immediately. She locks it again.

"Uh …" I stammer as I turn around to watch her scurry into the room.

"Oh, no need to tell me anything, miss. I already know." Her voice is eerie. Dark. It makes my skin crawl.

"You know …?"

"Yes," she says, glancing back at me before hurrying her trolley to the bed. She starts taking off all the sheets and putting on new ones, while I stare at her, unsure of what to do. Unsure if I should try to pry the key from her hands and make a run for it, or grab something sharp to stab her with.

I don't know why I'm getting this sudden urge to attack a woman I don't even know. Maybe it's because of this room. Maybe it's because I don't trust her. Or maybe it's because X told me everyone knows and nobody cares. Maybe he paid her to shut up. Maybe she's in on it. She knows everything.

I grasp for the bedpost, as wonky as I am on my feet. My life feels like a thin thread that could be severed at any moment by anyone. Everyone's my enemy. No one is safe. X is always one step ahead of me.

Except, when the cleaning lady takes her trolley to the bathroom, she forgets one thing. Her phone.

It's on the trolley with all the other items, but she herself has disappeared into the bathroom with a pile of fresh towels. An idea sprouts in my head, growing in my brain as I realize it's my only shot at freedom. Reaching someone from the outside world, out of X's grasp, is the only solution.

Sliding across the room as quietly as I can, I slip closer to the bathroom. I hear her scrubbing something, and when I turn my head around the corner I spot her cleaning the toilet. She's faced away from the trolley. A perfect opportunity. One chance I can't blow.

I reach for the phone and snag it away as fast as I

can, tucking it deep into my ass crack. Yeah, that's the only hiding place I have, unfortunately.

She gets up, and I spring back, pretending to look at the painting. With squinted eyes she gazes at me, waiting. I break out in a sweat. It's like she knows.

Then she grabs the trolley and pushes it past me, going straight for the door. She hasn't even noticed her phone has gone missing. All she's doing is looking for her key, prying open the door, walking out, and closing it again after glancing at me one last time.

When it's quiet, I get the urge to freak out.

But I don't. I have to calm down. Keep my cool. Take a breath. The phone is in my possession, and it's my only way out.

I pull it out from my panties and clean it with a towel before attempting to dial numbers. My fingers are trembling as I retype the numbers after pressing the wrong one from all the stress. It's the first and the only number I memorized, because it's the only thing that mattered to me before … this.

When I'm done, I hold the phone to my ear. Tears spring into my eyes as I hear her voice. "Hello?"

"Hannah?" My voice is croaky and broken.

"Jay? Oh my God, Jay! Where are you? Why haven't you called? We've been worried sick about you! Well … I have, at least. You know how Don is."

"I … I …" I run to the window.

I suck in a deep breath and begin my sentence.

"I need your help. I'm in a hotel. It's near some

street called … um … I don't know! I can't tell, but I recognize the Interstate thirty-five. There's a Shell gas station right next to us. From the looks of it I'm in Austin … maybe the Sheraton."

But before I can blow out my breath, the door slams open. The sound of his shoes is enough to make my heart beat like thunder roaring in the skies.

"His wings are gray and trailing, Azrael, Angel of Death, And yet the souls that Azrael brings Across the dark and cold, Look up beneath those folded wings, And find them lined with gold" - Robert Gilbert Welsh

CHAPTER 8

X

FRIDAY, AUGUST 16TH, 2013. 9:30 A.M.

My cell phone buzzes, and I check the message sent by Antonio.

You fucking asshole, what the fuck do you think you're

doing? Where the fuck are you?

I don't respond, but focus on driving instead. That fucktard has some explaining to do as well. I don't give a shit if it takes me all day, but I will find out who gave that order. Antonio might be gone from the scene now, but I know where he's at. His hideout this week isn't too far away from mine, which is unfortunate for him, but lucky for me. Especially since I didn't tell him where I'm staying. He won't be tracking me down, but I'm going after his ass. That son of a bitch better have a good explanation for this or I'm gonna blow his head off too.

When I finally arrive at his wooden cabin I park my car right beside his house and take out my gun before stepping out. I check the area for hidden spies, but discover nothing out of the ordinary. It seems he thinks he can handle me.

Oh, yes, I know he's waiting for me.

He and I both know we had this coming for us.

Carefully moving toward his cabin, I keep my finger on the trigger. Sweat trickles down my forehead as I knock on the door and quickly move to the side. It opens, but nobody steps out. It surprises me. Not the fact that nobody steps out, but that he actually opened it. We normally run out the back or fire blanks at the door, so this is unusual behavior, even for him.

I take a deep breath before walking inside, gun pointed at every angle of the room, trying to find him.

When he pops up from behind the door, I shoot the wood in the wall.

"Jesus Christ, are you insane?" Antonio lowers his gun and places it on the floor.

Grabbing his collar, I lower my gun and shove him against the wall. "Did you arrange this?"

"What? What are you talking about?"

"Her! The girl!" I push my elbow against his throat. "Did you or did you not set me up?"

"No, I have no clue what the fuck you mean. That girl was just an assignment. Nothing more. You blew it, you know that? You fucking blew it," he scoffs.

"Like I don't fucking know that." I let him go and he immediately grabs his throat, rubbing it like he was choked.

"What the fuck were you thinking, huh?" he says after catching his breath. "Waiting while you have a job to do? Taking the girl? Killing our own fucking agents?" His voice gets louder and louder. "You're in deep shit."

"I don't fucking care; she wasn't part of the plan."

"What plan? You were supposed to kill her and you ruined it!"

"My plan!" I growl, stepping toward him again. "She is mine. Don't you dare lay a hand on her."

"And our agents? You dared lay a hand on them," he spits. "You know fucking better than that. You don't know what you got yourself into. They'll be going after you now. You defied the rules *and* you murdered some of our own."

"I don't give a fuck about them or anyone else!" I point my gun at him again, and he freezes. "Who gave you the order?"

"What's wrong with you, man? Why do you even care? You were only supposed to kill her. You've done all your jobs magnificently until now. What went wrong?"

"What's wrong is that you went after *her*."

"I. didn't." He places his hand on the gun. "It wasn't me who gave the order."

"Then who did?" I snap.

"Higher up."

"And?"

"I … We don't know who the client is. It's a class nine job. Nobody gets to lay eyes on the details. We were just supposed to take her life and that's it."

"Don't lie to me!" I say through gritted teeth. "You know who it was." I can tell from the sweat drops rolling down his forehead and the skittishness of his eyes that he's lying to my face.

"Why is it so important to you? She's just a girl. What does it matter? If you'd just gotten the job done you wouldn't be in this mess. I don't understand why you're getting yourself into this mess and why you're going through all this trouble to find out who did it."

"It doesn't matter. I told you, she's mine. She's *not* just a girl."

"Right, but you're blowing *everything* … for her."

"I don't give a crap about all that. I want to know who the client is. Now tell me who it is!"

"I can't."

"TELL ME!" I press the gun into his skin so hard it's starting to crack. "Or I swear to God I will put a bullet in your head."

I'm barely able to stop myself from pulling the trigger. This fucker lied to me. He knows who's behind it and he is keeping it from me. He used to be my friend. Now I know better.

"Okay, okay … I will … Just … calm down, okay?" He holds up his hands, trying to make me feel better about the situation, trying to give me the illusion I'm in control. There is no such thing as control. Only those who are killed and those who kill.

Taking the gun off his forehead, I let him move. He's slow and careful as I watch him like a hawk, walking toward the safe in the back of his bedroom. Unlocking it is tedious and takes its toll of my patience. "Hurry up!"

"I'm trying …" he murmurs. When a click follows, I push him aside, still keeping the gun on his throat. My eye darts between him and the mobile phone lying on the cold steel bottom of the safe.

"Is that it?"

"Yes, I'm afraid so." He sighs. "Are you sure? If you do this, there's no turning back."

"It's already too late," I snap.

He shuts up as I pick up the phone and start

scrolling through the names. Somewhere at the bottom is a name associated with the organization. I click his profile and a bunch of his messages pop up. One of the latest ones is a text message from Wednesday, August 14th, 2013. 12:00 p.m. A few minutes later I received a message to kill her. This is the one.

As my working eye scans the message, my lungs stop expanding. My teeth are clenched. I grip the phone so tight, it shatters in my hands.

I step away from Antonio, ready to start this war, but he grabs my arm. "Wait. Stop and think about this for one second."

"Think about what? I know who's behind this."

"So? Does it matter? It doesn't solve your problems."

"Killing him does."

"And then what?" He frowns. "Are you gonna kill everyone who stands in your way?"

"If I have to," I say, tucking my gun back in its holster.

Antonio squeezes my arm, trying to stop me. "Are you sure? If you do this … it could mean the end. For all of us. For you."

I glance over my shoulder. "They went after her. That was their first mistake. Involving me was their second mistake. I'm not going to let this go unpunished." I shake him off.

"I hope you know we can't let you do that," Antonio says.

"Oh, I know," I muse, walking away.

"I'm your friend ... I don't want to have to kill you."

"What's done is done, Antonio. I'm following my own path now."

It's quiet for a while, but as I open the door he says, "It'll cost you your life."

"So be it."

***

FRIDAY, AUGUST 16ᵀᴴ, 2013. 11:17 A.M.

My mind is filled with thoughts about killing people. Murdering them in cold blood. Splattering their blood all over the walls and floors. I want people to know I did it, and I want them to know why. I know exactly who I'm going to kill, and I'm already thinking about how I'm going to do it and what tools I'm going to use.

However, when I find Jay in my room with a phone in her hand, I freeze and all thoughts cease to exist.

The phone drops to the floor as she turns around and stares at me in shock. Within a second I pull out my gun, aim for the phone, and shoot.

She shrieks as metallic pieces skyrocket through the room, hitting the furniture. Scrambling away from me as I walk toward her, she runs to the bathroom and closes the door. As if that's going to stop me. She was fucking calling someone.

I shoot the lock, destroying it in the process, and tear open the door. She's in the back, hovering close to the showerhead. She picks it up and tries to use it as a weapon. "Don't come any closer!"

I laugh, march toward her and jerk the showerhead out of her hands, throwing it away. Grabbing her wrist, I drag her out of the bathroom and throw her on the bed. She struggles, but I keep her down with my body. There are metal cuffs attached to my bed that I installed myself and are there for a very specific reason, and I intend to use them right now.

I force her wrists inside and close the lock, taking the key, and then I flip her body around.

"What are you doing?"

"You disobeyed me," I growl.

She whimpers as I move down to her legs, spreading them wide, and restrain her ankles too.

"You called someone. Did I give you permission to do that?" I tear off her panties, making her squeal. "Answer me!"

"No."

"Then why did you do it? Do you like defying my orders?"

I smack her ass with a flat hand. Her squeal is raw. It's like honey to me.

"I told you not to anger me."

"I'm sorry," she whines. "I won't do it again."

"Damn right you won't." I smack the other ass

cheek as well. Her squeal is a little less high this time, but still very appetizing to hear.

"I also told you to get out of these clothes. You didn't. You have to be punished."

"What?" she gasps, lifting her head.

I move to her side and push her head down in the pillow. "Don't … look at me."

Fury is coursing through my veins, but it's not just her I'm angry about. She defied me, yes, but what I found in that cabin was far, far worse than I could have imagined. She's the one to pay for it now.

I know just the way. I don't intend to take her body unless she willingly offers it to me. Otherwise it's not a victory. No, I will make her see what she's done. Make her see the errors in her ways.

I slip off the bed and take off my jacket, draping it over the chair near the door. She turns her head and looks at me. "What are you doing?"

"Waiting."

"For what?"

"For the one you just called."

Her eyes widen, and it makes me smile. Oh, how I love seeing the dread in her eyes. She knows what's coming.

I take off my holster and place it on the chair. Then I slowly unbuckle my belt, slipping it out of the knots as she blinks. This is going to be fun.

***

Jay

FRIDAY, AUGUST 16TH, 2013. 11:25 A.M.

"Twenty."

He makes me count each time his hand comes down. When I don't count along properly, I have to begin again. He said he won't stop until I reach his number. Whatever number that may be. I've lost count many times. Sometimes I think it's because of the fact that I'm a prisoner on this bed. Sometimes I think it's because I'm actually starting to like it.

I'm losing it. I'm losing myself. My freedom. My body.

He's claimed it all.

Even when I say he didn't, I know he did. I'm lying to myself when I say I hate this. My body has begun to adjust itself to his touch. When his hand strikes, I no longer feel pain. All I feel is release. Release from the fear, the anxiety, the regret. I can let go and let myself be in the moment. I don't know why it has this effect on me.

He grabs the belt that was draped over the chair and folds it. My heartbeat rises as he steps closer. I can already feel the leather before it hits my ass. It burns and stings, but at the same time sets all my nerves on fire. It courses through my body like lightning, zinging on my skin. Even my pussy seems to come alive because of it.

I don't want it to, but I have no control. Not anymore.

His strikes are fast and wicked like the way he grins. I take the time to look him in the eye as he does this, showing him that I don't intend to give up, even if my body has. I know it's betrayed me, because I can feel my clit responding to the lashes. It's not a beating, but a punishment, and I realize that this is what he wanted. He wanted me to feel this way. This is his way of making me feel bad, because he knows I'll feel ashamed of my body. He won't damage his property; he just wants to make me feel.

And in this moment I realize he makes me feel because he doesn't want to feel. He's escaping his own emotions by forcing them upon me.

I won't give it to him. I refuse to be his puppet. He can have my body. I've dropped the idea that I'll ever get that back. However, he won't have my heart and mind. I won't allow it.

"Hmmm ..." He groans as his hand slips over my ass. "Red ... it's such a nice color ... it suits you well."

His hand moves from my ass to my back, sliding all the way up to my shoulder as he stands in front of me. "Can you see how much I love watching you like this?"

He bucks his hips, showing me the bulge in his pants. I try to turn my head, but he grabs my chin and forces me to look at him.

"You don't get to turn away."

He leans in and presses his damp lips on mine. I don't resist. I don't have the energy and I know it's useless. I'm under his command, and the only thing I can do is do as he says. If I let him think he has me under his thumb, he'll get easier with me, and maybe I'll get the opportunity to slip away then. Gain his trust before betraying it. But in order to do that, I have to give him what he wants, and what he wants is me.

So I give in to his lips and let him kiss me. At first I'm scared, repulsed, but as the seconds pass I notice a change. He's softer and gentle, his lips slowly coaxing me to open my mouth. He's much nicer to me now that I'm more willing, and it's a relief. That, and I recognize something.

This kiss, it feels so familiar, and yet I don't know why.

How can you recognize something you've never felt before? Was he speaking the truth when he said he knew me? Have I really forgotten it all?

But this kiss is so … soothing … and that's so wrong. Why do I feel this way? How is it that I feel relieved by his kiss? It makes no sense, and it pisses me off.

He retreats and licks his lips with a look in his eye that screams 'I want to fuck you.' But then he smiles and wipes his thumb along my lips. "Angry, little bird?"

"Hardly," I say, as blandly as I can. Angry is what

he's looking for. I won't give him that satisfaction.

"You say that, but you don't mean it. In fact, you hate it that your body loves this."

"I do not."

"I disagree." He slides his hand along my spine, following the curves of my body until he reaches my ass, and then he slips down my thighs. His hand is between my legs, feeling the warmth.

A devious smile appears on his face. "I can tell when a woman likes pain."

I clench my teeth, because I want to say 'fuck you,' but I know that'll only give him more strength. If I stop fighting him, I can give him the illusion that he's won.

He starts spanking me again. I hiss from the pain. After he passes thirty, he stops. It feels like my body is in shock, numb from the pain. Numb from delirium. The mattress dents under his weight as he steps onto the bed. The belt lands on my ass cheeks again, but this time it's soft. With it X caresses me, sliding it up toward my back. But then he wraps it around my neck.

I choke as he pulls my head back while he kneels on top of me, almost sitting down on my back. "Have you learned your lesson, little bird?"

"Yes …" I gargle.

"I can't hear you."

"Yes!" I wheeze.

"Good." His low voice hums in my ear as he hovers close. "Don't forget who owns you now. Every inch of you is mine. I possess your body, your mind, and your soul."

He jerks the belt over my head again, freeing me from the constraint around my neck. I cough and slurp in the air like a junkie craving drugs. I am an addict. Not just for coke, but for my life too. And now it's all in his hands.

X unlocks the cuffs around my wrists while still sitting on top of me. I can't move, even if I try. His hands slide from my arms down my body, so gentle that it surprises me. His fingers curl around my stomach, and he turns me around underneath him. The first thing I see is his scar. The burned skin around his fake eye. The hideous lash marks left on his face.

I hate the way he stares at me, so blank, so emotionless. His face hovers right in front of mine, so close I can feel his breath on my skin.

Then he locks my hands in the cuffs again. Adrenaline shoots through my body, heating me up, preparing me for the pain. With his hands still on my wrists, he comes closer and closer, his lips right above mine. I close my eyes, waiting for him to do as he wishes.

"Open your eyes, Jay. Look at me just as I have looked at you all these years."

My eyes burst open.

"Yes, Jay … Hate me. Loathe me. Despise me." He bites his lip. "Can you feel the burn from my hand and belt on your ass? Can you?" His command is harsh and loud.

I nod quickly, blinking away the tears as he comes even closer.

"Live the pain just like I have. Learn to love it, just like I was forced to." His tongue darts out to lick my upper lip like a snake scenting the air. "Hmmm ..." His eye rolls back into his head. "You smell of fear." When his head turns back to me goose bumps riddle my body. "Love it."

Suddenly a phone rings. I jolt up from the scare. A smirk quirks up on X's face, as if he's just been handed sweet candy.

He pushes himself off me and rummages in the jacket hanging from the chair. He fishes out a cell phone and takes the call.

"Yes? Oh, the girl is here?" X glances at me, smiling when my eyes widen. "Good. Tell her to come up. I've been waiting for her." He puts the phone back into the pocket of his jacket, all while keeping his eye on me.

"What are you going to do to her?" I ask.

He cocks his head and pauses. "I don't know. I haven't decided yet." His lips curl up into a wicked smile. "You know, I have this amazing new toy, I call it the mini-chainsaw."

Bile rises in my throat, but I swallow it down. "Are you fucking nuts?"

"Yes, hadn't we established that already?" he muses as he walks to the window.

"You can't do that! She's my friend," I say.

He fishes a key from his pocket and unlocks the handle, opening it. The cold breeze makes me shiver. He opens it wide.

"What are you doing?"

"You look a bit ill, Jay. You could do with some air."

When there's a knock on the door, his face darkens. His eye blazes with a devilish fire. He marches toward the door while I struggle with my bonds, trying to free myself. As he opens the door, horror settles in my eyes, but also hers.

"You?" Hannah stammers.

"Yes, me." X grabs both her arms and pulls her inside, slamming the door behind her.

"Please, X, no!" I scream as he drags her through the room.

"Let me go!" Hannah screams. "What are you doing? I did nothing wrong! We had a deal."

X's brows lower. "The deal is cancelled."

Deal? What deal?

"What? You can't do that!" Hannah snaps.

"Oh, but I can."

He pushes her toward the other end of the room. She isn't strong enough to fight back. Just like me, she's left to his mercy. "No! Don't do this, please. Don't hurt her," I beg, trying to make the blow softer.

However, nothing, *nothing*, prepares me for the shock.

He shoves her out of the window and steps aside, closing it before I can hear her body splatter on the ground.

"Seduce my mind so you can have my body, find my soul and I'm yours forever."

- Anonymous

CHAPTER 9

X

That rotten bitch got what she deserved.

Jay is screaming and crying at the same time, jerking on the chains that keep her where she belongs. She's out of it. I don't get why she's so hung up on that girl. She was not her friend. If only she knew.

"Why? Why?" she yells.

"Because I can."

"You killed her!"

"Yes." I lock the window again and turn around. "She had to die."

"Bullshit!" She jerks on the chains again in a fit of rage, spitting curse words.

"You'll understand."

"Fuck you! The hell I will!"

I clench my teeth. "You will."

"Why would I? She was my friend! And you … you threw her out of the window."

"Be glad that's all I did," I scoff. "She deserved to be cut, just like all those other motherfuckers."

Her jaw drops and she frowns. "What the fuck are you talking about?"

I can't believe what I'm hearing. Jesus, I thought she'd heard what we were talking about, but she really is clueless. It pisses me off that she doesn't see it.

"Don't you fucking get it?" I say, shaking my head. "I was fucking *merciful* compared to what I would have done to any other bitch if she'd done the things your friend did!"

"Merciful? Is that what you call murdering people?" she spits.

My self-control evaporates at her ignorance. "I gave her a quick death. A way out. You don't even fucking know what she did. You think you can call her your friend? Wrong!"

"What?" she gasps. "What are you talking about?"

"She. Was. A. Spy," I say through gritted teeth. "For me."

Her lips part and her eyes widen, but she doesn't respond. All she does is stare at me, her eyes watery.

Time has temporarily stopped for her. The realization of it all hits her like a brick in the face. I can almost see the cogs inside her head twist and turn at this discovery. It's a marvelous sight to see.

"She was the one who got you into that whorehouse. She was the one who got you addicted. She was the one who constantly set you up with difficult clients. She was the one who brought you Billy."

I can barely mention his name without wanting to rip someone's throat out. Hannah didn't listen to me when I told her what I wanted and how I wanted it. She fucked up every single fucking time. And now this. Of course I got tired of her.

Jay's lip quivers and a tear runs down her cheek.

"The world is not nice, Jay. There is no such thing as innocent people. Only evil ones and those who punish them."

"And what category do you fall in?"

Her question is wonderful. I grin. "Both."

Tears run freely over her face now, her eyes shining like glinting daggers. From her big sigh I can tell it must feel like she just got a dagger to the heart. I can relate to that.

"But ... she was my friend."

"And a liar," I add.

Her eyes narrow. "What did she want from you? Why would she resort to such things?"

"Let's just say I can be very ... persuasive ..." I

pick up the holster lying on the chair and show it to Jay. "Her life was mine, just like yours is now. She was indebted to me. She just paid it off."

"By dying?"

"Yes, well, that's what happens when you defy the orders you were given." I smile.

"I don't care. She was my friend …"

"Don't you fucking say that," I say. "She was *not* your friend."

"Oh, and you are?" she shouts. "All you've done is chain me up and hurt me!"

"You have no fucking clue how much pain I've been through just for you." I sniff loudly, taking in a huge gulp of air to maintain my calm. "All because of you."

I can't look at her anymore. Can't witness the disgust on her face. Don't want to see the unjust look in her eyes. I am not unjust. I do what must be done. The way she looks at me infuriates me. How she's forgotten everything ruins me. I hate her. I fucking hate her.

And I want her to be mine forever. Even if it costs me everything.

I will fuck her senseless until I've got my fill, and I will make her pay for everything she caused. She won't get out of this one with her soul intact. I'll claim it all. Her body. Her mind. Her heart. Her soul. She's mine.

I thought it was enough to watch her suffer from a distance.

I was wrong.

***

SATURDAY, JULY 12TH, 2008. 3:00 P.M.

The sun is hot and unforgiving. I'm baking like a cake in the oven right now, but I guess that's a price that must be paid for taking on a job for a rich family. At least I don't have to worry about not getting paid, but fuck, these politicians are nasty. I never expected *her* to become the target of their dirty games.

Something blocks my sun, so I look up and take off my cap.

"What are you doing here?" I ask, sighing. "Get back into the water."

"Aren't you grumpy," she says, and she promptly sits down on my wooden lounge bed.

"Where's your guard?"

She shrugs and dips her feet into the sand and gazes up into the sky, flaunting her chest. Of course I can't help but indulge myself with a look. They've grown. So has something else.

"Go do what you want and leave me be," I say, trying to ignore the flimsy red bikini she's wearing.

"Why? I want to stay here with you," she says, with a smile so cheeky it makes me want to grab her and show her why it would be a mistake.

"You wanted to go to the beach. Now go. I'm

staying here."

"Hmmm … you know I won't do that. You should be enjoying the water too."

"No, you know the rules. You have a guard."

"Screw the rules! Forget about the guard. Let's have fun. Come swim with me." She grabs my hand and tries to drag me up. Of course it doesn't work. She's no match for my strength. Instead, I pull back so hard she stumbles and lands on top of me. Her tits are right in my face.

For a moment I contemplate rubbing my face against them, kissing them, but then I remember. This isn't going to end well.

She pushes herself up on her elbows, a flush appearing on her cheeks. "Crap."

"My fault." I clear my throat. "Better get off me, now." And by now, I mean fucking now, because my cock is throbbing and I hate having to do something about it when she's around.

"Why?" she says, frowning. "Don't you like me?"

Hearing those words, I close my eyes and hold my breath. It's not a matter of liking her. She *can't* like me. I was born from monsters, so a monster I will become. Besides, I'm already well on my way.

Suddenly I feel something hover above my lips and then it crashes down on top of me. It's warm and luscious and so fucking good. My mouth parts when it shouldn't, my sinful mind taking control of the situation. I've always longed for this. I want more,

more. It's not enough. I need to taste it, but when my tongue dips out and my eyes open, I see it's her.

I can't. It will ruin us both.

I shove her aside and stand up from the lounge bed. My cock is fully erect and on display for everyone who glances at me. Not that I give a shit, but I can't allow anyone to see us together like this.

"What's wrong? I thought you wanted that."

"You have no clue what I want."

"If this is about …"

In my anger I turn around to face her. "Stop making it so fucking difficult. My life is on the line, and I won't risk it."

She just stares at me with a blank look on her face, her eyes getting watery.

"This is *not* happening," I say through gritted teeth. "Don't you get it? I'm not your guard. A guard protects people. I was hired to kill."

She swallows. "I know."

"Then stop pushing my buttons."

Tears run down her cheeks. Her tears are the last thing I want, so I cup her face and force her to look at me. "It doesn't matter what you want or what I want. We're not in charge. They are."

"So you let them control your life? You want me to let someone decide what I want to do with my life?" she says.

"You have no choice."

"Fuck that, there's always a choice!"

"There is no choice when you and I both know what's at stake."

"But why?" she says. "I don't understand. Why does everyone hate you so much?"

"Because I am a monster."

She shakes her head. "That's not true."

"It is. You don't even know half of it."

Her lips quiver as air slips inside. "I wish I did."

"Don't wish for evil. You'll regret it for life." I lean in and plant a kiss on top of her forehead, and whisper, "Forget. Forget about me. Forget everything. Live your life. I'll watch you from the shadows and keep you safe."

***

FRIDAY, AUGUST 16TH, 2013. 1:00 P.M.

I never thought she'd literally forget. I've watched her all right, but not to keep her safe. Not anymore.

Betrayed is an understatement compared to what I feel when I look at her. But at the same time I still feel the urge to keep her. To do all the things to her that my filthy mind thought of when she was in my face. All those years. She'll pay for what she put me through. I'll take her in ways she didn't even know were possible. Pain is just the first step; pleasure is the next. I'll take what I want and more, make her beg for me, beg for release. I'll drag her through hell and back. And maybe then … maybe … I'll keep her as a reminder to myself not to fall again.

I take my phone from my pocket and call the receptionist. "Special order number fifty-six. Yes. Yes, I want you to take care of it. Cost doesn't matter, just get it done. Good." When they hang up again a sour taste lingers in my mouth. It stinks that I have to get the hotel to clean up the mess Hannah left outside, but I'm much too busy with my captive to do it myself.

I put my phone back in my pocket again and cock my head to look at Jay. Her chest rises and falls quickly. Being chained to the bed scares her. I could do whatever I want, and she knows that. The fear oozing off her is so arousing. I have a burning desire to taste some more. I admit, I may become an addict. I don't care anymore. My life has only been about consequences, but now I say 'fuck you' to those consequences. I will take what I want and own it. I won't kill her yet. No, that's too easy of an escape. She'll be my seductress, my little bird, and I'll be the monster in the dark claiming her.

After locking the door again, I walk toward her. She's shivering, trying to move away from me as I come closer. I sit down on the bed beside her and caress her cheek. She stays still and lets me. Good. She's finally adjusting.

"If you do as I say, I won't hurt you." My thumb travels down to her soft lips again. I can't help myself. I need to touch her. Need to corrupt her. Need to control her every move. It's the only way.

I coax her to open her mouth and speak. "Tell me, Jay. What will you do? Will you behave?"

"I won't fight. I promise," she whispers as I briefly brush along her tongue.

A wicked grin spreads across my face. "Good."

I unlock the cuffs around her wrists, but she keeps her hands there, probably afraid to move. I adore that she doesn't try anything on me. That she finally realizes it's futile. Although I have to stay vigilant. Her mood could still change at any time.

I unlock the cuffs around her ankles too. She slides back and sits up straight, rubbing her reddened skin. I hold out my hand. "Come with me."

At first she glances at my hand, then at me, a distrustful look on her face.

"Do you want to live?"

She frowns, confused, and then nods.

"Then you'll do what I say." She takes my hand and I lift her up from the bed. Her outfit is dirty and ripped, and in need of changing. Although, I must say, I do like the rugged, edgy look of that red lace and shredded dancer outfit. It's very titillating, and I was already about to burst after what I did to her ass. Hmm … I can't wait until she gets under the shower. I wonder if she looks exactly like I remember: like a ripe fruit ready for plucking.

I take her to the bathroom, but when I see the mirror I freeze. The tape is gone.

At first there is disgust. Then there is anger. And then nothing. I'm blinded.

My fist lands on the glass before I realize it, and it shatters, creating a zigzag pattern across the mirror. Blood drips down my knuckles, but I don't care. I'm fuming.

"You …" I turn around, seething.

"I just wanted to look at myself," she stammers.

"Don't ever do it again," I growl.

"I'm sorry."

With squinted eyes I look at her, and then open the faucet and stick my hand under. I wash off the blood and think of a way to punish her for her actions. I think I've had enough of waiting around with her. I'm taking what's mine.

I turn on the shower while she stands in a corner, arms folded, like she's assessing the situation. As I step back, she looks at me with questioning eyes.

"Take off your clothes."

"What?" Her eyebrow rises.

"Is there something wrong with your hearing?"

"No."

"Then take off your clothes."

She clenches her teeth, and I can see her grinding them. Finally, she gives in, and starts taking off her top. She throws the flimsy thing on the floor and then unhooks her bra. It slides off her arms like silk, teasing me as it drops lower and lower, and when it's off, I'm done for. I've already forgotten about the mirror. Her full, round tits and perky nipples are a sight to admire. They always were.

"Underwear too."

"Why?"

"You'll see."

"What are you going to do to me?" she asks, her face emotionless, as if this is a test and she's not falling for it. How charming.

My lips quirk up into a half-smile as I lift an eyebrow. "Nothing. You are."

She takes a deep breath and then hooks her fingers around the fabric of her panties. She slides them down so slowly, so sensually, I think she's trying to seduce me. Maybe she is, maybe she isn't. It's working, all right. She might be tricking me, but it doesn't matter. Her seduction is exactly what I want, what I need right now.

As she steps out of the fabric, her shaved pussy is finally revealed. She's a fucking diamond. That body of hers can rile up any guy, no matter what she's wearing. And now she's completely naked, ready for the taking, and I'm holding myself back.

It's hard, but I know the reward will be much, much better. She'll offer her body to me as her last remaining choice, because nobody can resist feeling loved, even if it's twisted.

Oh, how much I love her body. I never stopped loving it. Yet, I only want it when she submits to me freely. Of her own will. Seeing her bow down and bend over, putting everything on display for me and only me … It'll be worth the wait.

"Once the blood has been spilled, the reaping can begin." – Notes of X

CHAPTER 10

Jay

I step inside the bathtub and get under the shower. The warm water feels nice on my cold skin. Goose bumps crawl over my skin as I wrap my arms around my body, trying to keep him from seeing all my private parts. Not that it's any use. He's still standing there, watching me. His dark eye takes in my body like cake, his tongue dipping out to lick his upper lip. I can see the bulge in his pants growing fast.

Great. This means he's in a good mood.

Quieting down was a brilliant idea. He must think I'm still in shock from Hannah's betrayal. Hell no. I'd have thrown her out of the window myself first if I'd found out she spied on me. Although, I have to admit that it scares me that I'm so indifferent. I'm in constant survival mode, but I refuse to become a victim. I refuse to give in to any trauma whatsoever. I'll get out of this unscathed and sane. I need to.

To X I might seem like a weak lamb right now, but on the inside I'm still boiling with anger. However, I know my fury won't get me out of here. First, there's the belt hanging from the sink in full view as a gentle reminder. Then there's the fact that he'd shoot me before I had the chance to reach the door.

No, the way to go about this is by being calm, assertive, and above all obedient. It's not in my nature to be willing, but if that's what he wants, that's what he'll get. Not because he deserves it, but because it's my one shot at freedom. Giving him anything he wants will make him think I'm easy. It will make me seem conquered. It will make it much easier to betray him once his guard is down.

I'm not a fucking moron. I know how to play this game. Pretending is what I'm good at. Men always want my body, so I give it to them and pretend to like it. Now I'll do the same for X. I'll do everything he asks until he's so far gone in his fantasy of controlling me that he slips up, and then I'll seize the moment. I'll be waiting as a silent captive … he'll never see it coming.

I turn around and look at him. "Now what?"

"Wash yourself." He points at the soap bar lying on the rack next to me.

I grab it and turn back around again, facing the wall as I start scrubbing myself with the bar. My ass hurts and stings under the hot water, but I don't want to skip cleaning it. I feel dirty from top to bottom. Like I need to scrub myself with sandpaper. I don't want to feel disgusted with myself, so I stick my head under the shower and refresh myself. When I open my eyes I catch him staring at me. I didn't think he'd still be here, although it does make sense. I just keep forgetting. I feel violated by both his real eye and his fake one. Leaning against the wall, he keeps a vigilant watch, biting his lip when I bend over to soap up my legs. There's a dirty-boy smile on his face that I wish I could slap off.

For some reason I want to rub it in his face that he can't have me. That I'm here for the taking and that he's keeping his hands off me tells me he's waiting for me to come to him instead. Well, I have news for him. I'm not that easy. He'll have to come and get it, but for that to happen, one of us has to give in first. And using my body to show him what he's missing feels like a tool. He wants me, but then he doesn't want me. He's trying to resist. So that means I'm torturing him when I flaunt my body.

A wicked grin spreads across my face. Power. I have power over him. I need to use this.

With sensual strokes I start lathering my body in soap. My fingers are slow as I swipe them up my legs, pushing my ass toward him. When I stand up again, I turn around to face him with my breasts straight forward. Keeping my eyes locked on his, I spread the soap on my breasts and linger on my nipples, playfully nipping them with my index finger. As I slide my hands down my body, I gasp when I reach my pussy. X notices. His lips part and his black eye narrows. He cocks his head and scratches his neck, his fingers slower and slower with each scratch.

"You like to touch yourself, don't you?" he asks.

I suck on my lip and raise an eyebrow, shrugging. What can I say? I'm a tease. Especially with men I want to trick.

A half-smile appears on his face. "Go lower."

My hand reaches down into my slit but I keep it there without moving. Water rushes down onto my body, heating me up as my hand rests on my most sensitive part. It rinses away the soap while I keep my challenging eyes on his.

"Go on."

"With what?" I ask.

"Ask that again and you'll get another spanking."

"Hmmm …" I muse. "And who says I don't want that instead?"

He laughs. "We can play this the hard way, since you seem so intent on getting me hard." He points at his pants, which are fully tented now. I smirk and shrug again.

"Play with yourself," he demands.

"Or else?"

"Do not tempt me to bend you over, Jay. Because I will, and when it happens, I will make you beg for mercy." He unbuttons his pants and jerks down the zipper in one go, letting his pants drop to the floor. I'm amazed at his muscular legs, the thickness of them, but when my eyes reach his boxer briefs I'm struck with awe. He's fucking hung.

I almost forget this man abducted me. For some reason his cock is more appetizing than it is scary, considering it's one of the fucking reasons he wants me—so he can ram t*hat* inside me.

I swallow and force myself to divert my eyes, only to find out he saw me staring at his junk.

"It'll be all yours soon," he says with a smoky voice. "But first you need to learn to obey."

I squint as I await his order. My hand is still cupping my pussy, but I can feel it's already getting warm from seeing him. My body is lusty for him. I hate it. Why do some men have that effect on me? I never understood. Maybe it's because they offer me something else than just a quickie. Something permanent. Freedom.

"Play with yourself or I *will* punish you," he growls, balling his hand into a fist.

I swallow away my nerves and start sliding my finger up and down. At first I'm slow and hesitant, but I'm getting wetter and the slickness is helping me move faster. I can't help fondle my nub, as it's swollen and throbbing. His hand is on his huge cock, and he rubs it through the fabric of his boxer briefs. Seeing him touch himself makes me forget more and more who we are and where we are. I'm in the moment, feeling myself, loving myself, forgetting about everything and everyone. My free hand instinctively moves to my nipples, because I always like to tug them whenever I'm fingering myself. Heck, I like it whenever any of my lovers handle them roughly.

I close my eyes and take a deep breath as I slip my finger through my slit and try to enjoy myself while doing it. I know what he's expecting to happen, and I can't do it if I don't enjoy it. So I keep my eyes shut and pretend he's not there.

"Open your eyes." His voice is demanding. Harsh.

My eyes jerk open as if I've been pulled from a secret fantasy. I feel like I just got caught, which is ridiculous since he's been watching this whole time.

Frowning, I stop for a second. My finger is still slippery wet, and it makes me aware of what I was doing. I don't want to think about it. I just want to do it and not be reminded of it. But of course, that's not what we're going to do, because he doesn't like easy. He likes hard.

"Don't close them again," he says. "I want you to look at me while you fuck yourself."

"I can't do it then," I say.

"You will do it."

"I can't."

He pushes himself off the wall and reaches for the

belt. My breathing becomes ragged. Folding it double, he approaches. He's fast and merciless as he whips my inner thigh. I wince and struggle not to dance like there are hot coals underneath my feet. The burning mark the belt leaves on my thigh awakens all my nerves. Then another hit on the other, equally as painful, if not worse. It sizzles and sears as he pulls it away again.

"Listen to me," he hisses. "Use your fingers to fuck yourself. I know you've done it before. Now show me how wet you are for me."

He hits my outer thighs this time, and it stings so much I get the urge to close my legs again. Too bad he won't let it happen. Another painful lash ensues and I'm off to wonderland. My mind can't handle this shit. I've never been hit. At least, not like this. Sure, I've taken a slap or two to my face, but that was different. This is meant as a way to correct me. To train me. To make me obedient. To make me his. Somehow, I think this is meant to be erotic. And fuck me, my pussy even likes it. My clit keeps throbbing after every sizzle and I'm starting to wonder if I've gone insane too now.

"Keep them spread," he says.

"I'm trying," I say.

"Not. Good. Enough." He strikes me after each word, making me cringe and fight the tears. The belt leaves red stripes all over my thighs. He keeps looking at them and then smiles, like he's proud of making my skin look like blood. Twisted doesn't even describe this.

"Please …" I mutter after the tenth strike.

"Tell me you will spread your legs."

"I will."

He hits me again, this time letting the belt flip out and curl around my ass. "What's that?"

"I will, sir."

"Good girl." He grins. "You will address me properly from now on."

"Fuck you."

Another lash to my other ass cheek follows. I shriek and catch a tear with my tongue, trying to hide it from him. At the same time I spread my legs, because I know I have to do as he says. However, part of me doesn't want to stop. It always wants to rebel, even when it's not good for my health.

"Now pleasure yourself and let me see," he says, snapping the belt again. He flicks it a couple of time as he bites his lip, watching me with one raised eyebrow. It's as if he expects me to revolt again. He knows me too well.

So I decide to play along and do as he says.

I start rubbing my pussy again, painfully aware of the fact that the surrounding area is throbbing, putting even more pressure on my already engorged clit. No matter how much I fight it, how many times I tell myself I don't like any of it, I do like the sensation. It's wrong. It's so fucking wrong. But it's true.

Taking a deep breath, I continue caressing my folds and nub, trying to keep my legs spread at the same time. It's freaking hard, because I get the urge to close them when I get hot and bothered, but I can't. Each time I falter, he whips me again, reminding me to keep trying. I can't give up. It's either giving in to his wishes, or giving in to his displeasure. And I know better than to anger this man. I don't want to be thrown out of a window. Nope, compared to that, having to finger myself is stupidly easy.

I concentrate on myself and block him out of my mind, but then he opens his mouth again.

"Two fingers, not one. Fuck that pussy hard."

I sigh. "Yes, sir."

With strong, sturdy hands, he lets the belt loose on me again. This time on my nipple. I squeal, fighting to keep my legs spread.

"Don't you fucking smart-mouth me, little bird. Say it like you mean it."

"Yes, sir," I stammer.

"Now be a good girl, and show me how much fucking that pussy can take. I want to see what you're capable of before I take you, because when I do, it's going to be so fucking slow and agonizingly delicious you'll beg me to come quickly." He grins. "I'm not a sprinter, I'm a marathon runner."

It sounds like I'm an item, something you buy at an auction and have to check to see whether it was really worth your money. It's despicable, but at the same time it's oddly arousing to have someone boss me around like this. It's not often men are so clear on what they want. And Jesus, X talks dirty.

I don't know why I like it, but I do.

Now I've really gone insane.

"Make it nice and slick," he growls as he hits my nipple again. They are all puckered up from his whipping, painfully tingling. I dip two fingers into my pussy and swirl them around. Then I move back to my little nub and flick it, still pretending he's not there. If I'm going to do this, I need to forget about everything.

"Keep. Your. Eyes. On. Me." His voice is low and sounds angry, so I make sure to stare at him before I continue. I don't want to call out his anger more than I already have, although I do hate looking at him, knowing what I'm doing. I can't get the gun out of my mind, nor the belt, but fuck it, I'm losing it. My body is quivering, building up to the explosion, and I don't want it to go off. I know he wants it.

"Let me see you come," he says, rubbing his cock through the fabric. There's a wet spot on his boxer briefs. Looking at it makes it easier to cope with. Hell, it makes it easier to touch myself and get off, because his cock is nice; that I can't deny.

"You like this?" he says with a smug voice.

I try to ignore what he says, but he immediately reaches for the whip again, so I hurry to scramble an answer together. "Anything but your face."

Oh God.

He stops moving. Just one growl escapes his mouth.

Now I've done it. Oh, no.

He steps forward and grabs me by my hair, forcing me to look him in the eye. "Am I not good enough, Jay? Am I an ugly fucker? Is that what you're trying to say?"

"No, no, that's not what I meant."

A rumbling sound emanates from his chest. "The fuck you didn't. Look at me, Jay. Look!" he yells, pushing his forehead against mine as his free hand grips the hand I was fingering myself with. "See this fucking scar on my face? Do you know what kind of a motherfucker you have to be to get this kind of treatment? It's my name, little bird. Remember it, because it's going to be branded on your ass once I'm through with you. And then you'll be like me." He pushes my fingers down onto my pussy so hard it's painful. "Anything but my face, huh?"

"It's not your scar!" I blurt out. "I just don't want to be scared."

Frowning, he squints and pulls harder on my hair. "Scared of what? Me?" He laughs a little. "My face makes you scared?"

I don't answer, which makes him chuckle.

"Good." He grins and starts moving my fingers for me. "Did I say you could stop?"

I try to shake my head, but he grips my hair harder, making it impossible.

"Yeah, keep those pretty little eyes on me. Enjoy the burn on your ass and think of where it came from.

Look at me while you fuck yourself and make yourself come."

He lets go of my hand, but fists my hair some more, pushing it into a ponytail he can use to keep me in check. "C'mon, Jay, I'm not going to wait all day."

I flick my clit as fast as I can, trying to escape into a fantasy land, even with my eyes open. But it's no use. It's impossible. And as my climax approaches I realize there's no closing myself off, no turning away. I will have to look into his twisted coal eye and the mechanical one that suck out my soul as I come apart.

"Come. Now," he demands, keeping his eye locked on mine and his fingers entangled in my hair. He pulls it back while I reach the brink of ecstasy. In this final moment of bliss, at the edge of insanity, I find peace. Even in his single real eye, I see clarity, something more than just hate. Pain. Inconceivable hatred sprung from love.

An eruption courses through my body, stemming from my pussy as I convulse from the orgasm. *Whack!* A harsh, flat slap to my ass pulls me from my temporary euphoria. The pain sizzles through my body, actually intensifying the explosions taking place.

"So beautiful ... and so wicked ..." he mutters with a gruff voice. "You came hard, didn't you?"

I nod carefully.

A short, almost invisible smile tempers his face. "Hmmm ..."

He liked it. God, he seriously liked it. I've seen this

look on men's faces before and there's no question about it; this is what he wants. This is his weakness. Me.

I got him.

The more he pulls, the more he drags, the more he makes me suffer, the more he desires, the easier it becomes for me to seep into his bones like poison and ruin him. And then I'll be free as a bird.

When he takes his hand off my ass, I didn't even realize it was still there. Cocking his head back and sideways, he lifts his hand and brings it to my face, gently caressing my cheeks. I don't trust him.

"Such a good girl," he says. "If you listen, I will reward you."

"How?" My voice is still croaky.

"You'll see …" X holds out his hand and waits for me to take it. He helps me step out of the tub, but I still manage to slip on the stone floor. He catches me with his free hand and presses me close to his chest. I gasp, because I'm surprised he actually cared to not let me fall. That, and the fact that his cock is poking me. His hands are tightly wrapped around my body, and he buries his head in the nook of my neck. He smells me and then groans. "I remember this …"

His words creep me out.

Suddenly, his lips are on my neck. It's soft and warm, and so not what I'm used to. He leaves random kisses all over my skin, dragging his lips up to my earlobe. Shivers run through my body. Then he stops, hovering close to my ear. "So eager. So feisty. So yearning for the pain … You're a masochist, Jay."

"A what?"

"You enjoy my hand giving your ass a royal spanking."

"What?" I snarl, freezing, because I can feel his hands on my skin, feeling me up.

"You can deny it, but it won't change a thing. You and I both know what you are." His whispers make the hairs on the back of my neck stand up straight.

"You punish yourself when no one else is around to do it for you."

I'm shocked. I don't know what to say. I can't even bring out a few words. I'm totally and utterly flabbergasted.

And maybe a little ashamed, too.

He groans again, nipping my ear, biting it. "I'll be your provider. I'll give you pain as long as you give me your tears. Be wicked with me, Jay. Learn to love the monster that lurks inside you too. I know you've seen it. I can tell from your quivering lips and begging eyes. You need a man to control you, to temper your flame, and to make you feel alive."

He sucks on his lip, and it sounds like a hiss, making my skin crawl. Oddly enough, my clit is still throbbing, too.

"Blood, Jay. I want your blood. I'll strike you as long and as hard as needed until it turns your skin ruby and makes you so wet you'll spread your legs willingly.

My belt gives us both satisfaction. You'll get the burning sensation of leather, I'll get to draw your blood. But know this, little bird: you'll never be free of me. Don't think you were ever free to begin with, I've always been there, in the shadows, lurking, waiting to take my shot. Let me remind you again: I desire your blood, your tears, and your fear. I want it all. You can choose how. I'll give you that choice. My belt or your head. So you decide, which one do you want?"

My body is giving up the fight as I shake profusely in his arms. It's too much. I don't want to die, but if that's the only choice I have … would I pick a life of pain?

But then I realize I already made that choice long ago. I've been on my own ever since I left the hospital that day. The first day I remember after a huge blur. I've been wandering the streets like a lost lamb. I chose to trust the people, Hannah and Don, who betrayed me in the end. Always let people use me. Always abused myself. Pain is etched into my soul. He's right: I've never been free. Not from him, nor from myself. I'm my own monster, and now I've found an equal.

"I want to live," I whisper into the void.

I can feel him smile against my skin. "You'll make a perfect pet."

"The wicked envy and hate; it is their way of admiring." - Victor Hugo

CHAPTER 11

Jay

The warmth coursing through my body doesn't last long. Once the shower is turned off, X brings me straight back to the bed and binds my feet and hands again. I'm naked, spread for him to enjoy. He's admiring my body from a distance, scratching his chin as he observes my reaction. I shut off my emotions, because I know they would consume me if I allowed them to overtake me.

The belt in his hands makes me jolt up from the bed each time he flicks it. "Are you comfortable, little bird?"

"Yes," I mutter.

The belt comes down on top of my pussy, and it feels like I've been set on fire. He groans at my squeal.

"Wrong answer."

"Please …" I whimper, tears springing into my eyes.

"Please what?"

"Please, sir …"

A half-smile builds on his face. "So tell me, Jay. What do you want?"

"Anything. Just make this stop."

"Hmmm … you know it won't ever stop. You're mine now, and I intend to use you as I please."

A tear trickles down my cheek. He licks his lips when he spots it. "More tears, little bird. Give me more tears and I might release you."

"What?" I gasp, my eyes widening.

He chuckles. "Of course, by release I mean release you of the burden of having to feel so empty. That pussy of yours is begging to be filled." He bites his lip. "I know you want my cock. You'll get it soon enough."

My heart sinks into my feet as the promise of freedom is swiftly taken away again. He just dangled a piece of meat in front of a caged lion. Fuck him. I hate him for screwing with my mind. I'll make him pay someday.

"Now, stay right there."

"Where are you going?" I say as he drapes the belt over the bed and then turns around.

"I killed more than five people these last few hours.

You're not the only one who got a little dirty," he muses. He walks to the bathroom, turns around to hang his tie on the handle, and keeps the door open, giving me a full view of what he's doing. I raise my head, keeping an eye on him, because I'm looking for any possible way to trick him into releasing me. Anything that catches my eye. I need to see, need to remember everything. I keep telling myself to watch.

However, it's not that difficult when he starts taking off his clothes. Each button is carefully pulled without him taking his eye off me. His piercing stare makes it impossible for me to take my eyes off him as he takes off his shirt. A ripped, muscular body appears from underneath, his six-pack rippling as he hangs the shirt on the hook. In his right nipple is a straight metallic barbell, the glint catching my eye. His body is littered with tattoos; a skull on his abdomen and a wicked scythe above it. On his arms and neck are tribal tattoos. Together it's almost like a painting; a warning of the corruption that lurks under his skin.

And yet, it looks so sexy. It's so fucking wrong, but I can't stop watching him. He oozes masculinity. Dominance. Sex. Things I haven't experienced before. Or maybe I have.

I hate this confusion so I turn my head and look at the wall instead, trying to temper my arousal.

"Look at me, Jay. Did I tell you you could look away?"

I return to watching him, because I don't want to

call for another whipping. I don't even know why I think it's a choice, like I can avoid being hurt if I do what he says. As if pleasing him will keep me safe. My mind is spiraling into a darkness I can't escape. His darkness.

He turns on the shower and then continues to pull down his boxer briefs, giving me full view of his ass. Even from a distance I can tell all his parts are well-trained, firm, and without flaws. His ass is a prime example of one I would gladly squeeze. I have to keep reminding myself that even though he has a delicious body, his mind and soul are loathsome. I can't think about him like that.

Of course, it's no use. When he turns on the shower, steps inside the tub, and turns around to face me, my eyes gorge themselves on his erection. He has a Prince Albert: a circular barbell right on the head of his cock. To the side of the head is another barbell, pierced right through the top: a Dydoe. Damn.

X seems to revel in the fact that my eyes are drawn to it immediately, as he starts rubbing it with his hands, caressing the length of his cock slowly. With his other hand he strokes his body and bald head, letting the water run along his muscled abs and legs. I picture myself standing there just a minute ago and for some reason get incredibly turned on just by watching him right now. I feel so perverted, so disgusted with myself that it's happening, but I can't stop it.

The way he smiles at me, his dark eye glowing like a

marble, and the way he slides his hand over his shaft makes my juices flow.

Goddammit. He's got me exactly where he wants me.

"Enjoying yourself?" he asks, widening his stance in the tub as he increases his speed.

I just blow out some air through my nose, which I've apparently been holding back. My clit is throbbing at the sight of him, but I try to ignore it.

"If that pussy isn't wet by the time I get back, you'll be in a lot of trouble, little bird," he says with a grumbling voice that causes goose bumps to crawl over my body. "So feast your eyes."

Annoyed, I pull on the cuffs restraining me, but they're still too tight around my wrists to be able to break free. If only I could get more time to figure out a way to worm my fingers through one by one, I could grab the key and make a run for it. I know exactly where he keeps it: in the drawer beside the bed. The problem is, he's constantly watching me, always vigilant, which means I won't have a chance. He needs to be either gone or so far away I have time to free myself. I'll have to be patient and endure this.

After lathering himself up, he soaps up his cock a second time and makes sure to rub it some more before rinsing it off. Each time I struggle in my bonds, his cock bumps up and down. He actually enjoys seeing me fight my captivity. It's exactly like he said; he loves my flame and wants to temper it. What he didn't take into account is that his words and touch are gasoline to me.

He turns off the shower and steps out again, quickly drying himself with a towel before draping it over his shoulder. With a self-confident stride he comes back to me, still fully naked, and he positions himself at the back of the bed, right in front of me. I pull my knees together to deny him access, but he slashes down the towel on my pussy in a quick move. I growl at him as he playfully raises an eyebrow at me. Fucking jerk.

He slides the towel across my pussy all the way up to my belly button and then breasts as he moves to the left side of the bed. When he reaches my head, he leans down and pinches my nipple with his index finger and thumb. A half-squeal, half-moan escapes my mouth as he tugs it hard. Then the towel is suddenly shoved into my mouth and yanked on both sides. I try to squeal, but making a sound is impossible with this towel in my mouth. X lifts my head and makes a knot. Then he picks up a piece of the towel and covers my nose with it.

"Hmmm ..." he murmurs as he hears my muffled voice. "Go ahead. Make some sound. I like hearing your fading screams."

He pulls my nipples again, one after the other, until they are taut and swollen, and then he bends and sucks on them. His teeth graze my flesh, sensations shooting through my body, reaching all the way down to my slippery folds. When he bites I scream, but the sound is blocked by the towel. His teeth pull my nipple and then release again, leaving a bite mark on my skin as he retreats. I look down and spot a red lash mark around my breast. A small bead of blood rolls out.

"Hmmm … delicious," X whispers, and he licks his lips. He leans in again, encloses his mouth over my nipple, and sucks off the blood. He moans and rises. His hard cock is so close to my face I can see the veins pulsing. I swallow away the pain and tears as he starts rubbing it again.

"You want my cock, don't you?" he says.

I shake my head. He laughs. "Your pussy thinks otherwise, Jay. But I've decided I won't grant you my cock unless you beg me for it."

He steps away and walks to the back of the bed. Shivers run down my spine as his big hands wrap around my legs, right above the shackles. "Your pussy is dripping, Jay. You're staining my bed."

I frown, feeling insulted by his comment. Like I have a choice. As if he didn't want this.

"You're such a dirty girl, Jay," he says huskily, and then he rubs his cock again. "Even after cleaning up, you're still filthy."

"Fuck you …" I mutter inside the towel.

"Hmm? What's that? I can't hear you." X chuckles, making me even angrier. He picks up the belt that was draped over the bed between my feet, and folds it again, showing me the holes. "These little circles will be seared into your flesh when I'm done with you."

"No …" I mutter softly. My breath is faltering. The towel jammed against my tongue and blocking my nose is making it difficult to breathe.

And then he hits my pubic bone. "That's for trying to look away."

Tears spring into my eyes as the second lashing begins. My flesh is on fire, my legs shaking as he whips my thighs and pubic bone again and again. He growls, "Scream, little bird, scream. I want to hear you." The leather bites into my inner thighs. "Keep your eyes here, little bird. Look at me." I force my eyes open as he whips me again. "If you listen, I'll be a little gentler," he says.

It's a promise I know he won't keep, and still I obey. Still I keep my eyes on him, on his hand, as he flicks his fingers along the head of his cock. The tip is covered with pre-cum. He rubs himself so hard his skin gets as red as mine.

An overload of sensations hit me as he suddenly stops hitting and my skin is left zinging. My body becomes desensitized, and I'm moving further away from this world. Oxygen is limited and each time I take in a much needed breath, I smell him. I wince.

"Yes, Jay. I'm there, in your every pore. Taste me. Feel me. Smell me. Let yourself be taken, because you won't be able to resist once you realize you are mine completely."

I can't breathe … I can't breathe …

My mind is drifting away as he suddenly strokes me with the belt. It's a delicate balance between a gentle caress and the stinging of my red skin. I take a quick breath, expecting the worst. I can't take not knowing if he's going to hit me again. I hate not being able to do anything and being left to his mercy. And worst of all, it's exactly what he wants.

Out of nowhere he stops, and the belt leaves my skin. I'm left in confusion. Emptiness. Withdrawal.

The mattress dents as he steps onto the bed, towering above me. His feet are right beside me, his cock on full display. With a smirk on his face he starts jerking off again. He lifts the belt, so I close my eyes, expecting another hit.

Instead, the tip drops onto my nipple and wriggles around, tickling me.

"Eyes on me, Jay," he says gruffly.

His hand goes faster and faster, sliding over his cock with eagerness each time the belt slides across my breasts. My nipples become agonizingly taut and sensitive from his caresses. It's confusing, because it feels good, and yet I know it's wrong. Maybe that's why he's doing it. On his face is a wicked grin, which tells me he can see my confusion. He seems to love it. In this moment I realize he wants this. He wants me to feel agonized by the fact that I have no control. That I don't know when he's going to hurt me again. That I'm left to his every whim. He's still not sated, still not satisfied.

My breathing is ragged and uncontrollable as he teases me with the belt. I keep expecting him to hit me. The stress makes me cough through the towel as I try to catch my breath, but can't.

He grins. "Trouble breathing?"

"I c-can't …" I whisper.

"Good." He laughs.

My eyes widen. "No."

"Yes, Jay. Lose your breath. Realize there's no escaping me. Feel the air leaving your body. I'll be here watching you as your eyes roll back in despair."

"No …" I mutter again, choking as the air I breathe becomes less oxygenated.

As he jerks himself, pre-cum drips down onto me. It's an unwelcome warmth. He groans as I fight to keep my eyes open. I need to keep them open, because I want to know what he does. I don't want to drift. I need to be here. I can't lose consciousness. But it's too late; I can feel myself fade out. Not even the belt and his cock can keep me here. "No," I repeat softly.

"Beg me, you slut," he growls, jerking his cock like mad. "Beg me to continue and I might be merciful."

"Please …" I mutter. I can barely get the words out of my mouth.

He chuckles as he keeps rubbing his cock. "Please what?"

"Please … continue … sir …" It takes all my strength and willpower to get the words across my lips, but I make it.

"Continue what?"

In pain, I open my eyes, witnessing the bite mark on my breast. A tear runs down my cheek as I look at him, jerking himself off while he stands above me. The metal in his cock draws my attention, because the glinting reminds me of the stars and how they make me fall asleep. I don't even know what he wants from me anymore. I can't do it. I can't stay awake. It feels horrible. It's like I'm slowly dying.

"Beg me to come on you," he says. "Beg me to come, because you are a filthy girl. You're a whore, and you desire my cum so badly … don't you?"

I hate the word whore, but I can't say anything about it. I don't have the energy to do so. "Yes … sir …" I cough, fading in and out of this world.

"Say it!"

"I want your cum, sir," I say with my last breath. "Please, come on me."

X groans louder and louder, and then a huge roar escapes his mouth. He shoots his load onto my stomach and breasts. It comes and comes until I'm covered in it. But my body no longer feels anything. Not the cum dripping down my sides. Not the stinging from the belt marks on my breasts or thighs. Not the tears richly flowing down my cheeks. I'm numb and tired. I can sleep now. It's done. I'm free.

In the distance I hear his heavy panting and his groans as he settles down onto the bed and leans in to kiss my cheek. When he jerks the towel down and away from my mouth and nose I gasp for air. My lungs expand rapidly and I cough while sucking in much needed oxygen.

"Had a nice trip into subspace?" he asks.

I choke on my own breath and moan from frustration. With furrowed brows I say, "Fuck … you …" They are the last two words I manage to spit out before dropping my head back onto the pillow, but they're important and I damn well have to throw them out there.

He smiles. "Not yet, little bird. Not yet."

He tortured and pleasured us both. I'm confused by all of this. Confused by my body's reaction to his merciless assault. That I'm spent. That I'm sore all over, and that it gives me relief. My ass throbs and my nipples pulse with pain and satisfaction. He's taken and used my body, yet I won't give up the fight.

Fuck, he sure likes kinky shit. "You some kind of BDSM master or something?" I ask in a slur.

He laughs. "Me, a master? No. I just happen to love red asses and pleasurable screams. I don't follow rules. Safewords don't exist. I told you what I am. Sane is not part of the package. Kink is in my blood."

Like a happy crazy-ass person he gets up and jumps off me, striding into the bathroom, naked. He fishes his phone from his pants lying on the floor, and then dials a number.

"Bring up some pancakes and strawberries. Separated. Yes. No, no whipped cream. Have it up here in ten."

Placing the phone on the bathroom counter, he turns his head just enough to be able to gaze at me over his shoulder. "Don't move, little bird."

"Why?" I say, still breathing heavily.

"Don't want that cum to spill."

I gasp. Shit. This is another threat. I don't want the pain. I'll do anything to avoid it again.

"Keep that body slick and wet until I say so. Don't let my cum drip onto the bed or I *will* punish you for it."

Crap. He's going to make me do this, again? Fuck! I fucking hate him. I don't want another beating. Shit. I'd rather keep still to prevent that cum from rolling down my breasts and sides than get whipped again. His sticky hotness pools on my belly, filling up my belly button. It feels nasty, but right now that's the least of my worries. With his incessant evil games, X is toying with my sanity. Soon, I won't have any of it left.

After ten minutes, someone knocks on the door, and X proudly opens it. Without any clothes on.

I'm left in shock as the same woman from before enters the room with a tray filled with pancakes and strawberries.

"You can leave it on the table over there," X says.

The woman simply ignores me lying here in shackles, naked. It's like she's oblivious to everything around her. I wonder how much X paid her to keep her mouth shut. I wonder how much it cost him to have them clean up Hannah's body.

With a rigid face X watches the lady put the plate down, a hint of annoyance crossing his face. His eyes narrow as he catches her eyes while she turns around again. For a moment I wonder if he's going to kill her, too. With X, life is always uncertain.

But the moment passes and X lets her walk out the door. His fists are clenched, however.

"Why don't you kill her, too?" I ask with courage that appears out of thin air.

"She's useful, to some degree." He clears his throat. "Of course, I will still have to punish her someday for letting you grab her cell phone." He makes clacking noises with his tongue. "You've been a very naughty girl."

"Don't punish me anymore, please," I whimper. A yawn escapes my mouth. I'm so fucking tired, I can barely stay awake. I can't take another beating.

He smiles and picks up the tray from the table, bringing it to the bed. I try to move away, but then realize I have to keep the cum on my body, so I stop immediately. There's a devious smirk on his face as he sits down on the bed beside me and places the tray on his lap.

"Don't let it drip …" he mumbles as he plucks at one of the strawberries. Just looking at them makes my stomach growl. I haven't eaten since yesterday, and even though I'm disgusted with the idea of him feeding me, it's better than nothing. It's not like he's going to let me out of these restraints after calling Hannah.

"You must be hungry," X muses as he looks at my famished face. "Have a strawberry."

I'm surprised when he doesn't bring it to my mouth, although I shouldn't expect anything less from him. Instead, he hovers it close to my stomach. Then he drops it. My belly retracts as the strawberry lands in my belly button. In a puddle of his cum.

He picks up the strawberry and dips it in his own cum, dragging it up my body and along my breasts. Then he lifts it and holds it in front of my mouth. I get the urge to throw up.

"Open up, little bird."

"No!"

"Watch your tongue. You don't want to get punished again." His thumb presses down on my lip, coaxing it to open.

"Do you think I'm actually going to eat that? Are you crazy?"

"Yes, and yes." He raises an eyebrow. "I could eat them all myself, if you prefer."

"Oh, fuck you …"

"Such a potty mouth." He dangles the strawberry in front of me, pushing down on my lip. "Want to eat? You'll eat my cum or nothing. Your choice."

I think about it for a few seconds. Tasting his cum is the last thing on earth I want, but I'm so hungry and those strawberries are begging me to eat them. I can't resist.

"Fine."

"Hmm …" He groans as he places the strawberry on my tongue and closes my mouth with the tip of his finger. He seems to enjoy me cringing from the idea. Chewing only a little before swallowing, I force myself to think of something other than his cum slipping down my throat. X licks his lips as I finish swallowing.

"Such a good girl, eating my cum." He pats my cheek like I'm some sort of pet. "Keep that up and I might let you have a bite of those pancakes too. But first, another strawberry covered with my cum. You're going to eat it all up until you're clean."

After ten strawberries I've gained enough strength to start a conversation again. Each time he looks at me, more questions spring into my mind. Why does he know me? Who is he? And why am I the target?

I don't understand any of it, and my heart needs the answers to be able to cope with it all. So I ask, "Why?"

He stops cutting up the pancakes and looks at me. "Why what?"

"Why me?"

He frowns. "I thought we'd been through this already? People want your head. I chop off heads for a living. That's it."

"Who wants me dead and why?"

He puts the knife down on the plate and sighs. "Do you think, after all the crap you've done in your life, I'm the only one with a grudge against you?"

I frown and look down at the sheets, feeling guilty

all of a sudden, although I have no idea why. It's not my fucking fault I'm in this mess. He can't make me think that. I won't allow it. "You were the one who came to kill me. It's you who wants me dead the most."

"Correct. I could still kill you any time I wish, if that's what you want to hear."

"Then why haven't you killed me yet? Why am I still alive?" I say, grinding my teeth.

A smile slowly creeps onto his face. "Because I'm not done yet watching you suffer."

"Innocence does not exist, as we are born into a world of unjust." – Notes of X

CHAPTER 12

X

THURSDAY, MAY 17TH, 2007. 1:00 P.M.

"Governor, how do you feel about your daughter's involvement in the recent drug scandal?"

Of course they're bringing it up. She's been doing nothing but partying and getting involved with people she shouldn't be at this age. Rebelling against oppression. Must be tough, growing up with such a douchebag of a father. I sigh and shake my head. This girl …

From a distance, I watch the governor's face grow tighter and blank as he opens his mouth. Before anything comes out, his assistant cuts him off.

"That'll be all. Additional questions can be sent to the PR agency. Please, no more questions." He picks up the microphone while all the reporters scream through the crowd. They want juicy news they can fill their pathetic magazines with. My parents are at his side as the governor is escorted off the stage to the parking lot. They're surrounded and followed by photographers and journalists who keep asking questions. Keeping his mouth shut, the governor wades through them. It makes me chuckle a little, knowing that he's pissed off at all these people. It's funny, because he asked for it. He's the governor; governors don't have mishaps. They don't make mistakes. Certainly their daughters should be nice, well-dressed and always busy with charity and helping others. Of course, that's not reality. The governor just wants it to be.

He's such a hypocrite. As if he's such a great man himself. I mean, our family is looking out for his 'best interests' for fuck's sake. It can't get any more wrong than that.

I blow out the smoke from my cigarette and throw it onto the asphalt. Suddenly, a scream rises up from the crowd and my attention is drawn to it immediately. My hand reaches for my gun while I run toward it. As I come closer, I see the governor hurrying away, heavily guarded. His face is covered in yellow sludge from an egg; on his head lies the shell.

With my hand I keep the laughter from spilling out

as my family scours the area. The governor yells something at my mother, his face red from anger. She nods as the governor is brought to his car. His daughter is trailing behind him. I stay near the car and watch. My ears can't help but catch the conversations going on inside. The car door isn't shut yet, and his daughter's foot is still hanging out.

"Get out," the governor yells.

"What?" she says.

"You heard me. Get the hell out of my car."

"But …"

"No buts. You're a disgrace! How dare you humiliate me like that!"

"I can explain …" she says.

"You're a useless excuse for a daughter! You're only standing in my way. I've had about enough of it. Clean up your act or get out."

She slowly crawls out of the car and slams the door shut, sniffing. I can hear the muffled commands of the governor as he instructs the driver. Then the car shoots off, leaving her alone in the parking lot. She turns her head away and watches the crowd disperse. They only came to photograph and interview her father, and now that he's gone, nobody cares anymore. She brushes her hand along her cheek and sighs. Then she turns toward me.

A flush spreads over my cheeks as she looks at me. Really looks at me. Her eyes are still the same as I remember, and they still have a magnetizing effect on me. Before, it was all fun and games. Now, it's dead serious. I can't let this get to me.

Closing my eyes, I turn around and call my father. "Where are you?"

"We have him. In the alley, just around the corner."

"I'm coming," I say, and I put the phone back into my pocket.

Suddenly there is a hand on my arm. I stop and turn around to see her looking up at me.

"Please, don't go."

"I have to."

"But why? We had fun before. Why are you ignoring me?"

It's like a stab to the heart when she says that. I'm not ignoring her. On the contrary, I'm forced to be near her and her father against my will, all because of my family. I don't want to watch her waste her life. I don't want to watch her get hurt by her father's comments. I don't want to watch her kiss other guys.

"It's not like that," I growl. "Yes, we had fun before." Fun … whatever that means. Hanging out with her was fun, for a while, until it wasn't enough anymore. It was never enough. I should've known this from the start. Our time together has never been anything but a threat to us both.

"Come hang out with me then. I could use a distraction," she says, putting up a smile. She's doing her best to persuade me, but I'm not convinced she really wants that. She doesn't want fun. She wants to forget. That's what she always wants and why she does all those things. And I'm supposed to be the one to catch her when she falls.

I refuse. I can't do it. Not anymore. This has gone too far already. I should have cut it off when I had the chance.

"No. I can't," I say.

She frowns, so I turn around and start walking again. Instead of accepting her defeat, she stomps in front of me and puts her foot down. "You're not leaving. You work for us. If I say you stay and hang out with me, you do exactly that."

I laugh and shake my head. "You don't get it, do you?" I lean forward and grab her shoulder. "I'm. Not. Hanging. Out. With. You." I tap her chest. "You don't pay me. Your father does, and not at all for the reasons you think. So you can demand all you like, but it's not going to happen."

"Why not? What changed? Stop being such an asshole! You know I need someone to talk to right now."

"I know, but I'm not the one to lean on. You shouldn't, *ever*, lean on me. I'm not that kind of person." I grab both her shoulders and push her forward.

"Then what kind of person are you?" She folds her arms.

"Me and my family ... we are not your protectors. I am *not* a good guy."

She raises one eyebrow and lowers the other as she steps closer to me. Too close. Her hands are on my hips and the way she pouts as she looks up at me makes me want to cup her face and kiss her.

But I can't. I'd rather hurt her than be hurt myself. Life is cruel. I'm even crueler. I have my family to thank for it.

"But you are. We used to hang out all the time … I don't remember you being anything but good and fun."

"Stop living in the past!" I shout. "I can't do it anymore. You don't fucking know me, at all."

Tears spring into her eyes. "Don't say that …"

"You think I'm here to protect you? To be your friend? Wrong. You don't even know what my family does for a living. You don't even know why we are here in the first place."

"Then why are you here?"

I lean in even closer. "Did you see the man that threw the egg?"

She nods, holding her breath as I hover next to her ear. "My parents are with him. Do you know what that means?"

She shakes her head.

"He's probably lost all his fingers by now."

Her swallowing tells me she finally gets the picture.

I lean back and look her straight in the eye. "Run. Go to your friends. Go to the club. Do whatever you like. Live your life. But do not *ever* turn to me for comfort."

Shivering, she backs away from me, and then turns and bolts away.

If only she could stay away …

***

FRIDAY, AUGUST 16TH, 2013. 5:00 P.M.

Gasping loudly, I shoot up from the bed, eyes wide open. I must have fallen asleep after our little lunch break. I have been running on nothing but fury these last couple of days. No wonder my body decided it was time to sleep. I didn't think a short nap would hurt, but it turned into hours.

When I drop my head to the side, my captive is no longer there.

For a second, I stop breathing.

The bed is empty. Jay is gone. Every trace of her is missing. Not even her scent is here anymore.

Fuck. Fuck!

I look at the shackles and notice they're still there, firmly attached to the bed. She must have slipped out of the cuffs somehow. She wasn't that skinny, was she? Did she fucking work on this while I was sleeping? I rummage in my pocket, and, no surprise, the key to unlock the door is gone. No fucking way.

Scrambling off the bed, I grab some clothes and jump into them before running out the door with my gun locked in place. My cleaning lady is in front of a different door, fiddling with her key. I approach her. "Have you seen my girl pass by? Long, dark brown hair, chocolate eyes, you know what she looks like."

She nods. "I saw a girl running down the hall a minute ago, but I couldn't tell who she was. Did your girl run off?"

I don't answer and pass her in a hurry, jumping steps as I storm down the stairs. I'll catch that little bird. She can't have gotten far.

As I open the emergency door, I look around the hotel premises. The parking lot is empty, but there's only one thing out of the ordinary. A girl dressed in nothing but a bathrobe, frantically opening up every car door she can find. My little bird.

"There you are," I say.

In shock she turns around and shrieks. "Stay away from me!"

She runs from one car to the next, hiding behind them as I step closer. "Fly all you want, little bird. You can't escape this cage."

"Fuck off!" she yells from behind the car, and then she throws something at me. Dodging it, I look back and discover it's a hotel slipper she probably found somewhere and put on her feet. I catch the second one she throws.

"Stay away from me, you son of a bitch!" she yells.

I'm lucky the parking lot is empty at this time, otherwise this would make quite a scene. I might have had to actually kill every witness. Even her, if she doesn't shut up.

"Now, how did you free yourself, little bird?"

"Like I would tell you," she sneers.

I smile. "It seems the cuffs weren't tight enough after all." I check out her wrists and hands. There are bruising marks all over her left wrist and fingers. I guess she managed to wriggle herself out and take my key from my pocket while I was sleeping to unlock the rest. Clever girl. Must've hurt a lot.

"You can't keep me here," she says.

I take my gun from its holster and shake my arm, wrapping my fingers tightly around the trigger. "Yes I can. You can run, but you can't escape me," I say with a low voice. Trying to be calm is hard, but I don't want to unnecessarily damage my property, or my car.

"Get over here right now or I will shoot," I say.

"You won't!" she yells, running away from the car.

I aim for the asphalt right in front of her feet. She shrieks and jumps up and down, then bolts in another direction. There, I shoot as well. Each time she turns, I shoot in that direction, causing her to feel disoriented. From a distance I can see the panic flowing through her, the sweat dripping down her forehead, and her long legs dancing to the rhythm of my gunshots.

"That's it, little bird, flock to me and it will stop." Each step I take makes her more skittish, more eager to run. She's trapped, and she knows it. No matter where she runs, I will find her.

"Come to me and you'll be safe."

She shakes her head, tears forming in her eyes. "Safe? With you I'll never be safe."

"I won't harm you as long as you obey me," I muse, flicking the gun to get her to come to me. However, she remains unmoving.

"You want to hurt me," she says, her voice croaky.

"Hurt. Such a strange word. I see it as punishment. And another part of the spanking is lust." I take another step. She backs away. I point the gun at her abdomen and watch her eyes dart to the metal. She shuffles backwards.

I'm starting to lose my patience. "You will come back to the room with me. Now."

"No. You're a monster."

I don't have time for this nonsense. Grinding my teeth, I storm toward her. She launches her fist at me, but I evade it, and then poke her in the stomach with my gun. "There is no choice."

She shrieks. "Stop! What are you doing?" I grab her arm with my free hand. "Let go of me!"

Pulling her back toward the hotel, I check my surroundings carefully, always on alert. They could be anywhere, anytime, watching us, ready to shoot. They don't care about her life or mine. We'd be dead in a second if they saw us. Goddammit, why did I let her escape? This is fucking dangerous!

"Take your fucking hands off me!" she yells.

I drag her to a corner in the shadows and push her up against the wall of the building. "Are you fucking insane?" I tell her. "I told you, you would *die* if you went out there."

"I went out there. I didn't die."

"Don't mock me," I snarl. "Have you already forgotten what I told you? That I'm not the only one who came for your head?"

"Yeah, well maybe I'd rather be taken away by them than spend one more second with you!" She spits in my face, so I push the gun further into her stomach as I wipe my face with my sleeve.

"You'll fucking pay for that," I say through gritted teeth. "You have no fucking clue how much you need me."

"You must be joking," she scoffs.

"There are men after you. Men that are exactly like me; murderous sons of bitches. Nothing will stand in the way of their killing you. Do you hear me? Nothing. Not you, not me. They would kill us both in the blink of an eye." I hold up my finger for her to see, press it to her forehead, and then make a gunshot sound. Her eyes blink rapidly and her lips part, but nothing comes out.

"I'm the only one who can save you from them. The only one who knows how to protect you."

"I don't want your protection …" she mutters.

My finger drifts down her nose to her lip, dragging it down as I linger on her chin and nudge it up so she'll finally look at me. Really look at me. So she'll see that I'm the only thing keeping her alive.

"Your life is in my hands. It doesn't matter if you escape; they would still find you and kill you. It's their job and they'll do anything to get it done. Don't you get it? There's no going back. You are on the hit list. It won't end. Not when you run. Not when I die. It will never end."

Her eyes grow watery when she finally realizes she has lost her freedom. Not to me, but to the world.

"But I can't …" she whispers. "I don't want more pain."

"Pain is what you get when you don't listen. Pain can be avoided if you do. Whether you want it or not, you are mine now. I saved your life. I will keep it safe, so long as you do what I say," I murmur. "Anything. Everything."

The gun is still in her side, and when I move my hand a little, she gasps. Air leaves her mouth in short breaths. I can almost taste her panic. Her fear. Her downfall.

A sigh escapes her mouth. Her shoulders drop, and her defensive stance disappears. She loosens her muscles and opens her eyes again. She's defeated.

"I don't want to die. I'll do anything."

I take a deep breath. "I am the one who keeps you alive. No one else. You live because of me. I can take it away just as quickly."

"I know."

"I could kill you right now if I wanted to. Nobody would care. Nobody would even know. You'd disappear."

She sniffs. "Please don't."

My hand slides up her face to her cheek, caressing her. "What will you do? Run and die or stay with me and live?"

"I don't want to die. I'll do anything. Please … I'll do anything."

A slow smile builds on my face. "Good."

A tear rolls down her cheek as I lean in, tentatively waiting for her reaction. My approach is slow, but she doesn't object. Her lips are ready for the taking, and so I plunder them with greed. They're finally opening up to me, allowing me to take what's mine. Her mouth, her tongue, everything. I probe her mouth with hunger, because I want her more than anything. I've always wanted her.

But I also want her to pay. This is how I'll have my revenge.

"The torture of a bad conscience is the hell of a living soul." – John Calvin

CHAPTER 13

X

FRIDAY, AUGUST 16TH, 2013. 5:30 P.M.

She sits on the bed, her legs crossed and her hands on her lap, waiting for me. Waiting for my order. Finally obedient. It's what I always wanted. What I always deserved.

Except, now that I have it, it still isn't enough. I want her, physically as well as mentally. I will do anything to have her completely.

I sit down beside her on the bed. She stiffens and her eyes flash to me in fear. I raise my hand and lift a few strands of hair blocking her face from my sight. My finger slides across her cheek as I tuck it behind her ear. I lean sideways and whisper, "Are you hungry?"

She sucks in her lip. "N-no."

Maybe she's had enough strawberries for today. As I caress her cheek, my other hand crawls under her robe, sliding over her leg. She twitches.

"Please, don't."

"Why do you still resist me?" I murmur, nipping her ear, biting a little. She hisses when I bite down a little harder. A drop of blood oozes from the puncture wound. I lick it up and swallow her taste. She tastes like a whore. My whore.

That little bird who danced and flocked to men like they were her only feeders now belongs to me, and only me. I will be the one feeding her now.

"Anything, Jay."

She shudders. "Anything."

"But you will offer it to me freely."

She shuts her mouth as her body starts shaking. I grab a blanket from the back of a chair and wrap it around her body. "I'm not just a monster, I'm your monster. I take good care of what's mine; you can trust me on that."

Jerking on the blanket, she draws it closer to her and pulls away from me. I guess she won't hand it to me freely just yet. But she will, eventually. I'm not in the mood for fucking anyway. Now that I've released my seed onto her, I have a clearer mind on what to do next. I will make her my pet and I will have my revenge. They aren't mutually exclusive. On the contrary; having her in my possession will take its toll on her. I can take pleasure and pain from her, and it will destroy her, just like I planned.

I can't help but chuckle a little.

"Why are you laughing?" she asks.

"It's funny, because I always wanted you to be mine, but only on my terms. And now I finally have you." I grab her chin and lean in, pressing a kiss on her lips. "I don't intend for you to ever get away, you know that?"

She frowns, but lets me kiss her anyway. Her soft, succulent lips make my cock stiff again. I love how she despises my taste and still lets me kiss her. My tongue traces the seam of her mouth and then dips inside to take her, making her gasp for air.

Her hand suddenly shoots from under the robe, away from the blanket, and she throws herself on top of me. I'm thrown back onto the bed as we wrestle for power. Her hand is almost on my gun, and she shrieks with rage. With one hand I hold her down on my chest, and with the other I grab her wrist. She tries to jerk loose, pounding my chest with her fist.

"Let me go, asshole!"

I laugh seeing her struggle. "Jay, how many more times are you going to try this?"

She rages like a madwoman as I pry her fingers off the gun and force them away. She is lying on top of me now, her hands behind her back, her eyes on me like a hawk.

"Why do you keep insisting on fighting me?"

"Because I can," she snaps.

"And then what? If you manage to take my gun, which you won't, then what? Killing me won't help you, I already told you that and you know damn well I'm right. You've seen the others. They will come after you."

"I don't care."

"Even if you know you won't survive?"

She slams her mouth shut and frowns heavily, almost making me laugh.

"I told you, your only chance of survival is with me."

"Yeah, well if I hold the gun, I can protect myself just fine."

I shake my head. "You can't even protect yourself from your own mishaps, let alone me."

"What's that supposed to mean?" She starts wriggling on my chest again. "Let me go!"

"Only if you tell me you won't try it again."

"Fine. I won't. Happy now?"

"No. On the contrary, I'm rarely happy."

"Oh, and why's that?" she jests. "You always seem so fucking happy."

She's still such a child sometimes. It reminds me of long ago when I might still have been a little happy and she was too. When I wasn't as fucked up as I am now.

Sure, I've always been pretty fucked up, but that's normal, considering my family. But now … after what happened to me … yeah, you could say I'm fucked up like no other.

I push her off me and help her sit up. I keep a close eye on her as I release her from my grip. She rubs her wrists, flashing looks at me like she's warning me. It's cute.

"Whatever you're planning, I hope you realize it won't work," I say.

Making fists with her hands, she turns her head away from me.

"You'll never be able to take this gun from me. Hell, even if you could, you'd never be able to shoot me."

She snorts. "Yeah, right."

"It's true. Not because you can't shoot. Oh, I don't doubt that." Her eyes drift back to me, curious as to what I have to say. "I know you can aim at people. You just can't shoot me. You're still a rookie."

"Rookie?" she scoffs.

"Jay, you have no idea what it takes to use a gun."

"Oh, fuck you … I've used a gun plenty of times."

Oh, I've seen her use that gun of hers all right. Like a trembling little girl. "As a means to threaten someone, yes, but have you ever killed someone?"

Her silence tells me enough.

"You haven't, which is why I'm telling you, you have no clue. Holding a gun is one thing. Using it is another. Unless you've experienced that yourself, you won't know how to protect yourself or use it against others."

"Whatever … I don't believe it."

"Trust me, I know. I've killed plenty of people in my life."

"How many?"

"Too many to keep count, but if I had to guess, I'd say over a thousand, give or take."

Her eyes widen as she takes a sharp breath, and she blinks rapidly a couple of times.

"I've been killing people all my life, little bird. It's what I do."

"You can't be serious. You've been killing people all your life? That's bullshit. Sure, adults kill, but kids don't. Everyone starts out innocently."

"Being a kid doesn't mean you're innocent. There's no such thing. Not in this world. Not when you're born into my family." Family. Whatever that means. I hate talking about them. As a matter of fact, I don't even know why I'm talking to her about this. I clear my throat.

She sits up straight, wraps her hands around her legs, and leans her chin on her knees. "So you had family? What were they like? Were they just as monstrous as you are?"

"Worse," I say as I sit up, too. I try to cut it short, but for some reason, she can't seem to let this rest.

"Hmm … I can relate to that."

I chuckle at that comment. She has no fucking idea what she's talking about. "No, not really."

She turns her head toward me and waits. Silence speaks where words are missing. After a while her lips part again. "There is more than one kind of evil in this world." She sighs. "My father being one of them."

"Now I can relate to that," I joke.

It is rather funny, however. She thinks she's safe. She thinks she can talk about him to me. She thinks that just telling a tiny bit, but not the entire story, keeps her secrets hidden. She's wrong. I already know everything.

"Hmm … I guess." She sighs again. "At least you had a family."

Yeah, right. "If you call that a family."

"Did you have a mother?"

"Yeah, and what a bitch she was."

Jay shrugs. "But at least she was there." She turns her head away again. "I never had a mother. She should've been here to protect me."

The words pierce me like a blade.

She never had a mother. That's what she says. It's all she remembers.

I remember differently.

***

TUESDAY, OCTOBER 17TH, 1995

It's like she has super speed. She runs so fast, I can barely keep up with her. Racing like a bird through the sky, she jumps up and down and spreads her arms like an airplane as she storms through the house. Even though I'm older, she's still faster than I am.

Sometimes I hate her for it.

I can never win this game of chase. Somehow she always manages to evade me. That's why I don't like playing tag. Not that I have a choice. She forces me to play with her, and who am I to say no? Besides, my father would tell me the same. Whatever they want, happens.

People in the room adjacent to the stairs are talking loudly. I can't help overhearing words, even though I was specifically told to stay out of it. It's not for children's ears, or so they say. Well, whatever. I don't even want to be part of it.

Her mother's voice trumpets over all others as she curses through the house. I've never heard her curse before. Shrugging, I continue bolting through the rooms. I don't care. I'm not listening anyway. I'm not allowed.

I have my eyes solely on her, because I promised myself I would catch her today. I am going to win this game, and when I do, she'll beg for mercy, because then it's my turn to be the boss.

As I fly out of the room, I forget to look around, and ram straight into some lady's legs. She screams. I fall down to the floor, trying to grasp her leg. It's too late; her feet are already slipping down the staircase. And then the tumbling begins.

Each thud is another bone shattered. *Thud. Thud. Thud. Thud.* Down the stairs she goes.

Time stands still. My eyes widen in shock, tears forming in my eyes as I scramble up from the floor. I peer over the edge of the steps. A body lies on the floor down below, her dark brown hair flowing richly onto the wood. Her eyes are on me, but they are vacant. Blood pools underneath her.

The girl comes to stand beside me, her jaw dropping, her eyes tearing up. And then the shrieking begins.

***

Jay

FRIDAY, AUGUST 16TH, 2013. 6:00 P.M.

I cough and feel my body heating up again. I know this feeling all too well. My body needs drugs, and I hate the fact that my stash is gone. The urge to find some drug, anything, is strong.

"Don't," X says as he looks at me from across the room.

"What?"

"I know what you want."

"And what is that, exactly?" I say, frowning.

"Drugs."

Shit. Is it that obvious? The withdrawal must be clearly visible this time. Dammit.

"I'm not going to let you take that anymore."

I gasp. "What? But you can't. I *need* it!" I yell, stampeding toward him.

He stands tall and proud in front of me with that fucking infuriating smirk on his face. "You will get through this withdrawal and then you will no longer need them."

In my anger, I try to push him aside, but he grabs my wrists. "Look what it does to you." He leans forward. "You become a raging woman just because you need your sniff. You're not in control. The drugs are. Time to change that."

"Fuck you ..." I hiss. I don't want to admit it, but he's right. I need this, and I hate it. But this withdrawal is worse than anything else I can imagine.

"The first few days are the worst, but you will get used to it."

"I can't," I say in desperation.

"Shhh ..." X places a finger on my lip. "You will learn to deal with it. I will be going now, and you'll get some rest. Go to sleep for a while. You're tired, I can tell, and the withdrawal is taking its toll."

"I don't ..." I say, suppressing a yawn. Fuck that.

He chuckles. "Being stubborn won't get you

anything, Jay. You will not get drugs from me, and you will not leave this hotel room. Now, you can choose … behave and you can roam freely through the room, or suffer the consequences of your mischief. It's your choice, but as you might have seen, my discipline is not to be taken lightly." He tips his head downwards. "Sleep. Eat. Clean yourself and dress nicely. I might reward you if you do." He releases my wrist and I immediately take a step back. I hate that he wants to control me, but at the same time eating and sleeping seem so very tempting. He's right when it comes to my body … it'd be better if I took it easy to get this all out of my system. Still, my brain is telling me to go find the drugs. So conflicting.

I turn around and walk to the window, chewing my cheek. I wonder if what he says is true. If he'll be easier on me if I do as he says. I'll be treading into dangerous territory if I obey. It means the possibility of losing my own voice. Losing my strength and will to fight him. Am I strong enough to survive such a thing? If my survival is dependent on him and his desires, I should find a way to use it to my advantage.

I peer out the window, looking for Hannah's body, but there's nothing there. No body. No blood. There's not a trace of her left. It scares me, because it means X could discard me just as easily.

I close the curtain. I won't let that happen. I'll make him love me, so that even if I don't obey, he won't be able to kill me. And then I've won.

X is tying his shoes and buttoning his shirt. On the floor right below him is a suitcase filled with God knows what. I don't think I even want to know. All I want to know is how long he'll be gone so I know how much time I have to prepare myself for when he returns.

"How long until you come back?" I ask.

"As long as it takes."

"As what takes?"

He laughs. "You sound like a wife." He glances at me over his shoulder. "I do not have to explain myself to you."

"I know. I was just curious." I clear my throat and step toward him. If I'm ever going to start this game, it'll be now. "I wonder what you do with that gun of yours every time you are gone."

Silent, he turns around toward me and looks down upon me as I lift a finger. He keeps a keen eye on me as I straighten his tie. He watches me meticulously, like he still doesn't trust me. Of course, that wouldn't be the smartest thing to do, but it is in my benefit to gain his trust.

"A gun only has one purpose, Jay."

"It has two. One is to kill people. The second is to have power over them. Which one are you exerting tonight?"

He places his hand on mine and nudges it away from his tie. "Whichever is necessary to get the point across."

"And what point is that?"

He smiles. "Nice try. Now, you'll wait right here like a good girl until I come back."

"And why would I, exactly?" I taunt, raising an eyebrow. "Convince me why it's in my best interest to stay with you."

His eyes narrow. "Do you think you have a choice?"

"I do when it comes to fighting you."

He shoots me an annoyed glance. "Very funny, little bird."

"No, I mean it. I want to know why they're after me. Why you went after me but didn't kill me."

"Yet."

I roll my eyes. "Yet."

"Keep going, you might make me do it anyway."

I ignore him. "Why are they different? Why wouldn't they let me live if you have?"

He walks toward me, making me back up. Each time I take a step back, he comes closer again. "Someone wants you dead, Jay. Not just me, but the person who sent us."

"Is that what you're doing every time you leave the door? You didn't kill me, so now they're after you? That's it, right?"

A grumble comes from deep within his chest. "You have no fucking clue. I'm going after the ones who put this mark on your head."

I blink a couple of times. I did not expect him to

say that. Is it really true? "Why?"

"Because you are mine, and they are trying to take what's mine. I won't allow it."

I swallow when he walks closer.

"And who is it then? I must know them, right? I mean, what have I done that could make someone want to kill me?" I ask, still stepping back.

When I reach the wall, I'm trapped. X plants his fist on the wall and towers above me, his nostrils flaring. I've clearly pissed him off with all my questions, but I won't stop. I need to know. I will find out why this is happening and I will make it stop.

"You do not want this, little bird. Trust me on this."

"I want to know," I say with a soft voice.

A snort escapes his mouth. He shakes his head and looks down at the floor.

"What? Who is it then? Is it one of the drug dealers? Someone at the club? What am I not seeing here?"

"Everything," he mutters.

"Everything?"

The look in his eye when he lifts his head again, so volatile, pierces my soul. "Tell me, what exactly do you remember, Jay?"

I frown. "What do you mean?"

"I mean exactly what I say. What do you remember?"

I raise an eyebrow, still confused. "You mean about

the club?"

"Before that," he growls, impatient.

"Before the club? Well … I think I was on the streets … I was constantly high, so I don't remember a lot about it."

"Do you remember anything from before that time?"

His question has me confused. Not because I don't understand, but because I truly don't remember. I feel lost for a second. My brain is working overtime, trying to figure out what is going on, but nothing comes through. All I know is that I was in the streets, hustling, selling my body, and then I was taken into the club thanks to Hannah. Focusing on his scar, I drift into my memories and find little to nothing. Except a bed … beeping … blinding lights … someone in a doctor's outfit.

"I was in a hospital."

"And?"

"And what?" I don't know what else there is to add.

He chuckles. "See, this is what I don't understand. You seem to be under the impression your life started about seven years ago."

"No, I'm not! I know I had a childhood … somewhere." I clear my throat, pushing back the impending tears. I don't want to think about it. I don't want to feel it. I don't want to know that I don't remember. It means that I've been a fool.

"What *do* you remember?" he asks. I flinch when

his hand reaches for my face, but when he suddenly starts caressing me I'm even more confused. I don't understand why. None of it makes sense.

"I remember a big house … cars, lots of cars … people asking questions … and my father, yeah, he was grumpy all the time."

"You remember bits and pieces. Not the whole story."

I look up into his eyes, horror settling in my chest, running deep into every pore in my body. I stand frozen, my fingertips suddenly cold to the bone.

"I don't remember," I mutter. It's silent for a few seconds. Then I ask, "But how do you know that?"

He shrugs. "Some things are better left forgotten."

***

X

FRIDAY, AUGUST 16TH, 2013. 8:10 P.M.

Jay is in the hotel room, alone. She didn't want me to leave, but I had to. I couldn't keep telling her things she should've known herself. Besides, her not knowing anything makes it easier for me. I told her she needed to eat and catch some sleep before I come back. She'll need the energy to take what I'm going to give her.

Besides, it's not like she'll try to escape again. I know she's seen what I can do, and it terrifies her. She knows I'll find her, wherever she goes. Death lurks at every corner. For her to be safe, she must remain in my room, where she'll be waiting for my return. My key is safely tucked in my pocket as I drive toward the house I'm meant to be at tonight. Yes, tonight will be the night I put a bullet through the head of the one who gave me the assignment to kill her.

Long, long ago I knew this asshole who worked for the same people I used to be in the service of. The same fucker who gave us the assignment to kill Jay. Unfortunately for him, I'm not in their service anymore. He probably still is. That motherfucker will pay for his insolence with every last drop of his blood.

I race toward the address that was in the text message Antonio showed me. My tires screech as they slip through the streets and make a turn. Biting my lip, I contemplate what toy I'm going to use this time. I brought my entire box of goodies with me, just for the sake of it. This bastard deserves every fucking thing inside it.

The guy lives in some trashy house in downtown San Antonio. If you can call it a house. To me, it resembles a dumpster more than a house. It's shoddy, badly maintained, has a crooked iron fence that's easily bendable, and a botched-up pick-up. Totally not the sort of guy I'd expect to be in service of *them*.

I guess priorities have changed over the years.

Luxury has made place for simple-minded folks who can be discarded easily. Quite a smart move, actually. It's untraceable. Well, most of the time. Sometimes there are people who get their hands on secret documents that can't survive the light of day. People like me who go after these secrets and burn them to the ground.

I park my car a few blocks away and jump out with my suitcase in hand. With a rigid face I walk through the neighborhood, checking each house for possible witnesses. If anyone is here watching now, they will be dead by morning. For their sake, I hope they aren't.

As I reach the house, I adjust my tie and knock on the door. It takes a while for him to open the door. It creaks as a scruffy bearded man slowly opens it a bit, peeking through the slit with squinty eyes.

When he looks up at my one working eye, his own eyes widen.

He tries to slam the door, but I place my foot inside, causing it to jam. I pull out my gun and hold it to his abdomen.

"Unlock it now or I'll blow you to bits."

"The fu—"

I push the gun further into his potbelly. "Now."

His lips tremble as he takes off the chain door guard and I burst inside. Silently closing the door behind me, I keep my gun on him at all times. He's walking backwards, tripping over a stack of porn magazines lying next to his chair. He struggles to get up so I haul him to his feet, the gun pushed into his meat.

"Al John … It's been a long time," I muse. "Listen up, fatty, I'll give you one chance to answer my questions. Fail or lie and I'll blow off a few fingers. If you don't listen, I might resort to cutting you up. Are we clear?"

He nods frantically, shrieking like a little girl when I push him toward the table in the middle of his crooked house.

"Sit," I say as I point at one of the plastic chairs. With a swallow he scoots it backwards and drops down onto it, almost breaking the legs.

"W-what d-do you w-want from m-me?" he stutters.

I smile and rub my hand with my gun while he sits there, staring at it.

"I haven't d-done anything."

Wrong. Words.

I shoot his finger off.

He screams, holding out his hands in total panic as his finger is blown to bits.

"Don't lie to me."

He tries to get up from the chair to run, but I flick my gun, making him stop. "Tut-tut. If you get up, you lose your foot," I say calmly.

He slams his ass right back down in his chair, his eyes frantically searching for a way out of this house. His hand is shaking and his face is so red it looks like a radish; red forehead, pale mouth. Like he's about to throw up. Pathetic.

The man leans back in his chair, clamping his hand close to his chest as he breathes heavy breaths. Tiny, pained moans escape his mouth. With one hand I grab the chair in front of me and scoot it back. He swallows again, his chubby throat shaking along. Abhorrent.

"Tell me another lie and I'll do more than shoot off a finger or two."

"What do you w-want?" Al says.

"You know damn well what I want," I say, cocking my head.

He shakes vigorously. "N-no. Please …"

Lunging forward, I grab his head and slam it into the table. "Head, meet table. Table, meet head." He sputters while I shove his face down a bit more. Rolling my eye, I release him from my grip and sit back down.

I raise my gun and point it at him. "Now, ready to spill?"

He squeals. "N-no, no, please! Do you want money? I can give you money. Anything you want."

Leaning forward, I pull out a knife from my back pocket and hold it close to his throat. "I don't want your fucking money, you dipshit. Did you or did you not order us to kill a girl named Jay?"

His eyes widen as he whimpers and gazes at me.

My smile is gone. "Answer me."

"I didn't—"

Seizing his arm, I lurch forward and pound his still unscathed hand down onto the table, jamming my knife through it.

He screams in pain and spits out slime. His head looks like it's about to explode. This man can't even handle a scratch. Pathetic. Hypocrite too, because he was so eager to hurt another human.

"Shut up," I say as he keeps on screaming. "Unless you're into more pain."

With tears in his eyes he answers. "I didn't w-want to do it," he mutters. "I was forced."

"By who?"

"I don't know …"

He sniffs and looks at me with big eyes like he's so fucking innocent. Of course he is. Men like him are despicable. They do something horrible, knowing full well what the consequences are, and still they try to get away with it once someone finds out. Low-life scum of the earth.

Regardless of the fact that he's a client of the organization and that he's the one behind the placement of Jay on the hit list, he needs to be punished.

So I pick up my briefcase from the floor and place it down on the table. The locks click, making him jolt in his seat as I open the lid. A variety of toys lie inside: a battery-operated screwdriver, some nails and a hammer, a pair of scissors, a bottle of acid, a flask of non-lethal poison, a short rope, a canister of petrol and some matches, a few of my favorite knives, an icepick, a hook, and a pair of pliers.

I take out the acid and screw open the lid. The man starts to wail. I pay no attention to it. Before he has a chance to get up, I squirt some into his eye. He screams and yelps, blood pouring from his eye as it dissolves.

"My eye!" he yells.

"Ah, who cares? You don't need your eyes. You have your mouth to tell all those lies for you anyway."

"Fuck you! You'll pay for this." He slams his fist onto the table. Not amused by his threat, I pick up the icepick and hammer and ram it into his hand, pinning him to the table. He screams some more.

"You can scream all you want, but it's not going to help you."

"Fuck off!" He lashes out at me from under the table, kicking with all his might. So I put a bullet in his toe.

"Stop fucking moving!"

He screeches some more, causing me to roll my eye and sigh. "Are you done yet?" I ask after a while. "I'm getting bored of you quickly." I yawn. "You don't want that to happen, trust me."

"P-please ..." he stammers.

"Tell me who gave you the assignment."

"I d-don't know his n-name."

"Bullshit!" I pick up a knife and jam it into the table beside his fingers. Whimpers escape his mouth.

"It's t-the truth."

I narrow my eyes and purse my lips. "Are you sure

about that?"

"Yes! I s-swear. I d-don't know his n-name."

"How did they contact you?"

"It's in the file." His eyes dart toward the cabinet across the room. "In the t-top l-left drawer."

Scooting my chair back, I flick the knife in his hand, causing him severe pain. A smirk appears on my face.

"Don't move a muscle," I say, laughing at my own morbid joke.

I walk to the cabinet and open the drawer. Inside is an envelope and the note is still inside.

Taking it out and opening it sends cold shivers down my spine. I knew it. I fucking knew it. It was him, all along.

Crumpling the paper in my hand, I shove it in my pocket and take out a packet of cigarettes and my lighter. "We're gonna have a long night ahead of us, Al…"

"Passion brings us just as close to insanity as killing does.." – Notes of X

CHAPTER 14

Jay

FRIDAY, AUGUST 16ᵀᴴ, 2013. 10:12 P.M.

For the first time in days I slept like a log. My body and mind were so tired they didn't need more than a few seconds to shut off. I must say that this bed is quite comfortable. This room must be expensive to have all these luxuries. X probably gets all that money from killing people. I wonder if he stays here often or if he moves constantly; if he has a home.

Whatever the case, I won't find out by dawdling. If I want to discover more about him, worm my way into his heart, I need to please him. As much as it still disgusts me, I know I rely on him to keep me from harm. I saw those guys that tried to kill us … me … they'd kill me in a heartbeat. X hesitated, which means he has double motives. He wants me, and I have to use it against him. Making him desire me is the first step; betraying him is the final step.

Besides, X is going to kill the ones who are after me. I might seem like a cold-hearted bitch, but I'm actually rooting for him. Their deaths mean that X no longer has an excuse to keep me prisoner. My cage is my safety. When the enemy outside has been vanquished, the cage is no longer needed and I will seek my freedom. I think X knows this, so he wants me broken and submissive before he's finished the job, just to make me stay.

Oh, I will be what he desires … but only until it's no longer needed, and then I'll escape.

I get out of bed and open the closet. The cleaning lady placed a stack of fresh clothes there this evening when I was still asleep. I pick up a velvety see-through babydoll and stockings. There's a matching pair of high heels on the bottom. Rolling my eyes, I put it on and look at myself through the broken mirror in the bathroom. Without makeup I look horrible, but there's nothing here I can put on except some red lipstick that's on the shelf. So I pick it up and smear it on my lips. It's an ugly color, but it'll have to do. I'll just have to work my magic to seduce him. Oh, I'll wind him around my finger. Just wait … he wants a twisted girl?

He'll get a twisted girl.

I take a few sips of water to make sure I'm hydrated enough to be able to go without for a while. I have a hunch I won't be able to drink for a while when he comes home. Home. Such a funny word. This is not home. I shouldn't even allow the word to come into my head.

I step back into the hotel room and take a deep breath. In the middle of the floor I sit down on the back of my heels, my hands in my lap. This is a posture I am familiar with, but don't use often. It's a sign of submission; something not a lot of men crave, but X is an exception. Waiting for him like this will make him weak for me. At least, I hope.

Patiently I wait until the lock turns and the door is opened. Holding my breath, I look up at him. For a moment he stands in the doorframe, observing me. A hint of surprise flashes in his eye, but it's quickly replaced by wariness. With soft steps he treads inside and closes the door behind him, his eye still locked on mine. His hands drop beside him. Only then do I spot the red stains on his shirt and hands. His nails are black and crimson and his knuckles are bruised. Oh God. I wonder who he tortured now and why.

I swallow away the fear as he takes a few steps forward. Anticipating his approach, I close my eyes. But his hand never lands on my skin. My breath falters as I open my eyes again only to watch him walk into the bathroom. I turn my head and watch him wash his hands, the cold water rinsing away the dirtiness. He grabs a scrubbing brush and scrubs his nails and hands with soap. His teeth are clenched, groans of annoyance escaping his mouth as he throws the brush into the sink. I can hear him taking long, deep breaths through his nose. His nostrils flare as he rolls up his sleeves and looks at himself in the mirror. And then he just stands there, watching himself as his hand drifts to his eye and touches his burned skin. For a split second I feel remorse. Pity. But when he shifts his eye to me, it's gone as quickly as it came.

His heavy steps make my heart thump out of my chest. He looks at me, his eye running over my curves. As he stands in front of me, looking down upon me like some king of the universe, I calm down by reminding myself why I'm doing this. It's the only way to ever escape his grasp. Make him need me, fall for me, and even love me. And then he won't be able to deny me my freedom anymore.

Tapping the floor, his feet are right beside me, making me nervous. "What's this?" he says with a low voice that rumbles through my ears.

"You said I would be safe if I was obedient."

He cocks his head, a half-smile appearing on his face. "I did say that."

"And that you wouldn't hurt me," I add softly, pinching my own fingers, hoping it'll be okay.

He starts taking off his tie, each meticulous slip of his fingers making me more uneasy. "Do you want to be punished?" he asks.

"No."

Suddenly, his hand wraps around my hair, jerking my head up. The roots are pulled so hard it hurts.

"Say that again."

"No, sir," I say.

He releases me. "I think you do."

"No, sir, why would I?" I ask, biting my lip from anxiety.

"You love the pain," he says, flicking the tie in his hand. "Your pussy loves my hand coming down on your flesh. Don't you deny it, you whore."

I shudder at that word.

He leans in, cups my face and purses his lips. "Don't like that word, huh?"

"I'm not a whore," I mutter.

"Yes, you are. You don't fuck for love. You fuck for money. For drugs. For freedom. You're a dirty little whore." His finger traces the seam of my lip, pushing further with each stroke until he's inside. "Suck."

One look at the gun glinting in its holster is all it takes for me to do as he says. I suck on his finger so hard his eye rolls into the back of his head. I can see his cock growing in his pants. When he takes his finger from my mouth, he grabs my face with both his hands and smashes his lips onto mine. He's hard and rough as he laps me up like there's no tomorrow. His licks are furious and fast and uncontrollable. Like a wild beast he takes my mouth. I can barely breathe.

He plunders my mouth with his violent kisses, and I let him. His lips are eager and taste like strong alcohol. They entice me. Even if I don't want to feel anything, I still do. These lips—I remember them.

He stops as I gasp for air. A wicked smile rests on his face as he wipes his lips with his hand and smears the lipstick across my face. "You're my little whore."

After he's done he stands up again, his pants tented. He walks around me in circles, wrapping his tie around his hand like a boxing glove. It hurts just looking at it. "Face down on the floor," he commands.

I lower my head and hands, but can't seem to reach it.

"On. The. Floor."

I put my hands beside my body and place my head sideways on the floor. I hate this position, because it gives him a full view of me. That, and being face-down on the floor sucks. Somehow the wood smells like cum. I shiver.

"So here you are, waiting to be tamed. Offering yourself freely to me. Begging for my cock." He pauses. "You're such a naughty girl, thinking you can seduce me like that. You just want to taunt me into spanking you again. You like having your skin red, don't you? Did you see the marks on your flesh when you dressed up for me? Did you?" X's hand comes down on my ass in a swift, hot flash. I squeal in both pain and desire. His hand sets not only my ass on fire, but my pussy too. After the first hit, he gently caresses the cheek before slapping again, this time a little closer to my pussy. When his finger grazes my folds, a short moan releases from deep inside me.

"Answer me."

"No, sir." I must admit, I haven't looked at it in the mirror. I avoided it on purpose. Looking at it makes it real, and when it's real it hurts, so I refuse.

He makes clacking sounds with his tongue. "We'll definitely do something about that."

Whack! I jolt up from the sudden hot flash on my ass. He hit me, but it wasn't with his hand. As I look up, the tie dangles between his fingers. He used it as a whip.

"Ass up, little bird."

I push my knees toward my chest, perching my ass up as high as I can. I tell myself I can do this. I can let him take my body without handing over my soul. When the tie hits my pussy, I suspect I won't be able to. I hiss from the stinging and the tie being slid up and down my sensitive parts. He's toying with me, and he knows I dislike the thought of surrendering. I'm fighting with him, his mind against mine. This is not a struggle of power; this is a struggle of will. He won't break me. I won't allow it.

"Such a wet pussy," he muses. I can hear him sink to his knees. "It begs to be filled. Would you like that, Jay? Do you want me to fill that pussy?"

I don't answer, because he wouldn't like my response.

The smack that follows has my ass shaking. "Say you are a filthy slut, Jay. Say it."

"I'm a filthy slut," I mutter.

"Louder." He jerks the tie from my slit and whacks it on my ass cheek. "I won't ask again."

"I'm a filthy slut!"

"I know you are. Your slick hole is waiting to be pumped. Tell me how much you want it. Tell me how badly you want my cock."

"I want your cock, sir."

"Hmmm …" He groans. I feel his legs push up against mine, and then his tented pants. His cock pushes against my pussy while he slides the tie through my slit and takes it out. It's an odd, but gratifying sensation.

"Is this body mine?" he says.

"This body is yours, sir," I murmur, trying to keep my sarcastic voice at bay.

Splaying his fingers on top off my ass, he spreads my cheeks. "Who does this ass belong to?"

"You."

The slap that follows stings so badly I squeal and bite my tongue.

"Say that again."

"You, sir. It's yours."

"That's right, and this pussy is mine too, and do you know what I do with things that are mine?" he says. His fingers hook around my G-string, tugging it down my ass, exposing my flesh. He moans with approval. "I take them and use them for my pleasure."

Without warning, his finger dips inside my pussy, taking me by surprise. Drawing circles inside, he pushes in and out, heating me up to my core.

"So wet for me ..." he murmurs, pushing another finger inside. I feel him inside me, feel him claiming me with his fingers. His other hand grabs a firm hold of my ass as he drives his fingers inside me over and over again. His strokes become increasingly fast, making me delirious with need. I've told myself to accept the fact that this is happening; I already made peace with that. I just need to make peace with the fact that I'm actually starting to like it. When I don't struggle, X is much more lenient, and it becomes much less painful for me to endure. I shouldn't fight it. I'm in this now ... might as well enjoy it.

He retracts his fingers in a flash. For a moment I'm actually disappointed, even though I hate feeling that way. But then he slides his fingers down my folds and finds my clit. I gasp. I think I just died.

"This little clit of yours has been throbbing so badly, hasn't it?" he says. "It's swollen and wet for my touch. You want this so badly. Your treacherous body wants me more than you can handle."

He flicks my nub with fervor. His finger is rough and big as he puts pressure on it, just the kind I like. He knows exactly how to make me squirm. Especially when he lifts his other hand and slaps my ass again. With each whack, I falter, trying to keep my legs upright, but his hand is still on my privates, supporting me, lifting me up again. With his dexterous finger X keeps stroking me, keeps smacking my ass until it's numb and tears sting my eyes. He groans at my squeals.

"Don't come, little bird. If you come, I will punish you. That is not a threat, it's a promise."

I'm having trouble staying in the moment. It's such a mixture of sensations; my clit is being teased until the brink of ecstasy, while my ass is enduring a relentless assault.

Then, all of a sudden, he's gone. I'm left with wantonness and growing need.

I hear his footsteps as he comes to my face and goes to his knees. Grabbing my hair, he jerks my head and says, "Open your mouth."

When I do, he stuffs the tie inside.

"Taste yourself, Jay," he says, licking his lips. "Keep that in there or you'll be in trouble." I grumble through the cloth, but it sounds more like gargling. Tasting myself is strange, yet arousing. He steps away again, back to my behind, and I'm left nervous, wondering what he's going to do now.

When I feel his finger stroke my folds again, I moan. He groans with me as he dips in and out of me, smearing my wetness on my skin. Then he disappears again.

A zipper is pulled. A packet is ripped and thrown aside. Something is rolled out. A condom. "Are you hungry for more, little bird?"

"Yes ... oh, God, yes," I moan feverishly into the tie. I'm lost. Gone from this world. My body has been taken and still I experience pleasure like never before. When the tip of his cock teases my entrance I'm done for.

"Beg for my cock ..." he says with a dark, low voice. "Beg for it like your life depends on it."

It does. My life depends on his satisfaction. I spit out the tie. The words roll over my tongue like sugar. "Please ... give me your cock."

"How much do you want it?"

The warmth of his tip pushing against my pussy sends me over the edge. "I want it badly," I whimper. I've betrayed my own morals. I'm not okay with it, but it's inescapable. He has me, my body, my freedom, but he will never have my heart. This is only lust.

He lets out a short laugh. "Good girl, finally admitting to your desires. I'll reward you for it. I'm going to fuck your brains out." He smacks my ass again. "You've been so fucking naughty, fucking all these clients of yours during your time at the club. I'm not going to take any chances with you. Protection will have to do for now, but you *will* visit a doctor soon and you *will* be tested. And then the real fucking will begin." A groan-like laugh escapes his mouth. "But first I'll fill up this greedy pussy of mine."

When he pushes his cock inside I moan loudly. His cock is thick and throbbing as he enters me, pushing further, painfully slow. I can feel the ridges of his piercings rub my inner walls, a sensation so delicious I moan. He's inside me completely, and I love the feeling it gives me. So full. So satiated. Just what I needed right now, but totally did not want. At least, not like this. That's what I'm telling myself.

He is slow and steady, just like he promised. Each time he thrusts the piercings add an extra layer of sensitivity, which sends me into delirium. I want to beg him to ride me faster, to pump me with all he's got, and to shoot his load quickly, but I know it'll only pleasure him if I start begging. He told me from the beginning he'd take it slow. He said he'd make me beg; he was right. This is so agonizingly slow, like he's savoring the moment. Like he wants me to be on the verge of exploding. My orgasm is under his control, and he's loving it.

Suddenly, he grabs my hands and pulls them back. His thrusting becomes harder as he uses my arms as reins. I'm already on the edge when he drives in deep and hard. A loud moan escapes my mouth as his cock pulsates against my walls. And then he retracts again, slowly, all the way to the tip before slamming into me once more. He repeats this over and over again, pushing me toward bliss.

"Don't you fucking come until I say you can," he growls, slamming his cock back inside. "This pussy is mine and it'll come when I say so."

"Please ..." I say, moaning as he drives into me.

He lets go of my hands again, dropping them to the

floor. Instead, he grabs my ass, using it as a handle while he fucks me senseless. A quick but harsh whack and I'm off. I can't stop. The wave comes and comes and shatters me completely. I can't hold it back; it's that powerful. My legs shake as I fall apart from his thrusting.

All of a sudden, he pulls out of me and slaps my ass so hard my legs collapse underneath me.

"I told you not to come."

"I'm sorry, sir," I say.

He grabs my hair and jerks back my head. "You'll pay for that. You need to be disciplined."

"Please, no," I whimper.

Suddenly, a slap to my pussy rips me from my still lingering orgasm.

"Whose pussy is this?" he growls.

"Yours, sir."

"Then it'd better do what I say or this will be a hard lesson to learn."

My eyes widen. Shit. This is bad. Why couldn't I stop it? Goddammit, I've never had this before.

I hear him take off the condom. He steps in front of my face, grabs my hair again, and says, "Open your mouth wide."

The more my lips part, the closer he comes. His cock is right in my face, pushing against my lips, greedy to get in. I'm hesitant, but I know that if I refuse, I'll only be worse off. So I let him enter my mouth.

However, he's not slow this time. He shoves his

cock inside, making me gag instantly.

"Take it," he says gruffly. "Suck my cock like the little whore you are."

He pulls it back again, giving me only one second to breathe before plunging back in. He forces himself inside, over and over again. His piercings feel like cold, hard steel as they bump against the back of my throat. Sometimes X holds his position deep inside my throat, causing me to choke. Just before I sputter, he pulls back out. He slaps his cock against my face and jams it back into my mouth.

"Bad girls don't get cock in their pussy. Bad girls get face-fucked," he growls.

My eyes fill with tears as he grabs a hold of my head and thrusts his cock into my mouth again. Red lipstick smudges create rings around his cock. His pre-cum seeps into my mouth, the saltiness arousing me against my will.

"Lick it," he demands.

I swirl my tongue as much as I can, even though his cock prevents me from moving. I've had them deep before, but not by someone like him. This feels like he's enjoying the fact that he's using me for his own pleasure. That's why I don't understand why my pussy is still throbbing.

"I'm going to fill up that filthy mouth of yours with my cum."

His dirty words cause a strange mixture of emotions in me. This heavy fucking is so intense, so surreal, it pulls me away from reality. The smell of pants as my face is jammed against it while he pumps his cock into my mouth, his dark eye looking down at my face, the zinging skin on my red ass, the salty pre-cum dripping down my throat as he fucks my mouth; it's all-consuming.

He holds my head in place as he fucks my mouth, pushing me to the limit. My breaking point is near, but he doesn't stop. He pushes and shoves and takes me like no other. He takes from me what he desires with no holds barred. I am at his complete mercy. His cock pulsates on my tongue as he forces me all the way down to the base.

"Fuck!" he growls, and then the throbbing begins. He groans as he thrusts into my mouth once more, shooting his load. I can feel the cum spurt out of his cock and land in the back of my throat. With his hands on the back of my head, I can't move back, but I can't breathe either.

"Hold it. Hold it," he says, filling me up with his cum. "Swallow."

I do my best, but with his cock in my mouth it's hard. Eventually, I manage to take it all down. After letting out a big breath, he pulls his cock from my mouth. I gasp for air. X slaps me with his cock and wipes the excess cum on my cheeks.

"Eat it all, little bird." He only lets me catch my breath for a second or two before shoving his cock back inside my mouth.

"Clean it."

I lick his cock until he is satisfied. I feel used, and at the same time a flame ignited inside my core the moment I felt his orgasm. It's as if I did my job, like it's exactly what was supposed to happen. When he says, "Good girl," I know for sure.

X steps back and looks down upon me. His hand reaches for my face. I fight the instinct to lean away, because I know that's not in my best interest. His finger nudges me underneath my chin, directing me to stand up. "Come with me."

And then he does something that astonishes me. His fingers trail down my arm and reach for my hand. With his smoldering eyes focused on me he latches onto me, entwining his fingers through mine. This moment is intimate in a way I haven't experienced in a long while. It takes my breath away as he leans in and presses a kiss on my neck. His lips drag up to my ear, and then he whispers, "You are my possession, my fixation, my enslavement. You're bound to me forever."

"Pain and suffering grants us unimaginable power." – Notes of X

CHAPTER 15

X

TUESDAY, AUGUST 20TH, 2013. 09:18 A.M.

The razorblade is blunt, but it'll have to do. I've ordered a new one from the assistant I have here in the hotel, but she's rather slow in getting her shopping list done. While shaving, I contemplate whether I'm going to give her another chance or kill her and get a new one. Of course she can't quit; that would mean she could talk. Nobody talks about me. I do not exist. Therefore, they do not exist either.

When I'm done I rinse the razorblade and put it down. Noise in the bedroom alerts me. I step aside and look. Jay is still tied to the bed, and when she sees me looking, she raises a cocky eyebrow. I used a rope this time, but it seems to do the trick. She hasn't tried to escape in a while, but I keep expecting it to happen. Having her tied up relaxes me, because I know she can't escape and be killed. For some reason that thought angers me. I wanted her dead myself more than anything, but now that I have her, I don't want anyone else to kill her. That right is mine alone.

Except, I don't just want that anymore either. I want her completely. Her body. Her soul. Her mind. I want to do with it as I wish. To do the things I never could when …

I sigh. It was such a long time ago. I don't even remember what it was like to claim her without having to chain her up. Of course, I've always been into the kinky stuff. She used to be into it too. If I try hard enough, she might remember and learn to appreciate it.

But the way she's looking at me now, with annoyance and boredom, it makes me feel abominable. I am not just that monster. I'm also a man who knows someone like her needs pleasure and fun in order to feel appreciated. And when she feels appreciated, she might be more inclined to submit to me, which is all that I desire. I want to see her offer her heart to me, willingly, and for that to happen, she must crave all of me, even the blackest pits of my soul.

I smile and shake my head, stepping back to the faucet to wash my face. Soul. What a load of nonsense.

As if I even have one.

All I crave is her. All I want is her, completely. I know she's only giving it to me because her life's on the line, but I want it to be more than that. I will make it so that she'll only ever want me, even when she can choose not to. That even if I were to free her, she'd still come back to me, no matter what. Utter devotion.

As I lift my head the mirror is my sudden opponent. I watch the beads of water roll down my face, across the hideous mark that covers the place my real eye used to be. I'm taken aback by the confrontation. The mirror shows me the broken man I do not wish to see. The man who lost it all because of the girl in the adjacent room.

That day was detrimental. A decision that never should've been made. Forbidden fruits that shouldn't have been plucked. That day I was forced to become the monster I am today.

***

MONDAY, JANUARY 23ᴿᴰ, 2009

For a month I have listened to the beeping of the machine keeping me alive. The constant sound is a painful reminder that I'm still here in this world. That everything they've done to me was real. That I'm really in a hospital, lying in a stone-cold bed, watching the world pass me by. I'm constantly in pain. My face burns and itches, but I can't scratch. A bandage covers everything. I'll never get used to this.

I'd prefer death over this place, because if there's a hell on earth, it's right here.

SATURDAY, MARCH 28TH, 2009

The doctors tell me it could take years to recover, but I don't allow myself that much time. Even with only one eye I will make it work, somehow. I will recover quickly and reclaim what's been taken from me: my dignity.

Today is the day they take off my bandage. The careful unwrapping makes me furious, because I'd much rather rip it off and be done with it. I want to see what's happened. I want to see what those fuckers did to my face. When he's finally done, I pick up the mirror on my cabinet and hold it in front of me. Terror flows through me, an inferno of rage setting my veins on fire. My eye is gone, my face destroyed. What's left is a vicious remnant of their attack. Loose skin and horrid scars running all the way up to my skull. My hair is split in half as it no longer grows on the burned skin. All that's left is ruin and misery.

I've become a monster.

I was burned to ashes, along with my soul, but I will rise and make them pay.

FRIDAY, JUNE 19TH, 2009

It'll take some time to get used to the fake eye they just installed. I keep looking at it in the mirror. Somehow it looks like I'm staring at a completely different person. Not just physically, but mentally too. I've changed. Not for the better.

I got into contact with an old partner of mine, who I know through my family: Antonio. He told me he could introduce me to the organization he works for. I'll be an assassin for hire with them. I've already said I'll do it. I want them to train me, teach me how to kill an assassin just like me. They'll train me for years to come and I'll earn some good money working for them. But I won't stop until I'm the fastest, most skillful killer alive. And then I'll murder them all.

***

TUESDAY, AUGUST 20TH, 2013. 09:25 A.M.

I smash the mirror to bits.

Over and over again until there is nothing left and blood seeps from my pores. I don't feel any pain, just anger. I am wasting valuable time here. After I interrogated Al, I thought about killing the one who's behind all this. However, I decided not to. Instead, I want to make his life miserable. And I just happen to have the perfect idea …

"What's happening in there?" Jay yells.

I grab the trashcan and shove the pieces of the mirror inside. Then I walk out the door and show her my bloody hands. Her eyes widen.

"See this? It's because you took the tape off the mirror," I say.

She makes a face, riddled with guilt. Good. Guilt is the first step toward pleasing someone, and I want to be pleased badly.

"It's quite despicable to make a man see his own scars."

"It's also quite despicable for you to keep me tied up."

I smile. "Touché."

"Even though you said I would gain more freedom if I did what you asked."

I walk back into the bathroom and rinse my hands under the water. I think about it for a second. If I give her a reason to be more grateful and content, she might be easier to handle, which is a plus considering what I'm going to do when I have my plan ready.

I step out of the bathroom and stand in front of the bed. "All right. If you will behave I will take you to lunch."

She tempts me with those daring eyes of hers. Crawling onto the bed, I move on top of her. Her breath falters as my lips touch her belly. My tongue darts out to trace a line all the way up to her chest. Her chest rises but doesn't fall as I reach her tits. She's wearing nothing but panties, and although I would love to ravage her right now, a promise is a promise. Besides, I'm getting quite hungry myself.

I raise my head to her eyelevel and lean in, licking my lip. Her eyes follow my tongue desperately. I wait, tentatively moving closer and closer, until my lips are on top of hers. My kiss is greedy, because I need to taste her. Her mouth is open, ready to receive me. Not long ago she refused to give me what was mine, but now … now she is ready. She lets my tongue in as I probe her mouth with eagerness. I lick the roof of her mouth and kiss her harder, my cock growing equally as hard.

A growling stomach interrupts us. I take my lips off hers and look into her eyes, which fill with confusion. Her desires are showing, and she hates it. A cocky smile forms on my face. I love to see it all. But then another growl follows. I'm not sure which of us it was, but it's definitely time to grab something to eat.

Oh well, I'll fill up her pussy some other time.

***

Jay

TUESDAY, AUGUST 20TH, 2013. 10:14 A.M.

I stuff the food in my mouth like a ravenous pig. I'm so freaking hungry and this sandwich isn't enough to quell the need for food. Maybe it's the side-effects from withdrawal, but I don't care. Anything to get my mind off the drugs is good to me.

X smirks as he watches me eat, whilst he's still cutting up his sandwich as if that's the most normal thing in the world. Who the fuck cuts up a sandwich into bite-sized pieces anyway?

Not that I care. I'm already glad I have some food in my mouth and that I'm finally out of that hotel room. I was dying for some fresh air. When I first saw the sun and blue sky again I felt the urge to run and never look back, but I knew X would shoot me in an instant. He doesn't feel for me yet, and I know he'd do anything to keep me exactly where he wants me to be, which is close to him.

I can tell from the gun he carries around everywhere he goes. It's a silent threat, even under the table. He'd pull the trigger anytime I even tried to make a move. Screaming wouldn't be of use either; X would kill them all. I don't want that on my conscience.

Oh well, guess I should be happy I even got out of the hotel. It's a good first step.

I'm in the midst of eating my sandwich when a man walks into the diner. His wild hair and scruffy beard immediately draw my attention. He throws a blunt into an ashtray on a table and walks to the cashier to make an order. He stinks of marijuana and alcohol, so I hold my breath. When he's made his order, he turns around and waits. His eyes fall on me. I stop eating. The sandwich drops onto my plate. The man just looks at me, but my legs are shaking, my eyes widen, and my heart thumps erratically.

"What's wrong?" X says.

My nose twitches and my lip trembles. Tears fill my eyes. X's brows lower as he follows my eyes and looks at the man that fills my head with screams.

So many screams. Nobody could hear.

I try to push it out, but it's no use; the memories come flooding back in. This man and his drugs; he was the one who got me to use them. The one who got me addicted. He kept taking my money, kept stuffing my hands with drugs, kept needing more, kept wanting more. Until I had nothing left to give except my body. I needed the drugs so badly ... but I wasn't willing to sacrifice my body. Not at that time. It was long ago, before I joined the club ... when I was still in my teen years, wandering the streets. I don't remember a lot about my life prior to the streets and the hustling. However, I do remember this guy who picked me up when I was low. This guy ... the man who abused me and used me for his own pleasure in exchange for drugs.

I panic and shoot up from my chair.

"Sit. Down," X commands.

I shudder as a tear runs down my cheeks. This man

… his face is imprinted on my retinas. The urge to run is too strong. I scoot my chair back and step away, backing up slowly. X gets up from his chair, confusion preventing him from acting. He doesn't get it. I don't even get it. All I know is that I have to get away from the man at the counter.

"Get back here," X says through gritted teeth.

"I can't," I say.

He comes toward me as I keep backing up, holding out his hand while the other is firmly clenched around his gun.

"I can't be here," I say. "Please. Don't make me stay here with him."

X's eyes widen and then he looks back at the man in front of the counter, who is watching us with a suspicious eye. X glances back and forth between me and him, then grabs my arms and pushes me outside.

"You know him?" he whispers as we exit through the door. X hauls me into an alley behind the diner.

"Yes," I say. "But I don't want to talk about it."

I turn my head, but X grabs my chin and forces me to look at him. "Tell me what he did."

I swallow, my voice soft and croaky when I say, "He abused me … took me against my will."

X frowns. "What? When?"

I glance at the ground, feeling scrutinized. "Long ago. He was the one who got me drugs. After a while I couldn't pay anymore …"

X's face darkens, his eyes narrowing as he says,

"Then we'll make him give back what he took from you."

***

TUESDAY, AUGUST 20ᵀᴴ, 2013. 12:00 A.M.

I'm staring at the worst scum on this earth. This piece of shit defiled my body. He's tied to a chair in a warehouse on the other side of town. X managed to put something in his drink that made him sleepy. Before he passed out, he told the diner manager he knew the guy and would take him to a bus stop. Of course he didn't. He's here now, and will be punished for what he did to me.

X steps aside when he's done tying him up. The man screams his lungs out, but the sound doesn't penetrate the cloth stuffed in his mouth. Seeing him like this makes my blood boil. Crazy thoughts run through my head now that he's unable to move. Thoughts about cutting him up and taking from him what he stuck inside me. Vicious, murderous thoughts.

It's wrong. This is not me. I don't want to be like that.

X walks toward me, his eye glistening with joy. A gratifying smile rests on his lips. He rummages in his pocket and takes out a knife, flipping it open. "I carry this one around all the time, just for occasions such as these."

He holds it out to me. I stare at it, wondering what to do. One part of me wants to take the knife and ram it in the man who sits in front of me. The other part wants to use it to threaten X and run away forever. Sweat drips roll down my forehead. What do I really want?

Taking my hand, X puts the knife inside and closes it. It's heavy and full of implications. I don't move. I can't. X walks around me and places his hands on my shoulders. His warm breath tickles my ear. "Look at him."

My eyes dart from the knife toward the man screaming in the chair. The scruffy, red-eyed, broken-toothed man sitting in front of me. I see the things he did to me, over and over again.

"You hate him so much, don't you?"

I nod.

"Hate gives us power, you know," X continues. "Hate makes us strong and invulnerable. Hate gives us a goal. Hate is what you use to get what you want," he lisps. "And you want to punish him."

X's fingers dig into my shoulders. His words are like poison seeping into my brain, consuming me. I look down at the blade. It's trembling in my hand.

"You want to slice him up, and make him pay for what he's done to you. The son of a bitch deserves it, doesn't he?"

"Yes … but I can't," I mutter. The words get stuck in my throat.

"Don't let the fear take control," he whispers. "Take the reins."

The knife drops from my hand. Bile rises in my throat. "I can't cut him up."

"Then what do you want, hmm?" he asks, looking over my shoulder. "Do you want him to pay or not?"

"Yes …" The word comes out in a single breath. The man screams inaudible words, but I know it's because he heard me say yes. The look in his eyes tells me he remembers what he did all those years ago. He knows what's coming for him.

X takes his hands off my shoulders. The sound of metal being pulled out of leather rings through my ears. When X's hand reaches forward to show me the gun, I hold my breath. He takes my hand and places the gun inside. Turning my hand to the side so the gun is aimed at the man in front of me, he lifts my arm and leans his head on my shoulder.

"Do you want this, little bird?"

I gasp, not knowing what to say. A part of me desperately wants this to end. Another part screams to pull the trigger.

"There's a bullet in there that'll go straight into his heart if you'll allow it. He'll be gone from this planet."

"But … I don't know."

"You do." X puts my fingers on the trigger. "You know how to use a gun."

He helps me aim. Sweat beads roll down my face as I face the man who used me. He's begging me with his eyes not to do it, shaking his head. He whimpers, but I feel no pity. Not for him. In full force the memories of what he did to me flood back in. Pain, so much pain. Not just physically, but mentally too. I was torn apart. A girl used and abused on the streets. He took advantage of me. He made me feel like shit, and I remember all of it. It hurts. He deserves nothing less than the same. I want him to feel it.

X pushes down on my finger. "Kill him. End your suffering."

My fingers do the rest.

Bam.

The gun fires. One shot, right through the head. His eyes turn blank, his head drops to the side. Blood seeps from the wound between his eyes. And then it's done. It's over. He's gone. My mind and body are set free from this nightmare he placed upon me.

My hands are shaking as X pries my fingers loose and takes back the gun. I'm still gutted by what just happened. Not just because of meeting this man again. Not because of all the things he did to me. It's because he's dead now, and I was the cause of it.

"I've never killed someone," I mutter.

X smiles, stifling a laugh. "Now you have."

"Fear nothing. Expect the worst." – Notes
of X

CHAPTER 16

X

WEDNESDAY APRIL 18TH, 2007. 10:00 A.M.

"What is *he* doing here?" the client yells from behind his desk as he notices me come inside.

"Sorry, sir, but in order to protect you, we must use all our available forces. Even if it is against your wishes," my father says. "These last few attacks have been putting a strain on our ability to protect your legacy."

"I don't need *him*. I told you before. Keep him away from me and my daughter."

"We can be of much better service to your cause if you let us choose who we use to protect you. You did re-hire us for that purpose, of course," my mother says.

"I re-hired you to do as you're told," he snaps. "Don't make me regret that decision yet again."

"As you wish, sir," my mother says. "We will not disappoint you."

I try not to take it personally, but I know it's meant as such. I know what I did. I remember what happened years ago, and he still holds it against me. I can't blame him. I would much rather stay away from this house as well, but unfortunately my parents decided they needed me on this job. Apparently this client will pay them double what they'd earn with another client. Multiply that by the amount of years we've worked for him in the past and the years we'll be working for him now ... it's *a lot* of money. So long as we don't screw it up.

Which is where I came in last time.

I sigh as we turn around and walk out the door. When we're out in the hallway, my father takes me aside. "Did you hear him? He doesn't want you near him or his daughter, got it?"

"Yes, Father," I say, rolling my eyes.

He slaps me on the back of the head. I don't care. It doesn't hurt anymore. "You fucked it up last time, so don't you dare do the same now. You'll obey the orders you're given, understood?"

I nod, but keep my mouth shut tight.

Suddenly, he shoves me against the wall, grabbing

my shirt with his fists. "You don't talk to them. You don't do anything. You just shoot when needed. That's it."

"What if they talk to me?"

"Then you cut it off and leave!" he snaps. "Your only job is to fire that gun whenever they're threatened. You bleed for them. Die for them if you must. But do *not* let anything or anyone hurt them. Understood?"

"Yes …"

His hand is suddenly around my throat as he pushes me up the wall. I struggle to breathe. I'm stronger than him, but if I defy him, they'll kill me. "Not good enough!"

"Yes. I won't defy your orders," I say.

"Good." He lets go of me, letting me catch my breath.

"This job is too important for us. We have your aunt to thank for a good word she gave to this man about our family so he'd hire us again." He grabs my chin, his fingers digging into my skin. "We lost it once because of your foolish actions; don't make us lose it twice. If you fuck this up, I swear to God I will cut you."

"I know you will," I hiss, frowning, warning him not to take it too far.

"Don't talk to them. Don't even think about them. Be invisible."

My father looks me in the eye for a moment, a silent threat of what's to come if I ever disobey him.

Then he pushes himself off me and walks away.

***

TUESDAY, AUGUST 20*TH*, 2013. 1:00 P.M.

Now, I find myself beside her, regardless of what my father told me. I guess I disobeyed him anyway.

I take Jay back to the diner, where we attempt to finish our meal in peace. I'm still fucking hungry and I'll get my fucking food before I go anywhere else. Sometimes I just like to go somewhere else rather than eat at the hotel all the time. That, and I want Jay to get used to being outside with me. She needs to get used to the fact that even if she's away from her usual surroundings, I'm still there to keep watch. I won't let her slip away easily, which she should realize by now. There's no escaping me.

A bell rings as someone steps into the diner. I hear the rattling sounds before I hear their voices. I don't need to look to know I need to take cover.

Bullets fire as I shove Jay under the table, while I slide under too. At first she sputters and stammers, but when her eyes spot the suited men standing at the door she stops. Her lips tremble, her eyes widen. And then she screams.

I place my hand on her mouth while I take out my gun, pulling the slider back.

Gunshots fill the room with noise. First they shoot

the cameras, then the people. Customers scream and run for their lives, crying. Blood splatters flick onto the wall beside us. I have to keep Jay firmly down, because all she wants is to flee. There's no flight or fight here. Flee and die. Fight and live. The choice is simple.

"We know you're here. No use hiding," one of them yells. "Does it feel good knowing these people are about to die because of you?"

I didn't expect the organization to find me this quickly. We must've been seen by some snitch here at the diner. They're fucking everywhere right when I don't need them around.

They fire at random, shooting holes into the diner like it's some sort of fucking Swiss cheese. When my sandwich drops to the floor below, punctured by a bullet, I growl. "Oh, fuck me. Don't fucking touch my sandwich." Now they've done it.

Lifting my head, I check where they are and perch my gun on the couch, aiming for their legs. I shoot once, hitting the first one in the kneecap. He groans and sinks to the floor like a sack of potatoes. One more shot to the head and he's gone.

The one behind him is much bigger and when he notices where the shots are coming from, he barges toward me, enraged.

"Stay here," I tell Jay.

The man approaches us, so I put all my weight into throwing myself into his path. As I slide down the aisle, I fire another shot right through his shin, but the giant keeps going, even though blood is gushing out of his wound. I fire a few more times while crawling under a different table. He drops to the floor after six bullets go into his chest. A pool of blood leaks from him. Jay looks at him with sheer panic in her eyes. With my hand I signal her and mouth to her to stay down.

"You fucking cunt," one of the men yells. There are two left inside. Fuck knows how many are waiting for us outside. I look to the back, where the manager has crawled under his counter, and find a door behind him. A perfect way out. I'll have to shoot those other two motherfuckers first though.

"Hiding under a table? Pathetic son of a bitch. I wouldn't have thought you'd stoop to that level, you know."

"Afraid?" I yell. "Three of you against one of me. Fuck, you must be so proud of yourself to stand there watching your buddies die."

He shoots at my table. "Shut the fuck up." He laughs. "Like you're the one to talk. You fucking betrayed us, man. All these years I've known you, and now you pull this shit."

His steps alert all my senses. He's coming, but I don't know which way. I check both aisles, but as soon as I stick my head out, a bullet zooms past me.

He's running now. Fearing for her life, Jay crawls close to the window, trying to hide, but it's no use. He reaches her in no time, so I point my gun and shoot. Except, nothing comes out, just clicking. Shit. Now's not the fucking time to reload.

I race to put them back in in time, but when I hear her screams I know I'm too late. By her hair she's pulled out from under the table, a gun pointed at her side.

"Let me go!" she screams, fighting her attacker.

"Feisty one," the guy says.

As I finish reloading I point my gun at him, but he uses Jay as a shield. Fucker.

"Move and she dies," the guy says as my finger lingers on the trigger.

"Take your fucking hands off her."

His hand is wrapped around her mouth, preventing her from screaming. Prodding his gun into her thigh, he makes my blood boil. He smiles and cocks his head. "Oh, you like this one?"

His hand slips down her mouth to her throat, grabbing her so tight she struggles to breathe. When he starts sniffing her hair I'm ready to blow all my shit. "Smells nice too," he says.

"Take your fucking hands off me!" Jay screams, her voice hoarse.

The guy laughs and then chokes her some more. That motherfucker. I'm the only one allowed to do that to her. He has no right to toy with her body. "Wanna see who's faster?" he says.

From the corner of my eye I spot her reaching for her pocket. She's slow with her movements and he doesn't seem to notice, so I distract him.

"You wouldn't even be able to hit me if you got three free shots."

He frowns and makes a face. "Stop your fucking jokes and let's get to business."

"Tell me, what business does the organization have with me?"

"You know damn fucking well what you did. Stop playing games!"

"Oh, and here I was thinking you wanted to play a game of shoot 'em 'til they drop." I purse my lips. "Such a disappointment."

"You wasted it all. And you did it for this girl?" he says, pushing the gun further into Jay's stomach. A knife appears from deep down in her pocket as she carefully takes it out, trying not to get noticed. My knife. She must've picked it up from the ground while I was untying our victim from before.

"*This* is what made you turn against us? She's a fucking whore!" he yells.

Jay grabs a firm hold of the knife, grinding her teeth. "I'm not a whore!" she says through gritted teeth. A quick jab backwards is all it takes to jam the knife into his abdomen. He groans and reaches for his stomach, releasing her from his grip. At the same time she jumps away I pull the trigger and shoot that fucker straight in the heart. His eyes roll into the back of his head as he drops backwards onto the table and slips down toward the ground.

She turns around, hesitating for a moment, gazing

at the dead body before her. I crawl out from under the table and watch her go to her knees and pull the knife from his belly. Making a face, she glances at the blood before quickly wiping it on his clothes.

"C'mon," I say. "Back door."

She nods, tucking the knife into her pocket, and follows me back. I keep my gun aimed, ready to pull the trigger if they show their faces. There's probably at least another two waiting to ambush us outside. We need to be prepared. As I open the door, I look around and clear the area before stepping out with her. She's right behind me, tiptoeing as we walk alongside the building. My knife is still in her pocket and I know she could pull it out and stick me with it at any moment. Except, she doesn't. Maybe it's the fear of being in the middle of a gunfight, but for now I don't think she'll attack me. She knows I'm her only way out of this mess.

I look around the barren land. The area is open, and there's nowhere to hide, meaning they're either all in their car or waiting for me at mine.

"What do we do?" she whispers.

"Get the fuck out of here, what else?"

"No, I mean, all your stuff is in the hotel room, isn't it?"

"So?" I glance at her over my shoulder.

"Well, if we go back there, won't they follow us?"

I sigh. She's got a point there. Hadn't thought about that. But I *have* to get back there. I didn't bring my toys with me; they're all still in my room. No way I'm ever leaving them behind.

"We're going back there. I'll figure a way to get us out of here … So long as I can fucking kill them all, they won't know where we've gone," I say as we approach the parking lot. Antonio's car is right next to mine. Great. Fucking fantastic.

"If you come out now, I won't hurt you," Antonio yells.

"Yeah, right. You're insulting my intelligence too now?" I scoff.

"Show your face and you'll see what I mean."

Leaning against the wall, I take a tiny mirror out of my pocket and use it to determine where he is and what he's doing. He looks at me and smiles like he knows he's got me. That motherfucker. I know he can see what I'm doing, but that's exactly the point. I'm not going to fucking stick out my head and risk having it popped off.

Antonio drops his shotgun to the ground and kicks it away. "See? All good," he yells. "I just want to talk with you, that's all."

I sigh while putting away the mirror.

"Are you seriously considering going out there?" Jay says.

"There's no other option. My car is our only way to get out of here." Rubbing my bald head, I think about it for a second. I know he's got more shit up his sleeve. The organization would never accept him coming back empty handed. This is all a trick. "There has to be a way to get to that car without him fucking blowing our heads off."

"Then use me as a hostage. Fake that you're going to kill me," she says.

"They want you dead. I'd be playing right into their lap if I did that," I say.

"Then why not just walk out with your gun pointed at him? I mean, we have the advantage now. He has nothing."

"We?" I say, laughing. "You're not my accomplice, Jay."

She chuckles. "I know, but as you say, you're the only reason I'm alive. I'd rather get out of here than lose my head."

"You sound like me."

"I learn," she muses.

I think about it for a second. If he's ambushing us, there's no way I'm going in with just this gun. I need backup, because he'll demand that I throw my gun away too. I'll need something to protect myself and her when shit hits the fan. "Hmm ... still got that knife on you?"

"Yeah."

"Good." I take a deep breath. "Stay behind me, but keep an eye out."

We walk out of the alley, stepping into the light. A smirk appears on Antonio's face as we make our way to the car. I keep a close eye on him whilst Jay checks our surroundings to make sure there's no one else to screw with us.

"Finally … the two lovebirds arrive."

"Shut up," I say, keeping my gun pointed at his face.

"Now, now … a little tense?" He chuckles. "No need. I'm unarmed, see?" He holds up his hands. "I'm just here to talk with you."

"Stop bullshitting me, Antonio. I know why you're here."

He rolls his eyes. "What does it matter? We're all going to die anyway; might as well end it here."

"Not according to my schedule. Wanna talk? Speak up or I'm leaving," I say as we move to the vehicle.

The look in his eyes immediately changes. "You know as well as I do this is not going to end well. You can't escape this. Why do you insist on keeping her alive?"

"Because she is mine," I say, grabbing Jay's wrist. "You can tell the organization to back off. I'm taking this one and I'm out. I don't work for you anymore."

He laughs. "Yeah, that was already established. But do you honestly think that will stop us from claiming her head? There's a hefty bounty for her, and I don't intend to let it slip."

He starts fumbling with his pockets. I don't like it one bit, so I keep my gun steadily pointed at him. I don't want to kill him, but if I have to, I will. I know it's exactly the same for him. Code before anything else.

If he's set on claiming the money, then fuck it, I'll make sure that money won't ever become available to them.

"You won't get that money," I say. "I'm going to kill the client."

Antonio frowns. "What? Have you gone insane?"

"No, it's the only way to stop this all. If I kill him, it's all over. He won't be able to pay, so you won't need to kill her anymore, and I'm off the hook since I'll be gone forever. Everybody's happy." We approach the door of my car while Antonio's eyes narrow as he watches us from his own car.

"I won't allow it." He pulls out a second gun from his pocket.

I shove Jay aside while dropping to the floor. The shot hits my shoulder so hard it flings the gun from my hand. Shit.

"It was a pleasure working with you," Antonio says. "But you know money always comes first." He aims for my head.

From the corner of my eye I spot Jay pulling the knife from her pocket and throwing it at Antonio like a dagger. It hits his thigh. He screams as he drops to the ground in agony. His gun is still in his hands, but he's too focused on the pain to shoot. I scramble to my gun and pick it up. One shot is all it takes.

And then he's gone. His flame has been extinguished. His limp body lies on the asphalt like a ragdoll, his eyes vacant, his muscles still twitching. For the first time in a long while I don't feel victorious. This was not the outcome I would've preferred, but it had to happen. Still, it's hard to swallow. Antonio got me into the organization. He was the one who let me in, who trained me in their ways, who made me even better than before … who helped me with my disability. He was my killer buddy; we always used to take on requests together. Just the two of us, off shooting some random people and returning with plenty of cash. We lived like kings. Now we die like street rats.

Such a shame.

I get up from the ground and watch Jay get up too. She wipes her clothes and checks her surroundings. "Are they all gone?"

"I doubt it, but I'm not curious about it either. Let's go before shit really hits the fan."

"Right …"

She gets into the passenger seat of the car and waits for me. But I can't get in yet. My precious knife is still stuck in his thigh, so I walk to his body and pluck it out, wiping it on his clothes. Before I turn my back on him, I pry the gun from his fingers and tuck it into my back pocket. Never leave spoils on the battlefield. Then I close his eyes and walk to the car.

"To live is to suffer, to survive is to find some meaning in the suffering." - Friedrich Nietzsche

CHAPTER 17

Jay

TUESDAY, AUGUST 20ᵀᴴ, 2013. 2:00 P.M.

Eyes, always his eyes. They are always watching me. They find me in the dark like candles on fire. They tempt me to walk a path unknown yet enticing. His touch lingers on my skin, even after only one brief moment of contact. Rugged fingers craving to feel me.

His gun glistens in the moonlight as he watches over me, day and night. He's always there. Screams and blood follow him wherever he goes. It does not scare me anymore. This is what he does, but not what he desires. In the shadows he hungers for me.

And I in turn yearn for him.

***

Sipping in the air, I feel like my chest is on fire. What I just saw was real, and yet it was all in my mind. Flashes of a life that was mine surge through my head. I can't remember, but bits and pieces trickle into my mind like droplets of water falling into a pond.

And then it's gone again.

I don't even remember what I saw.

X sits next to me, his hands on the steering wheel, his gaze sometimes darting to me to check up on me. My heart is pounding, but I try not to let it show. I won't show any weakness. I've seen so many people die these last few days, it's all starting to feel so unreal. They drop like flies. Every day I wake up thinking it was all just a bad dream. Except it isn't; I'm still in this car with X, still his 'prisoner,' still on the run from people who want to kill me for whatever reason.

I'm shivering from top to bottom, trying not to focus too much on the fact that I'm covered in blood. Someone else's blood. Someone who's dead now. So many bodies. So many injured. So much pain. I wish I could stop it all. I wish I had control. But I know X would never allow me to leave, not even to save those people. I might be a self-absorbed bitch, but those people shouldn't have died because I was there. They were looking for me, and now all the people at that diner are dead.

I take a deep breath and sigh my worries away while I look out the window. We're almost back at the hotel, and I'm wondering what X is planning to do. Does he plan on staying there? Or will we move again? And if so, will I have a chance at escaping then?

So many questions, so few answers. At times like these the first thing I think of is drugs. Yep, I'm so fucking addicted, it's not even close to fun. I don't want to feel this craving. It's just another layer of weakness I can't afford anymore. I have to strip away the vulnerabilities and close them off. Being strong is my only choice to survive this.

When we're finally at the hotel room and X closes the door, locking it again, I just stand in the middle of the room, giving everything that just happened a place. X is behind me, and I can hear him pull some buttons. The sound of cotton being draped off his shoulders is alarming. It frightens me, because I know what usually comes next. The beast in him must be released. Whenever he's killed someone he comes back to me and …

I swallow away the fear. I can't think like that. Can't let him see that he has this effect on me. I don't even want to think about it, because it's tearing me apart and I won't allow him to do that to me.

I hear him place his shirt and gun on the chair. His steps are heavy as he walks past me and goes into the bathroom. While he turns on the shower, I look behind me. His gun is the first thing that catches my eye. It's right there for the taking. Suddenly, I'm overcome with the overwhelming desire to use it.

One glance at X and I know he isn't looking, so I take a chance and walk toward it. I pick it up. It feels heavy, and my hands start trembling again. It's because I know what it's like to kill someone now. I know what I did and it terrifies the living shit out of me. I could kill someone. I could kill him.

As I turn around with the gun in my hand, X is suddenly in front of me.

I squeal and point it at him. "Don't come any closer!"

All he does is lift an eyebrow.

The gun is shaking vigorously. He shakes his head and a chuckle escapes his mouth. "You won't, because you know I'm the only one who keeps you alive."

"I don't believe you," I say, my voice croaky. "What does alive mean anyway when I have to spend my time like this?"

"You've seen them. They'd take your head in an instant. Do you think those men were the only ones? Wrong. The organization is larger than you can imagine. They're everywhere, and now they know exactly what you look like. It won't take long before word gets out. You would be dead by now if it wasn't for me."

He raises his hand to the gun, but I pull back and

do the unthinkable. I place it against my temple. "I'd rather be dead then," I say, my voice wavering.

"Jay …" He sighs. "You don't want to do that. You don't want to give up already, do you?"

"I want to live my life the way I pictured it." Tears form in my eyes. The way I pictured it is far, far from reality. Rainbows and sunshine don't exist here.

"Pointing a gun at your head won't help with that." He clears his throat and takes a deep breath. "Jay, don't do that. You don't want to hurt yourself."

"And what if I do? I fucking killed people, X! I killed them … I took their lives … and for what? To save my own? Is it worth it? My pathetic life is useless and I traded it for theirs. I'm a monster."

He rubs his lips together. "You did what you had to … to survive. It's a kill or be killed world. Fairy tales don't exist. Don't tell yourself they do. Take life for what it is and be happy you still have it. Some weren't so lucky." He holds up his hand, looking at the gun. "You have another shot at life every time I save your life and every time you save your life. Don't waste it by killing yourself."

My fingers tremble as a tear trickles down my cheek. Time is slow and irrevocably lost whenever I try to grasp for it. Everything is an illusion. My life, my happiness, my freedom. I can't even control my own destiny.

His hand is so close now that I just let him take it. I can't do it. As much as I want to put an end to this, I can't. I can't pull the trigger without knowing what'll happen. I guess I could never lose control after all.

He pries the gun from my hand and puts it on the table beside him. He's still right in front of me, gazing at me with a barely visible smile on his face. "You're mine now," he says, cupping my face. "I won't let anyone kill you. Not even yourself." He laughs. "Let us be monsters together."

I take a deep breath and wish the tears would stop running. I hate them. I hate weakness, but I can't stop them from flooding out of me.

"I'll protect you," X murmurs, wiping away the tears with his thumb. "I protect everything that's mine, because I won't allow anyone to take it from me. I'm a little selfish, you see. I tend to want more from people than they can offer. Lucky for me, you can handle everything I give to you." He leans in so close I can smell his cologne. His tongue darts out in a flash, sucking up my tears. Then he licks the seam of his mouth and grins. "Even your tears are delicious ... hmmm."

He presses his lips on mine and kisses me, hard. His lips are rough, but numb the pain inside. For a moment I drift away into oblivion and forget about everything. His warm mouth has a tantalizing effect on me, something I haven't experienced with any of the other men I've been with. This feels so comfortable and safe. At the same time that feeling freaks me out. It shouldn't be like this, and yet it is. I want him to kiss me.

And then he stops. His one eye glistens with desire as he grabs my arm and pulls me toward the bathroom. There, he waits. Slowly, he starts undressing me. One by one the layers disappear until everything is gone and I'm completely naked. I let him see all of me. Even though I've been naked before, it's never been this naked. This vulnerable. At my absolute weakest point, I let him overtake me and give me comfort when I need it the most. This man, a killer, comforts me right now. The man who abducted me. It's too stupid and insane to put into words, but it's true.

He throws away my panties and starts kissing my leg, starting at the tips of my feet. It feels good, but when I look down it's scary. I still fear he might turn against me at any moment and put me in severe pain. I don't want to have to go through that again. Upsetting him means receiving punishment, so I keep calm and let him do what he wants. I surrender my body to him so that I'll stay safe. However bizarre that sounds, it's the only way to survive.

His tongue drags all the way up to my hips, leaving little pecks as he reaches my pussy. I get the urge to close my legs and move away, but he slaps my inner thigh with the palm of his hand.

"Spread." His voice is guttural and sends shivers down my spine. He stands up again and takes off his belt, keeping his eye fixed on me. I dare not look away as he starts undressing again. My eyes drift down the inked ridges of his muscular abs and zoom in on his erection when it bobs out of his boxer briefs. Carefully taking my hand, he guides me into the bathtub and under the shower. The warmth of the water cleanses away my sadness, my fears, my sins. It feels nice.

As X steps into the bathtub I look down. The water turns crimson as it mixes with the blood of our victims. My body shakes when I see the droplets run down my hands and face.

X grabs my chin. "Don't look at it. Look at me instead."

He comes closer and cups my face with both hands before kissing me. His lips are soft and smooth, not rough like before. Each time he touches me it feels different. I feel different. I feel like both of us are changing, going toward a place we can no longer return from. I'm not sure if I should fight it.

The more he kisses me, the more I'm lost in him. The world around me ceases to exist. His mouth on mine is all that matters. He kisses away the hurt, kisses me until I can no longer think for myself.

His tongue darts out to dance around mine. He explores every crevice in my mouth, lapping me up with luscious licks that soothe the pain. My tears mix with the water of the shower, and I no longer feel the difference between them. His cock prods my thigh and it turns me on. It's happened so often now, I no longer feel ashamed about it. I don't know what this is, or where it's going, but I'm taking it as it comes. I'm not going to fight it anymore; there's no use. I'm already hooked.

When he takes his lips off mine I'm already leaning in to receive more. He squints, a devilish smile on his face. As he licks his lip and bites on it a little, he says, "You tempt me, little bird."

I suck in my lips. Treacherous little things, wanting more. "Tempt you?" I hint at a question.

He plants a single kiss on my jaw. "There are so many more important things to do right now," he whispers close to my ear. "But I can't stop myself from ravaging you first." He nips my earlobe, biting it until I hiss. Goose bumps riddle my body as he moves down my neck and sucks on my skin. Sinking his teeth into me, he leaves bite marks all over. He travels down to my sternum, still leaving rough kisses everywhere, until he reaches my nipples. With his index finger and thumb he hardens them.

"You turn out to be a good little slut after all," he says. "I don't regret claiming you as my pet." He pulls and tugs on my nipples until a desperate moan escapes my mouth. "It sounds as though you're enjoying this quite a bit, too." A groan-laugh rumbles in his chest as he places his lips over my nipple and starts sucking, hard. I writhe from the attention he's giving them, suckling them until pain settles in. Good pain. Pain that makes my clit throb.

"Hmmm … you like this a lot," X murmurs against my taut peak. His tongue darts out to circle around the crown, teasing me, awakening my desires. I'm not resisting anymore. My hands are on his back as I let him play with me. He seems to enjoy the fact that I let him do whatever. There's a big smile on his face, and he keeps looking up at me, as if he's wondering how I feel about all this. I don't care anymore. Only pleasure seeps in.

"A little too much …" he mutters.

Whack!

The sudden slap to my ass pulls me back to reality, back to this place, back to him. He sets his teeth on my skin and bites down. I scream as his teeth sink into my nipple while he toys with the other. When he takes his mouth off again, a red ring appears around my nipple.

"Gorgeous," he says. With his tongue he laps up a droplet of blood and licks his lip when he's done. "What do you think?"

"It hurts …" I say, frowning, looking away.

"Good." He grabs my chin, forcing me to look at him. "Do not take your eyes off me." His eyes narrow. "You don't get to deny me your eyes. You will watch me when I take from you, because everything that is you belongs to me now. *You* belong to me now. And you will accept everything I give you and thank me for it."

He slaps my ass again, making me jolt up. "Do you understand?"

"Yes, sir," I say.

"Good. Now don't forget it, or I will punish you

for it."

I shiver as he goes to his knees and taps my knees. "Spread."

I set my feet apart, feeling vulnerable and open as he gazes up at my pussy. "Let's see if this pussy deserves some attention."

My lips quiver as his own are planted on my thigh. He leaves short, luscious kisses on my skin, working his way up to my pussy. There, he stops, but his hand doesn't. Just his thumb presses down on my nub, sending shocks through my body.

"Oh … you like this?" he asks. I don't know how to respond, because there are two possible answers; neither are good for me.

With the pad of his thumb he starts circling my nub, leaving kisses everywhere except where my body craves them the most. He's never been this gentle, though, and it surprises me. I wonder if it can be like this more often. Wondering that is wrong, and I know it is, because I shouldn't even want to be thinking about that. But I am.

"I think this little pussy wants more …" He grins as he stops kissing and touches my entrance with another finger. I gasp as he dips inside and feels me. He groans as he slips it in and out of me, going faster each time. Driving his finger into me while putting ample pressure on my clit creates an overload of sensations. I struggle to keep my legs spread while he fucks me with his finger.

"Do you want this?" he asks.

I nod swiftly, biting my lip.

Suddenly he takes his hands away and I'm left hanging. My pussy is throbbing with desire and he knows it. A wicked smile curves his lips. "Tell me."

"Please … I want it, sir."

He smiles, and leans in, blowing hot air onto my clit. "Hmm … you've done well today, little bird," he hums against my skin. "This is your reward."

When his tongue touches my nub I'm done for. The heat is rising, and it's not because of the shower. His kisses are hot and make me moan in sinful pleasure. He laps me up with glee, licking me with just the right amount of pressure. From underneath his dark lashes he watches me quiver, his touch painfully pleasurable. His hands move from my legs up to my ass, gripping me tight as he buries his face in my pussy. With his lips he rubs my clit, and then dips his tongue into my entrance. I'm delirious with lust. It's been a long time since a man went down on me, and shit, he knows how to work it.

"Hmm … I'm so glad you're clean; now I can do all the things I was planning on doing."

I got tested a few days ago, because X wanted to fuck me without a condom. Guess he got his wish after all. I can't complain.

He swirls his tongue round and round, lapping me up like there's no tomorrow. He groans as I moan, his fingers digging into my skin. His teeth appear and he sinks them into my flesh. A rush of fear sweeps through me as I fear he might bite my most sensitive part. Except, he doesn't. Instead, he nibbles softly, pushing my limits.

Whack!

A strike to the ass pulls me away from pure bliss. "Don't you come unless I say you can, little bird."

"Yes, sir," I moan as he whacks me again.

"I won't allow you to disobey me again."

"I know, sir."

"Remember it."

"I will, sir."

"Good. Keep those legs spread. Place your hand on the wall and the other on the shower screen."

I do as he says and position myself to allow him more entry. That's what he wants, I think. I keep looking down at him, because that's what he wants, too. I keep doing everything he desires ... I'm turning into an obedient girl more and more ... his obedient girl.

"You like pleasing me, don't you?" he murmurs, lapping me up. "My little slut gets all wet for me."

"Thank you, sir," I moan. I know it's what he wants to hear.

"You're welcome." He slaps my ass again, mixing pain with pleasure. Each time I'm on the verge of coming, he ends it quickly. I keep rising and falling, and it's exactly what he wants.

"So fucking wet ..." he whispers, pushing his

tongue deeper and deeper until my pussy begins to throb so badly I can barely keep it together. "This pussy of mine wants to come so badly." He chuckles, toying with my clit while he looks up at me. "Are you ready to come for me, slut?"

"Yes!"

He whacks my ass again and I squeal. "Yes, what?"

"Yes, sir."

"Does this little slut want to please me? What will you do for me?"

"I want to come for you, sir."

He smiles, and sucks on my nub again, almost pushing me over the edge. "Beg me to fuck you," he murmurs against my flesh. "Beg!"

"Please … fuck me, sir." The words come out in a slur as I feel the impending orgasm. "Can I come? Please?"

He takes his lips off my folds completely. A flat-handed smack follows. I whimper and scream.

"You're not allowed."

"Oh, fuck you," I growl.

He laughs. "Ask me nicely, and I might."

I frown and turn my head while he turns off the shower. Suddenly, he grabs my arm and drags me out of the bathtub. I stumble to follow him, still a little shaken by what just happened. My entire body is still zinging when he throws me onto the bed and pins my hands down near the bedpost. I struggle to fight him, but anxiety takes control again. Grabbing the cuffs, he chains my wrists down, my worst fear coming alive. I'm a prisoner again. A toy to play with as he sees fit. And worst of all, I know this has to happen. In order to win his trust, I must accept anything and everything he wants to take from me, including my freedom. Is it going to be like this forever?

"What are you going to do?" I ask, pulling on the cuffs. They feel a lot tighter now. I guess he learned from my past escape.

His hands slide up the curve of my body. "Simple. You are mine and I intend to use you as I see fit. I will take your body over and over again until you can no longer stand. I will demand your wetness and make you throb until you beg me to come. I will fuck your every orifice and spank your flesh until you turn crimson. And maybe then ... maybe ... will I grant you your orgasm. And you will thank me for it, little slut." Desire and amusement glint in his eye. "Starting right now."

"Take what lies within your grasp." –
Notes of X

CHAPTER 18

X

SATURDAY, NOVEMBER 24TH, 2007. 11:30 P.M.

It's becoming increasingly difficult to stay away from her. Not because I don't have the discipline, but because I keep being sent out to kill someone who's related to her. For some reason she keeps attracting all kinds of bad attention. Heck, that could even include me. She keeps hanging with the wrong crowd, smoking pot and doing other drugs, getting into trouble with her supposed friends, doing fuck knows what with who knows where. She offers herself to every chump that wants to stick his cock into her pussy. Just the thought of it makes me so angry I could smash this glass I'm holding to bits.

I watch her dance with another guy on the dance floor. He's short and covered in tattoos and piercings. The way he touches her makes me want to punch him in the throat. He's got his hands all over her, and I don't like it one bit.

See, it's already too late for me. I haven't stopped thinking about her, even though I promised myself I would. I haven't stopped being around her, even though I told myself I could take other jobs and tell my family to go fuck themselves. Of course, they insisted and I prefer not getting a finger chopped off. When my family wants someone dead, it sure as hell will happen, whether I'm in or not. They won't stop until they get their payment from their clients, which is all that matters to them. If I refuse, I'll have to accept a fate worse than watching her get groped by some random dude.

Life's such a fucking bitch sometimes.

Her eyes find me, and a hint of surprise flashes through them before the devious sex-vixen comes out to play again. She knows I'm watching and revels in it. Grabbing a tighter hold on her date, she leans her head on his shoulder while looking at me. Her eyes beg me to step in and take over. She's such a fucking tease; always pushing everyone's buttons. I know she has a rough time with her father always gone, always disappointed with what she does, which is all the more reason for her to continue what she's doing. It's a vicious cycle she can't escape. She's trying to pull me in too.

I've been around for months now, always killing the ones she messes up with. Either it's her previous boyfriends talking shit about her and her father in the newspaper, or some drug lord claiming that she was a customer. Of course, it all happened. No doubt about it. I'm there when it happens all the time. Except, when you're rich, you get to erase your history and past mistakes with the snap of a finger. Her father is just like that. He and all his political buddies care more about their reputations than the happiness of their family and kids. I know she takes this personally. He blames her for everything … even her mother.

And that's why she keeps looking for a way to escape. Keeps ending up in someone's arms that won't protect her but hurt her instead. Solace can't be found in the arms of a stranger. However, I won't be able to offer it to her either. No matter how much she'd like me to. And she's not the only one who's been thinking about it.

I take a deep breath and blow it out while putting the glass on the bar behind me. Better put it away before I throw it at the guy's head. Seriously, if he doesn't keep his fucking hands off her ass I'm going to blow his brains out.

My parents enter the club and their eyes scan the room. When they find me, they nod. I cock my head swiftly, alerting them to her presence, and they take note. Communication during a hit job is usually done with our eyes, not our mouths.

They walk into the club and blend in with the crowd, making their way to the back. They're going after the local drug dealer who sold a story to the newspaper. Of course it involves her. Now he has to die. No bad reputation for her father, ever.

I stay here to watch her and make sure nobody enters the room in the back. I watch them disappear through the door. I check my clock. Fifteen minutes is all they get or I'm going after them.

When I look up, she's in front of my face. I'm taken aback for a moment, frowning, wanting to shout at her, but at the same time I have no fucking clue what to say to her. I know what she wants. It isn't happening.

"No," I say, loud and clear.

"Oh, c'mon. Don't be such a party pooper. You don't even know what I came to ask."

"Oh, I know all right. Don't you have a date or something?" I say, raising an eyebrow while looking at the guy in the middle of the dance floor who's waiting impatiently for her.

"He's such a bore. Can't keep his mouth shut about tattoos and piercings, and he keeps wanting to show every one of them to me. I've already seen them twenty fucking times! I'm kind of done with him." She puts her hand on her side and taps her foot. I look down at her with mild annoyance.

"So? Go on, find some other guy then," I say.

She pouts. "I want to dance with you."

She steps closer. I lean back.

"I'm on the job," I growl.

"You've been doing nothing for the past ten minutes. I don't think they're going to filet you if you have fun for a little bit."

She tries to grab my hand, but I snatch her wrist instead. I pull her closer so she'll know I'm serious as I look down into her eyes. "Your father would fucking kill you if he knew you were even suggesting such a thing," I growl. "You should not want to be hanging around with me."

She jerks her hand loose. "I don't give a crap about my father. He doesn't care about me either, so I'm going to do what I want to do, which is dance with you. You and I both know you want to."

"That doesn't change anything."

"Yes, it does. You can't deny there's something between us. You can't keep your eyes off me." She pushes her boobs up against me, making me flinch. I never flinch. For fuck's sake, she's really grown.

"Yeah, I've seen you watching me. And I like you too. So why not dance for a while?"

"You don't like me. Stop this shit. You don't know what you're getting yourself into. I told you what we are. We kill for a living."

She grabs my hand and places it on her waist. Her

body is round and nicely shaped, and I can feel her thong through her tiny black dress. I'm much too aware of that fact.

"C'mon, I'm only asking you to dance with me. Nothing more. You're not going to die."

I snort. "I might. You're giving me a heart attack every fucking time I see you."

She squints. "You're just jealous."

"Jealous? You're pulling crazy stunts and endangering your life, meaning we have more people to kill, and you think I'm jealous?"

"You are." She winks, and then grabs my other hand, placing it on her other hipbone. "And I like it. I like it when I make you jealous."

"Stop this."

"It's only a dance ..." She leans in and wraps her hands around my neck, pulling me with her. "I only want one dance. That's it. Then you can forget about me again."

I roll my eyes and groan. "Oh, fuck me ..."

Sinful desire is what persuades me. With her arms around my neck and her sweet, coy smile seducing me, I stop saying no. For once I give in to what we both want, but I promise myself the moment I step onto the dance floor that this is the only and final time I will ever touch her.

She pulls me into the middle of the crowd, far away from where I'm supposed to be, and starts swaying her hips. Her fingers play with my hair as she puts on her most sensual dance act right in my arms. My hands are warming up, the good kind of warming up, the kind where they're craving to feel more skin. I get the urge to slip them down toward her ass. But my instincts tell me to keep my cool and focus on something else. I glance at the door to make sure my parents are still in there and that they aren't watching us. Fuck knows what they'd do to me if they found out.

"I'm here," she says, nudging my chin to make me look at her again. Then I notice the beauty in front of me. The pain, the hurt, the anger, the regret, the sorrow, the happiness, all wrapped into one divine package. At such a young age she's already prone to the shadows, prone to a life of misery, and I don't want to put her through that. For once in my life I actually feel the need to protect someone, to make her feel safe. A flame dances in her eyes, hypnotizing me. She's like a candle, burning brightly in the darkness of the night, and I covet the light that guides me through. But I am the tsunami wrecking all in its path, extinguishing her flame.

"Do you see me?" she asks.

"I never stopped seeing you."

Her fingers twirl the black hair falling down my forehead. The way she parts her lips makes me zoom in on them. A maddening hunger to taste her courses through my veins. I mustn't.

"Do you remember that night on the roof?" she asks. "Where you stole the beer."

I snort. "Yeah ... a job."

"I know that now. I was just wondering about ..."

"About what?"

"Well, your eyes. They just struck me. It's like I knew you all along."

I smile. It still surprises me that she sometimes remembers bits and pieces. We were so young. I hardly even remember anything, except for that time with ... her mother.

I swallow and clear my throat. "It's such a long time ago."

"Yeah, it is. But I can't stop thinking about it. I can't stop having this feeling that you and I have danced like this before. That we were friends. That there was something ... something about us."

"Stop ... please," I say. "I don't want to talk about it anymore."

Her eyebrows lower for a second in a flash of confusion. Then she leans in and watches me up close. Her lips part again, but she keeps looking at me, keeps asking for permission before she continues. I can already feel her breath on my skin. I can't say no anymore.

When her mouth latches onto mine I'm done for. Her kiss is soft and subtle and everything I expected it to be. She tantalizes me, makes me think of taking her back to my apartment and screwing her on my bed. Her taste is unbelievable, so delicious, and her lips set me on fire. I can't help wanting more, so I wrap my arms around her and pull her closer to me, pressing her against my chest.

But when I open my eyes in a rush of ecstasy I spot my parents leaving the room. Luckily, they didn't spot me yet, or I'd be a dead man.

I pull my lips away, breathing heavily from her raging fire. The smile on her face tells me she thinks she won. Like a cunning artist she toys with my heart.

She'll be my end. No doubt about it.

***

TUESDAY, AUGUST 20*TH*, 2013. 2:00 P.M.

She is not just my end. I have thrown myself into her abyss. I take sinful pleasure out of the fact that I have her chained up now. I made the choice and live with the consequences. She'll be the death of me. But not before I fuck her senseless.

I know exactly what I'm going to do to change everything.

I will ruin the person who's behind it all. Suffering. Regret. Pain. Shame. I'll show no mercy. Once it's over, I will be begged to spare lives, and I will grant them none.

I open a box that was under the bed and take out the camera that's inside. I bought it a few days ago, and this is the first time Jay will see it. She doesn't know what I'm planning to do, but from the look on her face

I can tell she doesn't like it. Good.

"What are you going to do with that?" she asks.

Ignoring her, I set up the tripod and perch the camera on top. Once I'm sure it's focused on the bed and her, I turn it on.

"You're filming me? Why?" she asks, her voice raspy from fear.

"After I'm done with you I'd like to be able to watch back and enjoy it again ... and again ... and again." I smile when goose bumps appear on her skin. I don't get why she's so scared. After all, this is all too familiar to her.

From my suitcase I fish a bunch of ropes, and from the chair I grab my belt. Her big brown eyes are luring me in. I get on the bed, place the belt and rope beside me, and crawl on top of her. Her skin is moist from the shower, and when my hand dives between her legs, it's even wetter. I grin as she struggles in the chains. "Stop fighting me, little bird. Obey and I might give you what you want." My finger circles on top of her clit and then slides down to her pussy, spreading her slickness through her folds. "You want to come, but you're not allowed until I say so, got it?"

She holds her breath as I dip a finger inside. Then I slap her inner thigh. Her squeal makes my cock bounce, eager to squirt its load on her velvety body. "Do not come. Do you understand?"

"Yes, sir."

"Good girl." I take my finger out of her and she

lets go of the breath she was holding. I move further up, planting my knees right beside her head. My cock is pointed right at her as I grab her face and perch her higher. "You will suck until I say you can stop."

Pushing forward, I rub the tip against her lips. My pre-cum serves as a nice lubricant as she opens her mouth and lets me slide in. I go deep and make her gag on me, which makes me even harder. I plunge in and out of her mouth at a steady pace. She jerks the chains from the claim I lay on her mouth as I fuck it.

"Wrap your lips around my cock, little bird," I command as I bury myself deep in her throat. In her eyes I see both fear and excitement, and it riles me up even more. Her mouth is at the base of my cock, her saliva richly flowing. I grab a fistful of her hair and pull her away, then force her mouth back over my cock. Her tongue swirls around my cock as I take it out and thrust back in again. She only gets a few seconds to breathe. I like seeing her panic, seeing her on the verge of choking. Not to the point of death, of course, but just enough to make her cower and beg.

She pants when I take my cock out of her mouth and move back on the bed again. Leaning down, I lick her neck and stick my tongue into her mouth. She's still gasping for air when I take her mouth and kiss her hard. Her hands and feet still fight the chains as I grab her jaw and lick her tongue with mine. A loud squeal escapes her mouth when I bite down on her lip. A drop of blood seeps out and I lick it up, kissing her again.

"Why …" she mutters. Her voice is faint and it sounds like she's pleading. She's almost ready to give up.

"Bleed for me. Hurt for me. Beg for me," I whisper against her skin, leaving rough pecks on her neck. "Your blood entices me, Jay."

She muffles away a moan when I cover her nipple with my mouth and suck so hard it puckers up instantly. I jerk the other while going down even more. When I reach her pussy, I lick right above it. She moans against her will, and it makes me grin. I get up, leaving her deprived of pleasure. Her delicate flesh is raw and red, her nub swollen and probably pulsating too. She looks at me with half-mast eyes, hungry for more, but shamefully aware of it too.

"Do you want to come, little bird?" I ask.

Her lips quiver as she sucks in the air.

I narrow my eyes at her, which immediately prompts her to open her mouth. "Yes, sir."

"And how badly do you want to come?"

"Badly, sir."

"Bad enough to do anything for it?"

She swallows. "Yes, sir."

A wicked smile curves my lips. "You will not move unless I make you, do you understand?"

"Yes, sir."

One by one I take the cuffs off her ankles. Picking up the rope lying beside me, I grab her legs and push them up in a frog-like position. I tie the rope around her left upper and lower leg, and do the same to the right side with another rope. She struggles to stay upright in this most uncomfortable position. I lick my lips at the sight.

Her head turns to look at the camera and then back toward me. "I don't like this, sir," she mutters.

"I do," I say, and then I drag my fingers through her folds. "And that's all that matters. You know I am selfish."

I grin when an expression of satisfaction crosses her face as I rub her shaved pussy. She's wet and open for me, so I dip two fingers inside and press down on her nub with my thumb. She cries out in blissful agony as I swirl around inside and take them out again. "This pussy wants to be filled so badly … doesn't it?"

"Yes, sir," she moans while I flick her clit.

"What does this pussy of mine want most?"

"I want to come, sir."

I stop and slap the top of her pussy with a flat hand. A nice, heavy scream escapes her mouth. Her legs falter, trying to close, but I nudge them open. "Did I tell you you could close your legs?"

"No, sir," she whimpers.

"Try again. What does this pussy need?"

"Your cock, sir." Her body shudders at the touch of my fingers. I splay them across her belly and move closer, perching myself right in front of her. The tip of my cock touches her entrance, her moistness making it bob up and down. Fuck, I can't wait to be inside her.

"Please ... I want your cock inside me," she whisper-moans.

I smile. "Such a little slut. I guess I should be nice and give you what you crave so much." I push inside her, slowly. Air escapes her mouth in the form of a deep moan, almost making me explode this instant. I keep it together and dive further in until her pussy is at my base. My cock pulsates against her flesh; feeling her warmth envelop me is making me crazy with lust. But I'm not content with my work yet. I want to hear her screams before I'm ready to permit her to come and take my load.

So I pick up the belt and fold it. Her eyes flicker open and widen at the sight and sound. She shakes her head, worry settling in her eyes.

"You will learn to love the pain," I say. Then I strike her tit with the softer end. Her squeal is accompanied by a moan when I thrust in and out of her again. The belt leaves a nice red mark on her skin. I intend to make it last. I want her to look at herself and see who she belongs to. Who she's always belonged to. Who she gave herself to the moment she decided to seduce me. My mistake was loving her. Her mistake was inviting me in. We both should have known better than to play with fire. And now the burning never stops.

I whip her again, leaving a hot, searing mark on her other nipple. Her screams fill the room as I lash out, pumping my cock inside her each time she yelps. I love the sound she makes, love how her muscles contract around my cock when she does.

"You should know I thoroughly enjoy pounding your filthy, wet pussy," I growl.

I'm reaching the brink of ecstasy and I want to be able to enjoy it in full. So I throw the belt away and hold onto her legs while fucking her madly. Her body moves to the rhythm of my thrusts, her red and swollen tits bouncing up and down. Her face shows mingled gratification and unease, and it's a beautiful disparity. I want to see more of it.

Placing one hand on the bed beside her head, I wrap the other around her throat. She coughs as I plunge into her. I lean down to kiss her and steal her breath away. I want her on the verge of coming to an orgasm before I release her. Pain and pleasure aren't mutually exclusive; they're intimately woven and, when released, cause powerful euphoria.

As I tighten my grip on her neck, I lean in and lick her lip. "Come for me, little slut."

I fuck her hard and fast as she sputters out air. "Come," I command. "Now."

Her eyes strike me as they open wide. Her mouth opens in a perfect O, and her brows scrunch up. Air stops flowing through her, a silent moan on her lips. And then the convulsions begin.

Her body rocks against me, her pussy fluttering with desire. Her muscles clamp around my cock and pulsate. I can feel her coming with every pore in her body, see it in her beguiling eyes. "Yes, milk me," I say as I pump inside her. The moan that escapes her mouth when I release her from my grasp sends me over the edge. Grabbing her legs, I arch my back and shoot my load into her. My cum fills her to the brim as I thrust twice more, letting go of the primal need that's been haunting me for days on end.

Lying down on her, I pant like an animal who just finished off a kill. Her chest is warm and soft like a pillow. I could rest my head and fall asleep if it were safe. But I know we don't have much time. We have to get away from here as soon as possible. They found us at the diner, so there's no telling when they'll find out about this place too. I won't take the risk. One of the other hotels I go to will have to do. Besides, if I am to continue with my plan, I must get closer to his location. It's a few states away. Might as well make the trip now instead of later.

I take the cuffs off her wrists and look at her. Her eyes glisten and their beauty draws me in. She is a goddess, and I'm the wretched being that takes everything from her. For a moment I wonder if she takes any pleasure in this at all. I don't even know why I care, but I do. Maybe there is a hint of my soul left inside this tainted body.

Her hands lie splayed on the bed, unmoving, even though she is free. She could fight me. However, she doesn't, which surprises me. I lean in and steal a kiss. My lips linger on hers. I can't take them off. I'm addicted to her taste.

"Tell me …" I murmur, taking my lips off for a second. "Did you enjoy this?"

"Yes, sir," she replies like a puppet well trained.

"No … do you really enjoy this?" I ask. "You must tell me the truth."

Her lip quivers against mine as I let my lips reign free on hers again. I shower her in tiny pecks, nipping at her bottom lip, leaving suction marks on her skin. She shivers.

"Answer me," I say, not demanding, but soft.

"Maybe." Her answer comes out hesitantly.

"Why?"

She sighs. "This is … dark. Hard. Painful." Her lips stop moving, but I can tell there's more she wants to say.

"And?"

"Mind-blowing … relief."

I smile. "So you do find release in this."

She frowns and pulls her eyes away from mine.

"Admitting you want to be claimed is hard, but you did it before. You'll do it again. This is who you are. A fighter who loves to be taken and made to submit."

I press my lips on hers, seeking her attention with my eye. She looks at me and starts kissing me back. It's the first time she allows herself to feel me. To really let my mouth conquer hers.

I devour her mouth, taking more and more. I can't stop. My mind is consumed with lust, my lips craving more and more of her. But then her hands slowly slide up my spine, enveloping me in her warmth as she wraps her arms around me and kisses me back. She wants me as much as I want her. Her body acts on its own, demanding more of me as her fingers grasp my head. I feel her. Her naked skin against mine. Her fingers splayed on top of my skull, touching the scars on my head. Anger doesn't rush through my veins. Instead, I feel empowered. Her embrace heals the scars left on my soul.

I realize now that she is not the only prisoner in this room. She has stolen what's left of me.

I must not lose her. I will not accept it. After all these torturous years she's finally mine for the taking, to keep, and I don't ever intend on letting her go. Nobody but the person wanting her dead stands in my way. I will put an end to it all. I'll destroy him if I must. Then she'll be mine completely.

"We seek the truth and will endure the consequences." – Charles Seymour

CHAPTER 19

Jay

TUESDAY, SEPTEMBER 6TH, 2013. 07:55 A.M.

The new hotel room is even bigger than the previous one. A king-sized bed with red linen; oak tables and leather chairs. Breakfast in bed and a skyline filled with towers. I'm a queen imprisoned in a tower.

Every night I dream of X. I have visions of the past, but can't remember them when I awaken. All I know is that I've seen him before. This man knows me for a reason. He was in my life for God knows how long, and I just can't seem to remember. I wonder why.

Every morning I wake up and come to the

realization that I'm still here. That he never leaves, at least not mentally. Whether I want to be or not, I'm bound to him. I haven't attempted an escape since … forever. I can't even remember the last time. I don't even know anymore if I still want to leave or not. My body has been chained and taken over and over again. My mind has been drifting away. The more time I spend with him the less I can see myself being alone. Soon, I'll feel anxiety when he's gone.

I thought I could fight it, that I could stop it from happening, but it's already too late. I was always too late. Like he says, I was always his.

There is no difference between now and then. Time does not exist anymore. Only me and him, this room, my body, his cravings, pleasing him. Each reward is less pain received, and so I strive to be what he desires. A good girl. His little slut. More and more I become what I am in his mind. I can't even remember who I was before him.

No's become yesses until I don't know the difference anymore. His rule is law. I'm not allowed outside. Death is what follows when I don't obey, I know that. I've seen it countless times. And I want to live.

However, I'm not so sure anymore that I can live without him.

X watches the television with anticipation, his fingers strumming the chair. As I sit on his lap and place my head in the nook of his neck, smelling him, I feel empty. Ridden of guilt. Not even in this world. With his hand around my waist and my naked body tucked into his, I feel nothing. I just am.

But when the television zaps to a different channel, a glimpse of a man is all it takes to incinerate the melancholia in my heart. A big bearded man with bloodshot eyes comes into the picture, someone named Al John. The news anchor says this man had been shot in the foot and assaulted with a knife, and that he was doused in some kind of acid. But the fact that this man was tortured doesn't shock me. Or the fact that the night he was killed was the same night X went out and came back bloody-handed.

It's the fact that I feel like I know this man.

His face brings back memories of my father talking to someone just like him, instructing him to do a job. They are mere flashes, but it's enough to know I was right. I remember this man. And now he's dead.

This has to be X's doing.

X

FRIDAY, OCTOBER 20TH, 1995

Her father blames her for everything. All I hear is him yelling at her about why she had to do that, why she had to be friends with me, why I was even around. My parents have kept me away from her and her father ever since the accident with her mother. Even during the funeral, they wouldn't let me speak with anyone. I've been standing in the shadows, watching her, waiting for a chance to finally speak with her again. Nobody will allow it, but I must try. She's my friend.

***

WEDNESDAY, OCTOBER 25TH, 1995

I'm in the hall, waiting for Father to come out and talk to me. My mother told me to stay here until they were done discussing. They're talking about me, of course. I did something bad; I went to check up on her.

When my father steps out of the room, my heart throbs in my throat.

"Don't you ever speak to her again, do you hear me?" my father says, grabbing my chin so hard it hurts.

"Yes."

"You will not talk, you will not even look at her, do you understand?"

"Yes, Father."

He shoves me away and pats down his clothes. "You're a disgrace to this family. Have you any idea what you did?"

"It was an accident."

His hand comes down on my face before I realize

it.

My cheek stings and heats up. I place my hand on top, as if that'll protect me.

"It's time you learned why you are here, who you are, and what you're going to be doing."

I frown. "What do you mean?"

"You will learn to control yourself and others. Lives are in the palms of our hands and we must decide who deserves to live and who deserves to die." He goes to his knees and grabs my arms so tight it scares me. Narrowing his eyes, he says, "Accidents do not exist. Mistakes must be answered for. Come with me." He takes my hand and drags me down the hall to a room I've never been in before. The door opens, the darkness behind it filling me with terror. A long staircase is all that's visible. I have no idea what's down there, except I've seen my mother and father go there often. They never invited me to join them, up until now.

My father pushes me down. "You'll see what our family does for a living, and you'll learn to do the same."

***

FRIDAY, APRIL 11TH, 1997

My father presses the gun into my hand. I'm shaking from top to bottom as he raises it to point at the man on his knees in front of me. He's pinned against the wall with nails in his hands. I saw how they struck them through and heard his screams as he begged for mercy. He won't find any here.

"Go on …" My father nudges me forward.

My heart beats in my throat as I push the gun against his head. My finger lingers on the cold metal trigger. I've seen my parents do this countless times. However, this is my first time. Can I take a life? Am I capable of that? I'm only nine years old. I knew the day would come when I would have to kill someone, but I didn't think it would be this quick.

"Kill him," my father whispers behind me. "You know how to do it."

I swallow, looking at the man with tears in his eyes. "I can't."

My father leans down behind me. "Do you know what this man did?"

I shake my head.

"He beat his wife to death and then shot his only child because he couldn't live with either."

Holy fuck.

I've heard shit before, but never really what they did. I mean, my father always said they were punished for a reason, but usually it was a stupid one, like stealing money or unpaid loans. Not this. No, most of the people my parents work for are even worse than the ones we torture. But this guy … Wow.

"Do you think he deserves to live?" my father asks.

"No," I mutter.

My father places his hand on the gun and wraps his fingers around mine, right on top of the trigger. I close my eyes. "We do not deal in mercy, boy, only death," my father says. And then he pushes so hard I can't stop the trigger from being pulled.

***

THURSDAY, NOVEMBER 26TH, 1998

I can't stop going to her house and watching her from a distance. Even though I'm not allowed, I want to see her. I miss playing with her. She seems so happy, even after what happened. Always darting about the garden, playing with imaginary friends. Sometimes I wish I was invisible so I could play with her again. I miss the times when everything was still simple. Still innocent.

She's younger than me, so young, she probably won't even remember anything about that day when everything changed.

We don't work for her father anymore. After the funeral, we never came back to her house. I wonder if it's because of what happened to her mother.

Suddenly, I'm grabbed by the neck and flung back. I scream and groan when I land on the asphalt, head first. Before I have the chance to see who my attacker is, a bag is put over my head. I scream, but my mouth is jammed with a hand as someone drags me away.

"Shut your mouth," he says. The voice is vaguely familiar.

I'm thrown onto something soft, but it doesn't ease my pain. A punch to the face follows. A tooth dangles from my mouth, the taste of blood lingering on my tongue. I can't fight my attackers as they choke me and slap me. They're much stronger than I am. Tears flow from my eyes as they punch my stomach twice. I feel like I'm about to throw up, but then the hood is taken off my head.

The brightness of the lamp above me has me blinded. A few blinks and I recognize the car I'm in, driving away from her house.

"You had to go and visit her again, huh? I told you what would happen. Next time I won't be so merciful," my father says.

***

WEDNESDAY, APRIL 16TH, 2003

Screams fill the hallway, elating me to my core. I can't count the times I've tortured someone anymore. Yesterday a flaying, the day before that a brutal hacking. What happened before that is all a blur. As if I want to remember the things I do to people. I've become immune to the sounds. Heck, I've even started liking it. Every time I give someone a good beating, my parents give me more privileges and money, which is always a plus. That, and they don't punish me for making mistakes.

I've grown accustomed to messing with people. They are nothing but toys to play with and use until we're done with them. My parents let me do the dirty work while they come back from time to time to interrogate my victims. I love to see the looks on their faces when they don't give the answers my family is looking for and they know what's coming next. Me.

Powerful, that's what I am. I control their pain. I even control their freedom. I could set them loose, let them go, if I choose to do so. Except, I won't, because our family lives off these things. I live because I do these things, and I do value my own life. It's kill or get killed.

As my victim's blood splatters on the walls, I see the lady with the dark brown hair tumbling down the stairs again. It plays over and over in my mind. Each and every time I see *her* as well. The girl that used to mean innocence. The girl I can never see again, because if I do, I'll experience a fate worse than death.

When I was young I used to believe in love and happy endings. What a load of bull. It doesn't exist.

***

TUESDAY, SEPTEMBER 6TH, 2013. 9:25 P.M.

They will all pay for what they did. Just thinking about it makes the hairs on the back of my neck stand up. Looking at the USB with the video, I know this is the only way. Life will be nothing but hell for him after this. I'll keep bombarding him with shit he's not prepared for until he begs me to take his life.

I put the USB in an envelope and wrap it firmly before sending it off. Once it leaves my hands, excitement fills me. I can already imagine the look on his face when he sees what I've done with her.

I take a deep breath as I step outside the post office. It's a beautiful day. Perfect for ruining more lives.

I've brought Jay to the city she once loved so much but which is erased from her memory. It's been a long time since I've seen Atlanta, but I still remember every corner of every street. This is where both our histories were made. If only she realized how dangerous it is to be here.

I only have a few friends here I can truly trust. I'll have to rely on them to do my dirty work for me and keep an eye out for Jay during the times that I'm gone, like now. Not that it's needed. She's grown accustomed to following me and obeying me, and seems less set on escaping me every chance she gets. She's changed, for the better. At least, for me. Every once in a while a little voice inside my head wonders how she feels about this. It quickly dissipates as well.

I get inside my car and drive toward the hooker

part of town. I know where to find them; I've been here plenty of times before, either to kill their pimps or kill them. Or both. It didn't matter, so long as I got paid.

When I find a suitable one, I roll open the window and signal her to come.

"Hey, pretty boy," a woman with long blonde hair, walking in stilettos and shorts says. When she sees me for who I really am, a scarred, ugly monster, she winces.

"So um … what are you up for?" she asks.

"Not interested."

She rolls her eyes and sighs. "What the fuck are you doing here then?"

"I'll pay ten times what you're offered here."

Her eyes widen and her mouth shuts. Good. I was about to blow her jaw off just for talking to me the way she did.

"I'm listening," she says.

"Good. Get in. We'll talk specifics while driving."

As she steps inside, I light a cigarette. "Name."

"Natasha. You can ask, you know." She shakes her head in annoyance. "So, what's your name?" she asks.

"X."

"What? Just X?" she scoffs.

I raise my gun and point it at her in a flash of a second. She squeals, but I place my hand over her mouth. "Listen and you'll live. Don't and you're dead. Simple. Understand?"

She nods frantically as I remove my hand from her mouth, immediately locking the car afterwards so she won't get out. "Now, you will work for me, but you must do exactly as I say."

"Why the fuck would I work for you?" she yells.

"Because you value your life and money, and you'll get to keep both."

She frowns, sighing. "Whatever. Just get on with it."

"There's a guy; I want you to fuck him."

She starts plucking at some strings hanging from her shorts. "That all?"

"No." I wait until she looks at me. When she does, I take out a note with his exact address and where he'll be at what time. "You will be there to seduce him at this exact time and place. He will be there and you will not let him go until you've fucked him."

"Uhuh ..." she says with furrowed brows.

"Make sure someone sees you."

"Right ... Is this some sort of secret orgy? I'm not—"

"You will do this if you value your life." I hold the gun up higher again. "Now listen. Once you're done with him, you'll report to me immediately." I fish an untraceable cell phone from my pocket and throw it in her lap. "You'll call me and we'll meet."

"And then what? Do I get my payment or do you want more shit done? Do I look like a fucking business to you?"

"Shut up!" I say, pushing the gun to her head.

"Okay, okay!" She whimpers.

"You will do this, understand?"

"Yes, I will," she says.

"Now this is very important, so remember it. If anyone talks to you, tell them you were used and beaten."

Her jaw drops. "What?"

"Do not tempt me to pull the trigger."

"Are you kidding me?"

"No, and if you want your payment *and* your life, you will do as I say."

"Fine. Whatever. But it'll be ten times the price."

"Done. Fuck him. Tell people he took advantage of you. Call me. Meet me. Got it?"

"Yes, sir," she says, saluting me with a chuckle.

I hate, fucking hate, hearing that word get spewed out of her mouth. It's like she's trampling all over the respect I demand with it. The respect Jay willingly gives me, because she knows I'm right. She knows I will take what I need and give her what she desires. She knows she owes it to me.

But this woman … this one's playing with fire. I'm almost tempted to blow her brains out right here and now, except I really need a complacent, replaceable, unimportant woman right now. She fits the bill.

"Letting go doesn't mean giving up, but rather accepting that there are things that cannot be." – Anonymous

CHAPTER 20

Jay

SATURDAY, SEPTEMBER 14TH, 2013. 10:52 P.M.

His fingers curl around my upper leg, digging into my thigh as he hits the gas. Right there, below his hand, is a red belt mark from the lashings of last night. It wasn't harsh or painful. It wasn't punishment. It was sinful pleasure that brought him to do this to me. Before he fucks me he needs to see I'm his, needs to see his marks all over me. My reddened skin delights him. His smile means I get a treat. Nowadays, coming is the only release I have. He grants me this gift as a reward for pleasing him. This release is all I have left

… I'll do anything for it. I admit, I've become a whore to his commands. I don't care.

Like now, when I'm in his car, letting him feel me up. I don't know where we're going, and it doesn't matter. All that matters is that my life and body are in his hands, and that the only way to escape it all is by shutting myself off.

I can already feel my heart falling deeper and deeper into his trap. I yearn for a loving touch, crave his attention, because he is the only one who can give it to me. He's tamed me. It's against everything I ever stood for, and yet I let it happen. My body is his. My soul is his. My mind … and my heart is soon to follow. Nobody survives without love, and he is the only one willingly offering it to me. He takes me and kisses my fear away, wraps me in his arms and tells me I'm his, providing me with certainty. How can I not say yes?

I shudder when his fingers leave my lap and my skin is left cold and yearning for his touch. The car slows down and X parks the car in a deserted parking lot, close to a news station. He turns off the gas and waits. Glancing at him, I notice he's fiddling with his tie while grinding his teeth. He's waiting for something to happen.

The doors to the building open and out comes a woman in high heels and too-short shorts. Her long ponytail swings from one side to the other as she walks down the steps and looks around the parking lot. X's brows draw closer as he clears his throat and opens the locks on the door. My heart rate shoots through the roof as impending freedom awaits. The lock is gone. I could open the door, jump out, and run for my life. I could do it right now, while he's still distracted by the woman walking toward an alley beside the building.

My legs shake and my feet feel numb. Somehow I know I won't be able to flee. No matter how many times I try, X would always catch me. Or he'd kill me before I managed to get away. And even if for some miraculous reason I escaped, the organization that's after my head will never let me live in peace.

I'm doomed to spend the rest of my life here with X. My brain just keeps playing these malicious tricks on me that put me on edge, that make me hate the fact that I can't do anything about it. They keep reminding me that I'm robbed of my freedom, and I don't want to be reminded at all. I just want to live in the moment and take it as it comes. That's all I'm going to do. Yup. No more thinking. No more believing. No more hurting. Just be.

For a brief moment X's eye darts toward me, emphasizing the fact that I'm with him now. He opens the door and steps out, walking around the car to open mine as well. Holding out his hand, he looks down at me with a smug smile on his face. It's almost as if he can see what goes on in my mind.

I take his silky smooth hand. The gloves he's wearing feel eerily comfortable as I step out of the car and pat down my tight black dress. Sometimes I'm still amazed when I look down and see myself in this dress. I look classy as hell, even though I'm no lady. X buys all my clothes and decides what I wear and when. It surprises me he wants to see me in this. In the bedroom I'm his slut in a skimpy dress, but when he takes me out I look like some sort of glamour girl.

X even tells me what makeup to put on and how he wants me to look. I do my best to make him happy, because it means fewer problems for me. Except, when I look at myself in the mirror I can't help searching for the marks he left on me. Seeing them reminds me of my strength and will to survive. Feeling them reminds me that makeup won't hide the filth underneath.

As he wraps one arm around my waist and beckons me to walk with him across the parking lot, I crawl back into the role he's chosen for me. I look down as he guides me, his warm hand bringing about strange emotions. I won't allow myself to feel them, so I watch his gun instead, the metal that decides the course of my life.

"You're my precious little slut, you know that?" X mumbles as we walk toward the alley.

"Yes, sir, I know I am."

His hand drifts down to my ass and he squeezes it softly. "Good. Remember it. I'm going to be doing something tonight you will not understand, but I want you to watch, and I want you to remember everything you see."

My lungs feel constricted. This dress is suddenly

too tight to breathe in. "What are you going to do?" I ask.

"Something that must be done."

I look up to see the monster he's becoming again. In his eye resides a twinge of anguish, that exact look I despise. The look I've come to worship. Two conflicting emotions, two conflicting beings in one. It's the same look he uses when he bends me over and spanks me until his hand is seared onto my skin. It's the same look that tells me he owns me. It's a look that both terrifies me and vexes me. The look is not for me.

It's for her.

My breathing becomes rapid as we approach the woman in the alley. She shivers from the cold and eyes me from top to bottom.

"Who's this?" she asks, pointing to me.

"None of your business. Did you do what I told you to do?" X says, his voice gruff and demanding.

"Oh, I fucked him all right. And I went straight to your contact to tell him the news."

"Good." X turns to me and I cower under his murderous look. "Stand over there. Do not do anything unless I tell you to," he commands me.

Then he turns back to the lady … and punches her in the face.

My jaw drops in shock and I cover my mouth with my hand to prevent a scream coming out. The woman winces and tries to punch him back, but he grabs her wrists and pins them to the wall.

"What the fuck was that for?" she yells.

"I told you to make it look rough. You didn't look roughed up enough."

"Fuck you. I went to the news and I told them I was used. You said that was enough."

"Not good enough. Your story might be convincing, but your looks aren't. A few bruises might do the work."

"X? What are you doing?" I yell.

He steps away from the woman, taking a deep breath. Then he takes out his gun and points it at her face. She screams and tries to fight him off, but before she has a chance to escape, a bullet has already penetrated her skull. She drops to the floor, dead.

In shock I stare at the scene in front of me. A tear trickles down my face. He just killed some random lady right in front of me. Her life ended just like that. As if it was his right all along. As if he can play with anyone he wants.

"I—I…" I stutter. I don't know what to say. I can't believe my eyes.

X turns to me again. I panic, backing up into the alley, away from him, but he keeps stalking toward me. In the darkness his scar becomes even clearer from the moonlight shining down upon us. He truly is a monster.

"Why?" I mumble. "Why do you keep killing them?"

"She had to die."

"But she did something for you. You promised her something, didn't you? She would never have done it if this was the outcome."

"I did, except, I don't intend to pay hookers when they don't do their job. Her job was to make it look like she was forced. She didn't, so I took over that part."

"And you killed her for it?"

"She had to die." His voice is eerily dark as he approaches me. When my back bumps against a wall, I panic. I'm trapped.

I scream as he comes closer and grabs my arm, placing his hand over my mouth. I fight him with all I have, but it's no use; he's much stronger than I am. Tears run freely down my cheeks as I realize that he only brought me here to witness her death. To see the power he has over people and to threaten me with it.

"Calm. Down," he commands.

As he holds me in his arms, I twist and turn until my back is against him and I'm facing the wall. He pulls my arms behind my back and tightens his grasp on my wrists, leaning in to whisper in my ear. "It had to happen. I'm trying to protect you." He's holding me so tight I can barely breathe. That, or it's the adrenaline coursing through my veins. "I want you, only you, and I'll do anything to protect you from them—the people who want your head. Now ... will you be quiet or do I have to shut you up myself?"

I swallow and nod, forcing myself to forget the images of a woman being murdered flashing through my mind.

As X takes his hand off my mouth, I mutter, "You killed her … you kill everyone."

"She was a loose end."

"Fuck loose ends; she could've kept her promise! You didn't!" I kick back, trying to free myself from his grasp, but he won't let me go.

"Listen to me, little bird. I told her to fuck the one who's behind the target on your back, so I can frame him. I'm going to make his life miserable, so that when I'm done with him he'll beg me to end his life quickly. I will not let anyone stand in the way of me having you all to myself, or my revenge." He shoves me against the wall, keeping me there with just one hand. "I am not a good guy. I think I told you that many times before. I use people to my advantage until they're no longer useful to me, and then I get rid of them. She was no longer useful." His free hand drifts to the front of my body, where it slips under my dress. "Useful … like a puppet under your command," I mutter as X's pants begins to tent and his erection prods my back.

"Exactly. Do what I say and you live. Be useful and you live."

"Am I still useful?" I ask in a haze.

X's fingers slide up my dress, exposing my bare ass to his thick bulge. "As long as you give me what I want …" he murmurs, nibbling my ear. "You are mine, little bird, to use as I see fit, and I do want you to give everything to me. I will keep your life safe so long as

you're willing to do whatever it takes to please me."
When his hand reaches my thigh, I press my legs
together, but it's no use to keep him out. I'm already
melting from his touch. He takes hold of my naked
pussy, reminding me why exactly he told me not to
wear panties. He spreads my legs with force, sliding his
finger down my folds.

"Is this pussy mine?" he asks, licking my neck.

I nod. "Yes, sir."

X's fingers dip inside my pussy, causing me to gasp.
He swirls around, making me wet to the core. I can tell
he knows he has this effect on me. He chuckles and
grins against my skin. "Already wet and open to receive
my cock. So willing …"

His fingers are dexterous and skillful as he flicks my
nub, his other fingers edging close to my entrance. In
his arms I quiver as he rubs me fast. His grip on my
wrists is harsh and painful, and I can already feel it
leaving a red mark. The pain adds to the pleasure as he
continues to play with me. He's right. I am a slut. I tell
myself I don't need this, but I do. I need him so I can
live. I need him so I can feel alive. He makes me feel
everything.

"See what a little slut you are?" he says. "Don't
deny it. Love it. I'll show you what it means to belong.
Now come."

The orgasm comes out of nowhere, responding to
his touch and voice. It flows through me, setting my
body on fire. His command alone was enough to set

me off. He keeps toying with my nub, flicking it, even while I'm coming. My body zings from his touch. I can't get enough. I still want more, still crave his attention. He keeps offering it to me. With his hand on my pussy and his fingers rubbing me roughly, he gives me mind-blowing pleasure.

I'm on the verge again when he breaks contact and leaves me hanging, panting. I glance over my shoulder. The sound his tie makes as it slips off his neck sends shivers down my spine.

He licks his lips. "Arms behind your back, little bird. Do not disobey me."

I keep my arms locked together while he wraps the tie around my wrists and knots it. "Good girls don't fight. Bad girls get tied up," he says, kissing my shoulder blade. His kiss turns into a bite, and I cry out in pain. He puts his finger in my mouth and says, "Suck, slut. Show me how much you're willing to give me everything." It stings when he takes his mouth off my shoulder. My mind is playing with me, telling me to bite down on his finger, but I know I might die if I do. The will to live is stronger than the will to fight.

I can taste myself as he swirls his finger around in my mouth. He groans as his hand drifts down to my ass and jerks up what remains of my dress. I'm completely exposed now, and when I hear his zipper being pulled down, I know what's going to happen.

"This little slut wants a cock? She'll get a cock," he says. The tip of his shaft pushes against my entrance as he wipes it back and forth over my pussy and ass. I groan from the teasing, feeling tormented sexually as well as mentally. Gripping the tie, he enters and fills me up completely. Air escapes my mouth as I feel him thrust in and out of me, pushing me up against the wall.

"You like this cock?" he grunts, his breath becoming rapid and loud like a bull blowing off steam.

Nodding is not enough. He grabs my hair and slams my head firmly against the wall.

"Say it!" he growls.

"I like your cock, sir."

"Not. Good. Enough," he says, jerking harder on my hair while fucking me roughly.

"I want your cock, sir. I love it," I say, spreading my legs to grant him more so he'll be nicer.

"Yeah, I know you do, you filthy whore." He pulls his cock out. Fazed, I hear the sound of his belt flipping through the rings. Oh, no.

"Oh, yes," he whisper-laughs.

Did I say that out loud?

Before I have a chance to respond, he wraps the belt around my neck and fastens it. With his fingertips he nudges me down until I can barely stand upright. "Keep that position."

Twisting the belt until the loose end is in his hands, he pulls it hard, and then drives into me again. I can feel every little ridge of the piercings in his cock as he drives into me. I can barely breathe as he fucks me from behind, using the belt as some sort of leash. I feel like an animal, and yet this fucking is driving me mad. Madly into bliss. It turns off every bit of shame, emotion, remorse, hurt in my body and only allows me to experience what's happening right now. Him, claiming my body, over and over again.

His cock is rigid and pushes deep inside me as he pulls hard on the belt. It's the only thing keeping me from tumbling forward, and I trust him not to let me fall. He wants me in this position, to be the slut he wants me to be. And slowly but surely I am turning into just that.

My pussy is fluttering around his shaft, craving more of his pounding until I'm at the edge of ecstasy. It wants to come so badly, but I know that if I do, I might get punished. But I can't deny that his cock makes me insane with lust, that I'm losing control over my orgasm. That I have no say in whether I come or not. I just do.

"Do you want to come again, huh?" His voice is smoky and dark. "Does this little slut want to milk me so badly?"

"Yes, sir, please … can I come?" I say. He pulls so hard on the belt I nearly choke.

"No."

I growl and groan from frustration as he thrusts into me once more. It's hard to keep it together when his cock starts pulsating inside me. I can feel everything: his hot breath lingering on my skin as he leaves little bite marks all over my shoulder, the way he grinds me, how he groans and breathes like a madman overcome by sheer lust.

"You want my cum, you dirty whore?"

"Yes, please," I say, taking a deep breath to retain my calm.

He jerks on the belt and whacks my ass with a flat hand, making me scream. "Louder."

"I want your cum, sir."

"Beg for it."

"Please, give me your cum."

As I whimper and groan from his thrusts, he explodes inside me. His shots come out with loud growls as he fills me with his warmth. "Now come," he groans.

The command brings me over the edge. The explosion courses through my body, which pulses with need as I come together with him. My pussy feels warm and sated. When he's done, he slaps my ass again, leaving a painful sizzle.

Suddenly, he pulls his cock from my pussy and twirls me around. "Down. On your knees."

A push is all that's needed to bring me to my knees. I'm weak. Willing. Offering. Unlike me.

With the belt still in his hands, he starts rubbing himself. He jerks himself in front of me, looking down upon me with teeth jammed together as if he hasn't decided whether he wants to screw me again or screw me over.

He flicks the head and runs his hand along the shaft, then slaps me with it.

"Suck all of it off," he says, pulling on the belt to get my head closer. "Suck until it's clean."

I lean forward, but he pushes me hard into his cock. Even when half-hard, he still makes me choke on it. I lick, suck, and plead with my eyes until he's satiated. Rubbing his lips together, he groans as he takes his cock from my mouth and inspects it.

"Good girl. You lapped it all up." X grabs my chin and nudges me to stand. My breath comes out in short gasps as he takes off the belt. Suddenly, he leans in to plant a kiss on my lips. I'm taken by surprise as he claims my mouth, his tongue probing at the seams. He's eager and I can feel his desire to have me in every way possible, just from this one kiss. It's almost as if … No, that's not him. He could never want my heart.

With his lips massaging mine, he unties my wrists. He brings his hand to my pussy and dips it in, to my surprise. I gasp in his mouth as he speaks the words, "I want you to drip as you walk back to the car. Let my cum run down your legs and show the world that you belong to me."

"Forget the past. Only the future can be altered." – Notes of X

CHAPTER 21

Lay

SATURDAY, SEPTEMBER 14ᵀᴴ, 2013. 10:32 A.M.

Losing your soul comes at a price. A hefty price. Sanity.

Two shovels, one hole. A body on the bottom.

The clouds have gathered, raindrops falling down by the bucket. We're soaked and cold, but we keep going. Shoveling up the dirt, I try not to look her in the eyes as I throw it on her. X is on the left while I'm on the right, working our asses off to bury this body. My heels sink into the dirt and my dress is smudged. I feel like a criminal. No, I know I am. This is so fucking wrong, I can't even begin to describe it, but what else am I supposed to do? X handed me the shovel and told me to help him. I can't say no anymore. I lost that word long ago, when I tried fighting him. It's no use. He wants me, and X always gets what he wants. No matter what I do, he wins. He's spinning me around his finger now, winding me up like a doll that speaks, talks and walks as he commands. The worst part is that I don't care anymore. I've stopped caring. It's not going to get any better if I care. There's nobody that needs me around, or searches for me, or wonders where I've gone. Only him. He is the only one who truly needs me … who cares about me in his own wicked way.

Sometimes I think I'm starting to need him as much as he needs me.

But it's strange. Being around him has made me realize the world is much more complicated than I thought. That I'm more complicated than I thought. I'm doing things I never imagined I would. I'm helping him hide a dead body, for fuck's sake. It can't get any more fucked up than that.

I wonder why he goes through all this trouble just to catch the one behind everything. If it's really all about me having a target on my head. He wants them to feel misery and pain. Humiliating him is his goal, especially now with that hooker. There has to be more to it. He wouldn't just do that for me.

"Why are you doing this?" I ask in between shoveling up the dirt.

Frowning, he briefly looks up from under his brows, a grizzly look in his eye. Then he sighs loudly and continues.

"Whose life do you want to ruin?" I ask again.

He slams the shovel into the ground and wipes his hands. "Someone who destroyed not only your life, but mine too." He picks up the shovel again and slams down the sand on top of the grave. "And now I'm going to do the same to them."

Destroyed his life? Is he talking about after he found me? Or does he mean before that?

One look at him is all it takes to know what this is about. He's hiding his face from me again.

"Is this about your scar?" I ask with a soft voice, trying not to enrage him.

He throws the shovel away and stands there, panting. "That too."

I lick my lips, mulling over the words I'm going to say next. "What did they do to you?"

His eye drifts toward the ground as he stamps the grave with his feet. "You don't want to know."

"I do," I say, standing my ground.

He looks at me, a brief moment of silence passing between us. "You? You want to know about me?" he scoffs.

"Is that so odd, that I want to know who my captor really is? What he's been through? The least it will give me is the knowledge that I'm not the only one hurting here."

"Yeah, I reckon you want to use it against me. Because knowledge is power."

I swallow away the nerves building in my throat and stomach. God, why is he always one step ahead of me? I purse my lips. "Fine. If you don't want to tell me, then don't." I pat down the grave with my shovel while X throws on leaves.

It's quiet for a while until he opens his mouth again. "All right. I've decided I will tell you. After all, a pet like you should feel the need to please me. It might come easier to you when you know."

"Know what?"

"That I sacrificed everything for you."

***

X

TUESDAY, DECEMBER 9TH, 2008

Sweat drops roll down my face as I face what no man should ever have to face.

"You know why we have to do this," my mother says.

I twist and turn in the wooden chair, trying to free myself. The ropes are cutting into my flesh, but I don't care. Just the sight of that thing makes me want to stand up and run, no matter that I'm tied down. "Please, Mother, isn't there another way?" I ask. I never use the word please. Now I'll gladly use it.

"No," my father growls. "We told you what would happen if you defied our orders."

Darkness surrounds me, nestling in my heart. The room is lit only by the crackling fire right in front of me. My eyes dart back to my mother and what she's doing. A chill runs down my spine as I watch her play with the fire like it's all fun and games to her. The fun ended a long time ago.

I swallow. "I don't deserve that. Not for what I did."

"That is exactly why you deserve it!" my father yells. "Don't you see?" He grabs my chin and forces me to look at him. The shame and humiliation I feel are reflected in his eyes. I realize this is really going to happen.

The urge to flee takes over.

I get up, chair and all, and try to make a run for it, but my father captures me and puts me down again.

"No! You can't do this!" I scream.

He holds me down, grasping my arms and keeping my feet together with his shoes. The stern look on his face is unlike any other I've ever seen.

"You knew the risks. I told you what would happen if you continued."

"It wasn't me!" I yell. "I'm not the one who started it all."

My father goes to his knees in front of me, his eyes narrowing. I see my mother poking the fire, the sight making me sick to my stomach.

"You couldn't stop using those eyes of yours for all the wrong reasons."

"Who cares? You're a monster! You're all monsters!" I scream. "How can you do this? Are you crazy?"

I ask the question, but I already know the answer. I knew it since I was born into this fucked-up world. My family never was, and never will be, normal. Vermin. Scum of the earth. Shadowy protectors of the vile and killers of the innocent. We are everywhere and nowhere. We are nobodies. Our lives don't matter.

My life doesn't matter. Not even to them.

"Stop. This is what's happening. End of story. You had a choice and you wasted it," my father says.

"Choice? My ass! There is no choice between dying and *that*!" I grind my teeth.

My father smiles. It's disgusting. "There is always a choice."

He gets up again and takes a few steps back. My mother turns her head and raises the fire iron. The red glow sets a full panic attack into motion.

I wriggle and struggle to get free, but it's no use. Snapping his fingers, my father summons a few men to keep me down.

My father turns his back to me, clearing his throat. "You ruined us. Because of you we lost the same client yet again. It cannot be undone. This is your punishment. Accept it with dignity and grace."

My mother inspects the fire iron and then smiles at me. It horrifies me. When she starts walking toward me, I push back as hard as I can. It's no use. Within seconds she's in front of me.

"I love you, my dear boy, but this has to be done. You know the rules."

"Screw the rules!" I scream, fighting the ones that are holding me back.

"Even in our profession there are rules. You should have realized that before you attempted to break them." She lifts her hand, and I lean back, but it's not enough. She can still touch me. Her hand gently cups my face and caresses my cheek, like she's suddenly the loving mother she could never be to me.

I gnash my teeth, trying to bite her. She withdraws and chuckles.

"It was this or killing you. You know why we can't let this go." She raises the fire iron. "An eye for an eye."

And with those last words she sears my right eye. My lungs can't handle the screams that come from my body, the air that expands my chest so fast it feels like I'm bursting apart. My skin is on fire. Being stabbed doesn't compare to this. I can feel my warm blood flowing down my face. Closing my eye is no use. Red turns to black and soon everything is gone. My screams are ignored as she continues to carve me. It stings so badly that I want to cry with the eye I no longer have.

I'm in between fading in and out of consciousness, and at that moment I'm suddenly aware of the silence surrounding me, filling my head. It prepares me for the burden I have to carry, the hatred that has been scorched into my skin. I will make them pay.

When she's done with her savage attack, she steps back and takes a look. She's admiring her work. I gaze up at her with my one working eye, a small slit I can barely keep open, but I refuse to give up. I reject weakness. I will survive this, even if it costs me everything.

Frowning and clenching my teeth, I look up at her, seething. Pain runs through my veins, but I ignore it completely. Fury has taken over my soul. "What have you done to me?" I hiss.

"What you did to us. You scarred us for life. I returned the gift to you."

My father signals the men. He doesn't even look at me. "Take him away."

"I'll kill you for this!" I scream. I jerk around, but my strength is waning. I can't fight the ropes anymore. The blood and pain have taken their toll on me.

"You'll never see us again, never hear from us again, you'll never be welcome here again," my father says.

"Goodbye," my mother says as she wipes the poker on a white cloth.

I keep my eye solely on them as I'm dragged out of

the mansion. When the doors close I lose my will to fight. The pain has taken its toll on me. For a moment everything fades and turns to black. As I slip in and out of consciousness I feel like minutes have passed. I'm still being hauled, although I have no idea where. They take me to a forest, far, far away from anywhere, where they throw me into the snow, chair and all.

Their footsteps are the last thing I hear before there is only nothingness. Flakes of snow fall on my face, and I welcome the cool it brings to my withered skin. This place, in all its serenity, is a perfect resting place for a screwed-up person like me.

However, I won't surrender to this cold, to this pain, to impending death. I will survive. I will conquer and slay them. The promise I make to myself fuels the spark of life left inside me. One day I will come for their lives. I will be the devil that guides them to hell.

***

Jay

SATURDAY, SEPTEMBER 14ᵀᴴ, 2013. 10:40 A.M.

Frozen, I stand there, shivering in the rain. Goose bumps scatter on my body as my lips part and my mouth is left hanging. The shovel drops from my hand;

the sound of metal falling to the ground is loud in the silence of the night. I'm speechless.

Rain drips down his face, running through the grooves in his skin, the lines of his scars even more visible than before. The light of the moon casts an eerie darkness on one side of his face as well as light on the other.

Two conflicting emotions weave their way into my heart: disgust and pity. X's fingers curl up into a fist as he slams his mouth shut. We're both at a loss for words. The silence is killing me. I can't believe what I just heard. I don't even know what to say.

"Your parents?" I mutter.

He nods and frowns, cracking his knuckles.

"Holy shit …"

"You could say that again," he scoffs.

"But … why? What did you do?"

He purses his lips and then marches toward me. Panicking, I back up into a tree, but fail to move past it. He's right in front of me, seething, his nostrils flaring. His stare feels like it penetrates my skull.

"You."

I suck in a short breath. "What do you mean?"

Smashing his lips together, he looks down at the ground and sighs, closing his eyes. "You don't fucking remember." As he looks back at me, I'm shaken to my core. The way he gazes at me, like I'm his weakness, is unsettling. Not because I'm scared, but because I've never seen this before.

Or maybe I have.

Without thinking, my hand lifts to meet his face. He tentatively moves his head away, but still not enough to prevent my hand from touching him. As I place my hand on his face, he winces; his chest suddenly stops heaving from anger. I feel his scars, the ridges and dents on his eye. My fingers move to touch every crevice, every painful memory, all the pain and agony seared into his skin. This is what they did to him. They made him the monster he is today.

His hands reach up and grab my head. He leans in, placing his forehead against mine as he looks deep into my eyes.

"Remember," he says, his voice thick with lingering emotions. "Remember, little bird, remember!"

His voice. This touch. It rips everything apart, leaving pieces of the puzzle on the play board. And now I assemble them one by one. Memories of the past and present mix together until I can no longer form a coherent thought. Pictures and images of a past me spin through my head. A past with him.

I know him. I always knew him.

"The heart that truly loves never forgets."
— Thomas Moore

CHAPTER 22

Jay

NOVEMBER 3RD, 2006

I'm in the back of the office, pretending not to be here, so I don't get noticed. My father ordered me to be in this room, because he wants me to meet the new people who will be keeping us safe. It's not necessarily because he thinks my life is in jeopardy; more because he wants to keep an eye on me. I couldn't care less about all that. If it wasn't for the fact that he took my allowance I wouldn't even be here in the first place. I'd be off partying with my friends, drinking booze until we're passed out drunk. It's safe to say I don't like wearing dresses and pretending to be a nice girl. Especially not when my father bosses me around. I'm sixteen years old; I can decide for myself who I want to be and what I want to look like.

"Jay." The way he calls out my name makes it sound like an insult. I know he hates it. Not just my name, but me too. There's a reason I was named Jay; my father would have preferred a boy. Boys are so much better at politics. Women are only good to keep the men company. I'm not exaggerating; this is truly him in a nutshell.

"Tuck that frizz behind your ear. And pat down your dress, you look like a mess," he says gruffly.

"Yes, Father," I sigh.

"And do something about that attitude. We can't have that."

"They're only guards."

"They're not *just* guards." He coughs and clears his throat. "These people have worked for me before and I demand their utmost respect. I need you to look and act your best. I will not have them see you and lose respect for me. You will behave like a lady."

"You mean like a robot."

He briefly throws me a look, and then continues pacing around the room. "You are to listen carefully and introduce yourself properly." He walks to his desk and sits down on his black leather chair. "And if you do anything, I swear to God I *will* take everything from you for a month, and by everything I do mean *everything*."

I swallow, letting the threat sink in. I don't want to lose my internet, my access to the outside world, my friends, all my connections and fun. *Everything* means being locked up in a cold tower here … well, not literally, but it's still boring as hell and not fun at all. Of course, this is coming from past experience. I've never been on good terms with my father. Somehow I always struggle to do as he says. Maybe it's because he never gave me a good reason to do what he wants. There's nothing in it for me. Not even a shred of love.

There is a knock on the door, and our butler enters the room. "Sir, their car just arrived. Shall I escort them in?"

"Yes, yes, and bring them to my office immediately."

"Right, sir."

The butler tiptoes off again, while my father spends his time checking out his suit and combing what's left of his hair. He looks tired. His cheekbones seem even more hollow than before I got caught kissing a boy at a party. It's as if each time he catches me doing something I'm not supposed to, he ages a few years.

My playing, teasing, and reckless fun bring him shame. His shame makes me want to run, tease people, and have free-spirited fun. It's a never-ending circle of disappointment in one another. My father has always tried to mold me into one of his perfect shapes, and I never was what he wanted me to be. I'm not a leader,

I'm not calm and assertive. I'm not kind and sweet. I'm everything he never wanted, and because of that I rebel.

I sigh from the jumble of thoughts, but then my father's guests enter the room and I stiffen. A few men and one woman walk into the room. They're all in suits, except for her. In her high heels and long red dress she looks like a superstar on the red carpet. Her hair is tucked in a bun, and she has a beautiful birthmark on her upper lip. She briefly glances at me, striking me down with just a look. It's like a thunder strike, so bold, so swift, and deadly.

The men are equally as scary. With their shiny black shoes and clean-fitting tuxes they look like gentlemen, but they reek of evil. Power. Fear. It's their trademark. One look is all it takes to know they mean business.

My father steps away from his desk and holds out his hand, shaking theirs.

"We meet again …" my father says.

"We are delighted to have you as our client. You've made a good decision to hire us again."

"Don't make me regret it this time," my father says, eyeing me when he does. I feel creeped out by all of this.

"We will make sure of it."

"So long as you keep that boy out of it and away from us."

"We will, I promise you that."

"Great," my father says.

They talk some more, but I don't pay attention, because I'm taken by dread. These people make my skin crawl and the hair on my back stand up. Especially the way they seem to move around the room, so cautiously, so painstakingly aware of everything surrounding them. They're like hawks circling above the land, narrowing in on their prey before launching a vicious and calculated attack.

Are these the people my father hired to protect us? He must be insane. There's no way they can protect anyone. I bet they'd kill them first.

When I notice someone else standing in the hallway, hidden in the shadow, my breathing stops, and I think my heart does too, even if it is only for one second. A guy with hair as black as night is waiting outside. Someone I remember.

***

SATURDAY, SEPTEMBER 14^(TH), 2013. 10:40 A.M.

That someone was him.

Memories come flooding back in like a never-ending wave.

The boy at the party with his raven black hair came to work for my father. The killings were his family's doings. The boy I can't get out of my mind.

He knew me all along.

***

SATURDAY, DECEMBER 6TH, 2008. 10:13 P.M.

I can't take my lips off him. He's so damn delicious. I've never kissed someone like this before. Sure, I've had plenty of boys and guys, but not someone like him. He's a man. Someone who knows how to handle a girl. His kisses are rough and his little bites make me moan. I love how he nibbles on me, taking more and more of me, like he can't get enough of me either.

The lights in the hallway cast a gloomy light on him. His damp skin glows, drops of sweat dripping down his beautiful body. He's ripped and covered in tats, and I love running my hands down his chest. He groans in my mouth as I unbutton his shirt and slide my hands up his buffed chest.

"Fuck …" he whispers against my mouth. Hungry for more, he probes my mouth with his tongue, claiming me completely. I love how he just takes what he wants and owns it, no questions asked. After years of teasing and flirting back and forth, I've finally got him. He's all mine.

"You're such a fucking bad girl, Jay," he growls, biting my lip.

I moan when he drags his lips down my neck and sucks on my skin, leaving a red mark. The sizzle that accompanies the pain makes my clit thump with desire. God, I'm such a slut. I love it.

He comes back up and plants his lips on mine again, kissing me hard and rough. My lips are red and swollen when he suddenly stops and looks at me from under his dark lashes.

"Yeah … I think you've had enough," he says, a devilish smile appearing on his face.

"No, give me more," I say, pulling him closer again. He leans back, preventing me from kissing him.

"No."

"Oh, c'mon, stop fighting it."

"These nightly adventures should stop here."

"No. Why should they?"

I wrap my arms around his neck, but he grabs my wrists and takes them off again. A loud groan slips across his tongue when I steal another kiss. I grin.

"Because we'll get caught. You've been seducing me in your house, for fuck's sake. It can't get any more dangerous than that."

"Who cares …?"

"I'd like to keep my balls intact, thanks."

I giggle, pecking him on the jaw, dragging my lips sideways. "But I want you," I murmur close to his ear. "Take me."

His grip on my wrists tightens and he pushes me up against the wall. "You're a slut. You let yourself be fucked by any man and you don't fucking care. So why should I?"

"They're nothing," I say. "I don't want them. I just wanted their attention."

"And why would it be any different with me?" He purses his lips. "You're a seductress, Jay, but you look to me for all the wrong reasons."

I push my chest forward, showing him how taut my nipples already are through my top, desperation taking over. I need love. I need his love. It's my drug.

"I look to you because you're the only one who can give me what I want."

He squints. "You can get this anywhere. I'm not going to be your plaything and risk everything." He smirks. "I stole a couple of kisses from you, but that's as far as it goes."

"What you do ... I want it. You can give me something no one else can. I need it." I lick my lips, thinking of all the dirty things I've seen. Things I shouldn't have seen, but can't forget. Who'd have thought that sneaking around would let me witness such a hot scene.

"You don't, trust me," he says.

"Do me like you do them," I say, cocking my head. His eyes widen.

"Yeah, I've seen what you did to those girls. Don't worry, I won't tell."

"You've been watching me?"

I smile cheekily. "I might have stumbled upon a nice fucking session at the beach while I was taking a stroll ... I couldn't help myself."

"A stroll? You? No. You followed me." Shaking his head, he laughs. "You're a dirty girl, you know that,

Jay?"

Biting my lip, I say, "I want to be yours. I want to feel what it's like to be claimed."

With half-mast eyes he looks at me, his gaze drifting down my chest. "This body of yours can't handle me. It's not trained for pain."

"Try me," I retort. "I think you'll find I'm very flexible."

He leans in, his hands firmly planted on top of mine. His smell is intoxicating as he plants a kiss on my neck, right below my ear. "I like your courage, Jay, but when I do a girl I want to know I'm the only one."

Shuddering from his dark voice, I get close to his ear and whisper, "You are. Every time I fuck them, I think of you. Only you. I don't want them." His head tilts back to look me straight in the eye. He licks his lips and sucks on them. He's so very close to me, I could lean in and kiss him, but I know that's not what he wants. Not yet.

"I've been dreaming it's you all along. I fuck them and imagine it's you. Every. Single. Time." With my eyes I dare him. I dare him to take the leap and just fucking go for it. I've been waiting for it for so long. Now that I'm old enough to decide for myself, nothing stands in our way.

He releases my wrists, his hands drifting down my arms to my ass. My jeans stand no match against his tough hands. He grabs me so tight I squeal. "Shhh …" he whispers, his eyes playful. God, so sexy.

He plants a kiss on my neck, making me moan, but then it turns into a bite, and I'm shocked. I shut my mouth to prevent another squeal from escaping. I'm also fucking turned on. He just bit me, and I love it.

His hand leaves my ass cheek and then suddenly comes down fast and hard. His other hand quickly moves over my mouth, soaking up the sounds I make.

"You want this?" he says gruffly, rubbing my ass. His hand leaves my mouth and slides down my chest, grasping my breast firmly. I moan as he massages it and then dips into my shirt. My panties are completely soaked when he starts playing with my nipple and pulls it. But then he tugs so hard it makes me gasp.

"I'm not nice, Jay. This is just foreplay. The real deal starts when I have you in bed. Hard. Painful. Raw. Fuck." His tongue dips out to lick the seam of my mouth. An overload of sensations hit me when a rumbling sound comes from deep within his chest. So primal. Full of lust.

I'm anxious for more.

He groans. "I'll make you do things you don't expect. You'll do things to please me, and only me, and I don't take no for an answer. Do you know what this means?"

I nod, shaking as he spreads my legs with just his feet.

"You don't," he murmurs. "But I'll tell you. The girls I tie up don't have a safeword. They can't escape. I'm not fucking good to them. On the contrary, I use them for my own pleasure. I take and take until I'm satisfied. I fuck them so hard they can't stand for days. I take their breath, literally. I fill them up with my cum until they can taste it in their throats. After I'm done, they thank me for everything. And do you know what else?"

Shocked, I shake my head as he grabs my chin and forces me to look at him.

"I've got a confession to make. When I fuck them … I think of how I'm going to do the same things to you."

His words arouse me to my core. I'm swept away by his insane confession. It only makes me want him even more.

With a devious smile on his face, he slides his hand out of my shirt and down my belly, undoing the button of my jeans. He slips his hand into my panties. I hold my breath as his fingers dive in and cup my pussy. "Hmm … so wet already? My, my, you are a dirty slut."

"Yes …" I whimper, closing my eyes.

"Hmm? What's that? You sure you want more? There's no going back, little bird."

"More …" I open my eyes again. "Wait, what? What did you call me?"

He smirks and retracts his hand from my pants, leaving me breathless. "Too late, little bird. You're mine."

Swooping me up in his arms, he puts me over his shoulder. I yelp as he carries me all the way to my bedroom and opens the door.

"You teased me long enough," he says. "Time for you to pay for all that flaunting."

***

SATURDAY, DECEMBER 6ᵀᴴ, 2008. 11:43 P.M.

Fuck. I learned what he really meant by hard sex that day. He pushes my limits like no other. Jerking on my nipples while I'm tied to the bed. He used his belt and his tie for that. Such a turn-on, the way he's been rousing my body with slaps and tickling. His fingers are delicate and rough at the same time, a delicious combination.

He's been roughly fucking me and making me beg for mercy the last couple of minutes. I keep wanting to come, but he won't allow it. Each time, he pulls out and smacks my tits with his bare hand. I'm red all over. It's so intense, but I'm loving it. I've been yearning for this day to come.

He twists me around, my ass facing up, and then steps onto the bed and spreads my cheeks. Pushing his cock in, he starts fucking me from behind. I moan when he yanks my hair and makes me face the mirror in front of me. He placed it there. He told me he wanted me to look at the little slut I've become. Fuck, I love his dirty talk. I'm delirious with need. His fucking takes me to planes beyond my imagination. This one time will never be enough for me.

But then the door bursts open and my heart plunges to my feet.

He scrambles off me and pulls up his pants in a desperate attempt to hide his pre-cum-dripping cock. Then he quickly unties my hands. Unfortunately, it's not in time. In shock I scream as I turn my head and see my father walking into the room.

"What the fuck ..." my father murmurs, his jaw dropping. Surprise makes place for fury. Oh, shit. I fumble to grab a blanket and cover myself with it.

"You ..." my father says when he directs his gaze toward him. "I should've known."

"How the fuck did you know we were in here?" I yell.

My father frowns. "Jay, please, I know you've been taking boys back to your room. You refuse to behave like a proper lady, despite my warnings. I told you what would happen. I installed a camera." He points at my bookcase across the bed. "I've been watching you this entire time. Disgusting. Filthy whore. You are not my daughter."

My father snaps his fingers and in come two men, probably belonging to the same family. They grab him by the arms.

"No!" he yells. "Take your fucking hands off me!"

"You defiled my daughter!" my father yells. "Look what you've done to her!"

"She wanted this! She *begged* me for it."

The men drag him away from the bed. He

struggles, but it's no use. They punch him in the stomach, making him heave. Two against one … it's not fair.

"Stop, please," I beg, crying. "He's done nothing wrong."

Wrapping the blanket around my body, I get up from the bed and grab my father's jacket. "Don't take this away from me, please. I need him."

And then my father does the unthinkable. He shoves me away from him. His push is so hard, I stumble over the blanket and slip. My head hits the bedpost. Searing pain shoots through my body, and then everything fades to black.

"The phoenix hope, can wing her way through the desert skies, and still defying fortune's spite; revive from ashes and rise." - Miguel de Cervantes Saavedra

CHAPTER 23

Jay

SATURDAY, SEPTEMBER 14ᵀᴴ, 2013. 10:40 A.M.

All I remember is infinite passion between the two of us. Adoration and excitement that's survived through time and suffering. It started sooner than what I can remember, but that night ... that sinful night is one of the few bits of my past I saw. I remember. I remember he once craved me more than anything, and I remember that I desired him just as much. He was right all along. We both denied each other love. I needed his fucking to make up for the love my father didn't give me. He needed mine to make up for the love his family didn't offer. We're both victims of a cruel world.

"I remember …" I whisper.

"What?" he says.

"I do …" My eyes grow watery. "Us … the night in my room."

His pupils dilate. "How much?"

"All of it."

X grabs my arms and tugs me closer. I don't resist. I fall into his arms and let him hug me for the first time in what feels like a lifetime. His arms are warm and a welcome relief as he holds me against his chest. It feels like I always belonged here.

"My father … he …"

"I know. I saw all of it, but I couldn't do anything. Trust me, I would've cut them all to pieces."

"He wanted me gone, didn't he?" I sniff. "He hated me. I endangered his stupid campaigns. All he cared about was his image in the media."

His chest rises and falls as he takes a deep breath. "Yes. You did some things he did not agree with. I guess seeing us was the final straw for him. After you blacked out, he had you taken away. A few states away you were dropped at a hospital with nothing on you. I followed you all the way there. I came to check up on you once, but you couldn't remember what happened.

You couldn't remember me." He's silent for a few seconds.

"I remember bits and pieces now … but wait a minute, you followed me? I thought they took you away?"

He sighs. "I never said when."

Oh … "You mean after what they did to you."

He growls, and it fades into a sigh. "Yes."

"Oh my God." I slap my hand in front of my mouth. "They did that to you because of me?"

I look up and gaze into his eye, which is filled with regret. I lift my hand and place it on his face again, truly feeling him for the first time. Tears run down my cheeks as I look at X. His scars overflow with rain underneath my hand. I don't remember them being there when we had sex the first time. They burned him because he took their chance at my father's money.

Oh God … are they the ones after my head? They must be. Of course my father stopped working with them after they all found out about our affair. They must've been pissed off. And if I die … then maybe all their problems will go away and they can work for my father again.

Oh, fuck no. No wonder X is so intent on humiliating them and pushing their buttons until they beg for death. No wonder he went through all this trouble finding out who did it. He probably knew but didn't want to tell me.

And it's all because of the fact that we fucked. My

father taped it. Why didn't I see that camera? He could've been watching me for months. Of course, that's just like him.

I shudder. "That camera. I should have known. That's why ... you blame me. It's my fault." I push myself from his arms and let the rain pour down on me once again. I feel miserable. Not only because of what he put me through, or what I have forgotten because of that injury to my head, but also because I am the reason he was scarred for life.

Tears mix with rain as I stand here, feeling more dead than alive.

"Yes. You should have known," he says.

Each word he utters is another dagger to the heart.

"They murdered me."

It breaks me.

"I lay in the cold snow, dying over and over again, until I got up and swore that I would make everyone pay."

"And have you?" I say, wincing. "Have you made everyone suffer as much as you did?"

His lips twitch, but he doesn't respond.

"Have you had your fill of revenge?"

"Not yet."

It shatters me. He is still not done. Whatever he's doing, it has to end. At some point, neither of us will have a heart left to bleed from.

His lips part. "I hate you."

His words cut me like a knife. I don't know why I

dislike hearing them so much. Have I really grown to actually want anything but hatred from him?

He steps toward me. Enraged, I raise my fist and try to punch him in the face. Before it lands, he grabs ahold of my hand, pushes it back into the trunk of the tree, and slams his lips against mine.

I'm stunned. He's kissing me in full force, pouring every bit of regret, remorse, pain, agony, and … love into this. No, it can't be. I can't even pull away to think about this. My mind won't let me. This kiss, this all-encompassing kiss, tells me more than any words he could say. His hatred is strong, but not as strong as his wantonness. His lips smash mine with greed, not even taking the time to breathe. He wants me so much he can't even take a moment to catch air. This is what we are. Two broken souls coming together as one. I feel powerful and weak at the same time. I know what happened to me now, but I also know X never left me. Not physically, not mentally. We were always connected.

I feel his desire to be with me, despite what happened. Despite all the shit I put him through. Despite all the shit he put me through. I can't say no anymore. I don't want to. What I want is love, and even after everything we've been through, he is still offering it to me.

In his arms I was taken. In his arms I am reborn. Everything I was fades away. He breaks me down and builds me up again, piece by piece, just the way he wants me to be. He saves me from the people who want to kill me. He keeps me alive.

These words fill my mind as if they own me. They have been floating there for a while now, slowly creeping in, slowly taking over. Slowly, but surely, they become truth. Until there is nothing left except the unbreakable bond I share with him.

When he takes his lips off mine, they still linger as I gasp in air, catching my breath. I look at him, the scars that remain, the boy I remember him to be. They're one and the same. What was once perfect is now ruined. I can't live with that. I have to fix this. Everything.

I've been blinded by amnesia, but now I know. I won't stop reliving the pain until I remember everything. I owe it to X and to myself.

His lips part. A droplet of rain rolls into his mouth. And then he say three words that split my soul apart.

"I love you."

"Love, in all its shapes and sizes, is timeless. Nobody is ever ready when it comes." - Clarissa Wild

CHAPTER 24

X

SATURDAY, SEPTEMBER 14TH, 2013. 1:00 A.M.

Truth. Such a strange word. There's no such thing. Everyone has a different notion of what's right and wrong, so truth is a blurred emotional opinion. On her part, she thinks she knows the truth now. From my side it's completely different. She remembers only a few parts, only our flirting and fucking, but she still doesn't even remember my name. She knows nothing about the horrible things my family used to do to people her father deemed a threat. She doesn't know the full extent of my obsession with her. That the first thing I did when I came out of the hospital was find her. I followed her day and night, planning my revenge.

She has no clue about that. She has no idea about the horrible things I've done. Like killing her mother.

I walk down the aisle and grab a few bottles of liquor. As I near the end of the store, I notice a clerk spying on me from behind the counter. Narrowing my eyes, I contemplate whether I'm going to behave or blow his brains out.

Taking a deep breath, I choose the highroad and place the whiskey and wine on the counter. He gazes at me with a perplexed look on his face, his fingers shaking as he takes the bottles and bleeps them. I fish a few dollar bills from my pocket and slam them on the counter. "Keep the change."

I jerk the bottles from his hands and saunter out of the store. The zoned-out clerk follows me out with his eyes. Is it that fucking strange to pay for something once in a while? I could've killed him. He should be happy he got another day to live. Whatever. He can eye me all he wants, I don't care. I would shoot any other guy who did that, but I'm in a good mood.

I get back to the car and step inside. Jay is still here. The doors weren't even locked. It doesn't matter anymore; she won't run. There's no going back to where she came from. Now she knows why.

"Here," I say, handing her a bottle of wine. I take

out my keys and unscrew the cap. Placing the tip to her mouth, she drinks eagerly, her thirst insatiable. Damn, that woman can drink. With a smug face I open the bottle of whiskey and hold it up.

"Cheers."

"To this fucked-up world."

We drink to the pain until we're smashed and drunk from laughter. I feel myself caring less and less about what happens to us. This night is all about forgetting, and I'm quickly forgetting everything I promised myself to do to her as well as the one behind this all. It all just seems so futile. Now that I have her … now that she remembers the extent of our history … why go through all the trouble of hurting the one who took everything from me? I've already got what I want.

Turning my head, I place the bottle down between us and look at her. She's beautiful. I love and I hate her so much. I don't know why, but for some reason I can't let go of either. This is so fucking unlike me. I don't fucking get attached to anyone. She is an exception. A girl who kept escaping me, kept taunting me to take her, even though the consequences were severe. So severe I came to hate her for it. Yes, I blame her for everything. Maybe it's unfair. Too fucking bad. Life isn't fair. The moment they took my sanity was the day hatred was burned into my very being. I don't even think I'd be able to survive without it.

She throws the empty bottle behind her. I guess replacing one addiction with another isn't so bad. She gets to enjoy the numbness and not feel the craving for drugs. I get to forget about my need to punish. However, I just can't seem to let go of the thought of ruining her.

Fuck, this is really fucked up. I used to care about her, but somewhere along the line caring turned into contempt. She should have known that camera was there, and that her father was watching her every move. She tricked me into fucking her. She tempted me like the seductive little bird she is. She's my enemy, and yet I still can't help but want her.

Sighing, I lift my hand and tuck a strand of hair behind her ear. It's no longer a case of just wanting to have her body and fuck her any way I want. It's more than that. I need to own her. I will have her until I die.

I still want to punish her. I will never lose that lust for blood. I will always want to see the fear and the pain. I was born in it. I was raised with it. It's all I know. All I've become. A monster in love with pain and death. How pathetic.

"What are you thinking about?" she asks in a haze.

I snort. "I should be asking you that since you just remembered pretty much everything."

"I know …" She blinks a couple of times and frowns. "I'm not sure how I feel. I can hardly believe it's all true, but it's in my mind, so it must be."

"Is it hard to believe you once wanted me?"

She cocks her head. "No, but—"

"More than I wanted you?"

She gasps. "Pig."

I smirk. "That's sir pig to you."

She snorts so hard she has to cough.

I laugh. "You know, the noises you made when I fucked that pussy of yours for the first time were quite the turn-on."

"Fuck you … that's not fair."

"It is now that you remember."

"I only remember flashes, not my complete history." She swallows. "There's a lot I don't remember at all. Like my mother, for example."

I slam my mouth shut. For a few seconds I contemplate forgetting she mentioned her mother. However, something in the back of my mind tells me she has to know. If I'm going to make her stay, she has to believe I'm speaking the truth. I have to be honest with her. It's the right thing to do, even if it's just once.

My breathing slows down. "Your mother is dead."

Her jaw drops, her eyes flashing to me like she just saw a dead man walking.

"She fell down the stairs."

"What? How do you know?" she asks.

"Because you were right. We do have a history together, you and I. We used to play together in your father's house. When they were busy talking we used to run after each other a lot, playing catch. One time your mother came out the door right when I took a turn. I didn't see her and then…" I sigh. "I killed her."

Her face turns from pure shock to revulsion. I

expect her to try and hit me. Instead, she picks up the bottle of whiskey and drinks it until she almost chokes.

"Hey, take it slow," I say, plucking the bottle from her hand before she drowns in it.

"Like you fucking care," she spits.

I laugh. She sounds just like herself again. I was worried she might've lost her spark after everything I did to her, but I see it now. It's still there. Everything she was, everything she is. She's right here, right in front of me, ready for the taking. What I wanted so long ago is now my reality. I have her completely to myself, and she isn't running from me anymore. This is too fucking perfect. Especially considering the fact that I just told her I fucking killed her mother.

"I do care, actually," I say, putting the bottle away. "I will not lose my property to alcohol."

She snorts and smashes her lips together, nodding. "Property. Right."

I grab her chin, nudging it softly. "You are mine, Jay. You always were. You were never anyone else's. You didn't even permit yourself to think of anyone else but me, despite being a slut."

"Oh, fuck you. You might have my body, but you won't have my heart."

I cock my head. "Do you really believe that?"

She gazes at me in complete silence for a few seconds before turning her head away from me again. She knows what I mean. What I said was true. I do love her. She knows this. She knows I would risk anything to keep her. She also knows she can no longer resist the feelings tucked inside her. I've seen it too. Her eyes can't stop begging me to hold her, to kiss her, to fuck her. She's always struggled with the idea of giving in to me, because she feels it's wrong; she's been taught to fight and fend for herself. When that choice was taken away from her, she realized she didn't need it anymore. All she needed was love. It scares her that I offer it to her. That, and the fact that she probably never expected to like all of the kinky fucking.

Now that we're past that, I wonder if I can truly make her mine. Make her see that she wants me just as much as I want her.

I clear my throat. "You know, it was an accident. You never remembered. I never forgot. Your father blamed you for it."

"No wonder he likes me so much." She rolls her eyes in disgust.

"I do."

She laughs. "You? Like me?"

"Hmhm … contrary to what you may believe, I think we make a great pair."

"You just told me you killed my mother. It's your fault. And now you're telling me you like me? I'm sorry, I don't even know how to fucking respond to that."

"Actually we were playing and I bumped into her. It wasn't intentional."

"And that's supposed to make it all okay?" She

shakes her head. "Never mind, I don't even know why I care so much. I never knew her anyway. It's not like I feel anything."

"It doesn't. I did many things that anger you."

"You did."

I lean in closer, placing my hand on top of her leg. "I did. I punished you. I whipped you until you were red and sore. I tasted your blood. You tasted fucking delicious." I smile. She tries to lean away, but can't, because this is a car after all, and there's not much space. "Tell me, in all honesty, that you didn't like any of it."

Slamming her mouth shut, she diverts her eyes and balls her fists.

"I know you won't, because it isn't true. You do like it. Years ago you even begged me to do it to you. You crave the wickedness. It's in your veins. You waited and waited for something you didn't even know you needed: me."

I plant a kiss on top of her cheek, sliding her hair to her back. Shivering, her breathing speeds up, and her lips quiver.

"All I ever wanted was you. All I ever got was pain. Now you know what it feels like," I whisper in her ear.

My hand drifts closer to her inner thighs, moving up to the warmth between her legs. She shudders as I place a kiss on her jaw, dragging it to her lips. With my other hand I nudge her chin toward me.

"Stop fighting it, little bird. Ignore your conscience.

It makes you unhappy. Let me make you fly."

When I lock my lips on hers, she closes her eyes and lets me in. I kiss her softly and slowly, adding more pressure to her thigh as our kiss grows deeper. She tenses when I slide my hand closer to her pussy, but relaxes when I peck her softly on the side of her lip.

"Be mine, little bird. Give yourself to me. Let yourself go," I whisper against her soft skin.

Her lips quiver as she sucks in the air. "I need … love." The words come out in a slur.

I caress her cheek with my index finger. "I know, little bird. My love is what you get as well as my fury. But you can handle it. You're a strong girl." I press my lips to hers as they part, allowing me entrance. I cup her face and kiss away the fears she has left. Now is not the time to think. Now is not the time to be angry or remorseful. Now is the time to let go and enjoy each other's company. It's all we have.

Wrapping her arms around my neck, she kisses me back, licking my tongue. It feels riveting. My cock bounces in my pants, eager to feel her soft flesh again. Connecting with her gaze, I watch her chestnut eyes turn into a blazing fire.

Leaning in, she throws her legs around mine and inches closer. My hands drift to her tits as I lazily pull them from their holsters and play with her nipples. I tug and pull, alternating harsh with soft as she moans in my mouth. I love the sounds she makes when I'm a little too hard on her. Her pain brings me pleasure, and her pleasure brings me pain. I need both right now.

My mouth is desperate to feel her again. I remind myself why I loved her all those years ago, how much I ached to touch her but couldn't. Screw the fucking rules. I'm throwing everything out of the window now.

Lust overtakes me as I plunge my fingers down her folds. Silencing a squeal with my mouth, I ravish her, fondling her pussy until she's swollen and wet. My cock thickens, straining my pants. Fuck, I'm so hard for her. My lips travel from her mouth to her neck and down to her nipples, where I cover them with my mouth. Swirling my tongue around, I sink my teeth into her skin and pull until she screams with delight.

She doesn't fight me. Her hands are still around my neck, her fingers digging into my skin. My back burns from her scratch marks, but it only makes me hornier. So I play with her nub and push her to her limits before I pull her completely into my lap. Probing my finger inside, her snugness is what makes me mad with wantonness.

"Oh ... fuck ..." she moans as I circle around inside her, nipping at her tits at the same time. Bite marks are all across her chest and neck area, like a beautiful necklace to accompany that beautiful body of hers. I want to make her mine so badly I can't stop thinking about marking her everywhere. Knowing that she is mine and mine alone is what drives me to do the things I do.

I rip down my zipper and take out my cock. But

before I have a chance to lift her up, she grabs my face and kisses me full on the lips. It surprises me. I never expected her to succumb to me so quickly. Her neediness takes me aback, and for a moment I'm left wondering if she's just in the moment, if she really wants me, or if she's too drunk to care. Either way, I'm rolling with it.

Her hand drifts down her body as she gives in to the moment we're having. Her fingers find their way to her clit, rubbing it with fervor. Licking my lips, I slide my hand up her tits and grab her by the throat.

"Yes, little bird. Make that pussy even wetter for me. Go on." I clasp her throat tight, and she looks down at me with equal thirst. She's hungry for my power, eager to gain my approval. Her gasps come in short breaths as I tighten my hold on her neck, staring into her eyes as she flicks her nub.

"Do it," I whisper. "Make yourself come. I want you to spill it all over me. Show me how much you want this."

She rubs and rubs, her fingers crazy from excitement. Her eyes roll into the back of her head, her lips part to make an O, and her voice turns into a high-pitched noise. A moan slips out and then she bucks her hips, her body shuddering to the touch of her fingers. I groan and grind my teeth like an animal. I'm so fucking ready to blow inside of her.

"Well done, little bird."

She shudders, drawing in a lip-sucking breath.

"Thank you, sir."

I grin. "Now take my cock like a good girl."

The muscles in her legs tighten around mine, and so I take the opportunity to raise her and lower her onto my pulsing cock. The anticipation is visible on her face as she scrunches her brows and purses her red lips, making me want to kiss her. I can feel her heartbeat through her skin, increasing its pace as her body trembles above my cock. Eager and on edge. Exactly how I like it, and how she needs it.

Her expression is a mixture of agony and bliss as I bury myself into her snug pussy, coating my cock with her wetness. She has never felt this good before, so willing, so open to take me. Her skin is coated in a thin layer of sweat, drops rolling down her plump tits. I suck them off and circle my tongue around the crown. She moans, taking my cock even deeper. We're riding on the waves of ecstasy, fucking for the sake of fucking, but I'm loving it so far. I bet she doesn't give a shit either right now.

Sweat breaks out on my forehead as I plunge deeper into her. She bucks her hips, enclosing me around her as she rests her head on my shoulder. I grab her ass with both hands and pump into her again and again. Slapping her ass, I make her ride me like a good little slut. Finally she gives me what I've been craving all along. Her willingness. Obedience. Desire. Everything.

We're both in the place we want to be. Both our

needs fulfilled. My domination and her freedom. It's all in this one moment of mindless sex.

Her screams fill the car, fogging up the windshields as I bang her quick and dirty. No words are needed. She knows I am her only pleasure, her only release from this tainted world. She knows I give her an escape when she needs it the most. Fleeing isn't what she wants; she wants my cock to make her forget everything around her. We're both users. Two sides of a coin.

"That's it. Fuck me, little bird. Use me for your pleasure like I used you," I whisper in her ear, nibbling it, biting down hard.

Her finger traces a line down my tattoo, fixating on my nipple piercing when she reaches it. "Yes …" she mutters.

"Hmm … I know you want to. Ride my cock, Jay. Ride it because it's yours, like that pussy of yours is mine." My tongue moves back to her other tit so I can give it a good lick. I roll her nipple between my fingers, tugging and squeezing until she moans in my ear. Then I suck on it and bite down again, creating two identical red marks.

I move my hands back to her ass, spanking her with a flat hand. She bounces up and down each time, the extra friction a delight to my cock. Her skin heats up underneath my hand as I keep hitting her. Her brows draw together and she bites down on my shoulder in pain. I fucking love it.

"Fuck me …" she murmurs.

"Yes, Jay, let me fuck that pretty little pussy of yours. Keep riding that cock. Make me proud and I'll let you come again."

She leans back, planting her hands on the dashboard. She slips her wet little pussy over my cock with ease. So eager. I can't even fucking believe it.

"Hurt me then," she says.

I can't fucking believe my ears either.

"Give me the pain. I can handle you," she says.

I'm done for.

I rip my tie loose and throw it around her neck, holding both ends. I tie it around again and pull it, squeezing her throat. She gasps, her breath faltering from the pressure building on her neck.

"Yes, Jay, feel the air leaving your body as I fuck you hard. I want to see the blood leave your face while you come."

I caress her with the pain she desires so much. She struggles to keep going as I tug on the leash around her neck, but she still does. The innate desire to please me is too strong for her.

I slap her tit and jerk her nipple, her screams disappearing into nothingness as the air fails to push through her lungs. I bounce her on my lap, pushing her to her limits, her eyes darting all around, delirious from the high.

She is slick and hot as we cross the line between this world and the next. The sensation of being inside her, feeling her body against mine while she allows me to hurt her is riveting.

"Come for me, little bird. Show me how much you want to please me. Show me how much you love this cock buried deep inside you while I take your breath away."

The muscles in her pussy start rippling, arousing me to my core. Her eyes roll into the back of her head. And right at that moment, at the peak of her pleasure, I let go of the tie around her neck and pull her toward me, crashing my lips into hers. My tongue probes her mouth as she falls apart in my arms, convulsing heavily. Her heavy orgasm pushes me to the brink of ecstasy. Groaning, I come undone. A hot jet of seed spurts into her pussy. My release is edgy and fulfilling. As I unleash my load into her, I moan in her mouth, and she responds with a heavy sigh, filled with emotions. My cum seems to come in streams as it spills out of her pussy and onto my pants.

"Thank you …" she whimpers.

It sets the fire in me ablaze.

Panting, I wrap my arms around her warm body and press her tits to my chest. She's snug against me, her head resting in the nook of my neck while my spent cock slips out of her. Her skin is covered in marks; red, blue and purple. Colors I created. Mine. All mine.

I don't know why I care so much. I never did care for any of the girls except her. I suppose, even after all these years, she never left me. Not my heart.

I realize this could be my downfall. I am in love with her. I always was. It's exactly why I despise her so much. She made me weak, and in that one weak moment I faltered and was punished for it. I died that day my mother burned my eye. And Jay is the one who caused it all.

But having her in my arms like this, like a little girl, wanting to be loved … she can undo me.

Even after all the things I've been through for her, no matter how many times she's hurt me, I still need her. Denying it is futile. I've already fallen into her clutches.

I hate her. I love her. Those emotions cannot coexist. What follows now will be the end for us both.

"For there to be betrayal, there would have to have been trust first." - Anonymous

CHAPTER 25

X

Loud talking disrupts my shaving session. I drop the razorblade in the sink and walk out to see Jay watching the news. A dead girl is all over the news; the woman we buried together. They're talking about knowing who the killer is thanks to an anonymous tip. Of course they know, I sent it in.

"Turn it off," I say gruffly.

"Can I watch this, please?" she asks nicely. She's been trained well, but I know she's trying to push my boundaries.

I glance at the television again and when the reporter begins about a sex tape sent to the local news station my eyes widen. "No."

I march toward her and jerk the remote control from her hand. She pouts. "Oh, c'mon."

"Do as I tell you, little bird," I say. "Or do I have to remind you who's in charge here?"

Frowning, she swallows. "Fine."

I cup her face with my index finger and thumb, holding up her chin. "Get dressed." I smile, which lightens her mood a bit. I try to make her forget about the hard stuff in life. All she has to worry about is pleasing me. She's doing a wonderful job. It amazes me that she's accepted me so openly. I wonder if this could stay.

Once I'm done with my job and I've had my revenge, she will stay. I will make sure of it.

***

Jay

WEDNESDAY, SEPTEMBER 18TH, 2013. 9:43 A.M.

I won.

His heart is mine. He told me he loves me. Even though he also said he hates me, I can tell he wants me more than anything. Hatred and love aren't so far apart. He just can't stand that he wants me so much. Which means I've got him.

He's mine. He needs me. I'm there, already in his grasp, ready for the taking, just like he wanted me to be. I'm a filthy, obedient, lusty whore. He controls my every waking thought. To him this means power. To me this means he is weak. Every day I wake up realizing more and more that this man can no longer give me up. X's desire to keep me is stronger than his need for revenge, even on me. He can't kill me. I know it in my heart.

Every step I take toward the car means another step toward freedom. My heart is racing, my thoughts are a jumbled mess. My brain is telling me to run, to keep walking and never look back. He won't shoot me. I keep telling myself this.

But my body won't listen. I can't get my legs to move away from him. They follow him like meek lambs, listening to his every command. Sometimes I feel stupid. Sometimes I feel like this is where I belong.

Somehow, I can't let this go. No matter how much I wanted my freedom back, there is something here with him that draws me in. The memories that have been creeping back into my mind have changed me. All this time I had this feeling like I knew him, and now I know why. His kisses were magnetizing to me. I wanted his touch more than anything. Even then I knew what pleasured him, and that he got gratification out of whipping me until he drew blood. I still wanted it. I needed it. I needed to feel his overbearing love because that was all I had. My father never gave it to me. My mother was never there.

Or at least, I don't remember her. All I remember is him.

In the past.

In the present.

In the future? I don't know. I can't decide. My heart has caved in. Submitting to him was the ordeal that brought me from insanity to freedom. With him I feel safe, even though he still makes me bleed. I don't hurt anymore. Pain has turned into lust, and lust grew into feelings.

These past few days have only added to that.

If I even knew what I wanted, the answer would terrify me, so I decide not to think about it.

In the car, he holds me in place. His fingers are firmly curled around my leg as we drive toward whatever destination he has in mind. His possession over me lets me escape from reality. His inevitable desire makes him want to take care of me. It puts me at ease and gives me the illusion that I'm cherished. Maybe I am. The lines between reality and fantasy have blurred rapidly.

Is freedom still what I'm looking for? Or is it more than that? The more days I spend with him, the less I have the desire to run. After everything that's happened, he is the only person in my life still left standing. I don't know if I can survive being without him anymore.

His warm hand sends an electrical current through my body that I can't ignore. My skin tingles from his touch, desperate for more. A night ago he spanked me so hard it made me beg for his cum. The way he whipped me with his belt and wrapped his red tie around my wrists had me delirious. Especially when he fingered me to an explosive orgasm. God, I can still feel it burn. The pain seared into my ass delights me. Is it so wrong to like it?

I turn my gaze toward X. In his eye I see sorrow and regret, things I shouldn't see, but do. I can't escape his penetrating stare. Can't escape the memories I share with him. All those moments in time when I truly cared for him and wanted him to be near me. Even now, I still cling to him. I never lost that attraction. These last passionate nights have only made it worse. I might've won his heart, but I already lost the fight. He's claimed mine too.

***

WEDNESDAY, SEPTEMBER 18TH, 2013. 10:11 A.M.

We enter a shady building in the middle of town. Paint is crusted on the walls inside, the lights flicker on and off, and the banisters almost fall off as we walk upstairs.

"Why are we here?" I ask as we reach an old door.

"To meet someone," he says.

"Yeah, but why did I have to come?"

He smiles. "Because I want my little bird around wherever I go. Whisper sweet things in my ear, Jay, wherever we are." He licks his lips. "I'll reward you greatly."

A shiver courses through my body as he runs his finger up and down my arm. He smiles and turns toward the door.

X rings the doorbell and takes his gun from his holster. The metal no longer scares me. My mind knows it won't be used against me. He'll only use it against others to protect me. Why that doesn't bother me still eludes me.

A scrawny blond dude with a cap on opens the door. He squints when he sees us. "I thought you were coming alone?"

"Plan's changed."

X steps inside, nodding at me over his shoulder. It's a silent demand for me to follow him, and I do what he wants. X takes off both of our coats and places them on a table beside the door. Looking around, I gasp. The apartment's filled with computers and gadgets and all kinds of stuff I have no clue about. Loads and loads of equipment and buttons are on the desk opposite the door, including dozens of screens. I wonder why we're here.

"Name's Dale," the guy says as he grabs my hand

and shakes it. "Nice to meet you."

X growls, which makes Dale jittery. He immediately lets go of my hand and clears his throat.

"Did you get in yet?" X asks as we walk further inside.

The guy sits down on a leather chair in front of the computers. "Yes, in fact, I'm almost done with the transfer. All I need is the right signature."

"Transfer?" I ask.

"Yeah, we're transferring all the money from—"

"That's enough, Dale," X says gruffly. "I don't pay you for your mouth. Now get on it. I want it done now."

I frown, looking at the two staring at the screen. They're doing something I'm not supposed to know about, according to X. Why else would he shut him up so quickly?

I step closer, trying not to make a sound, and peer over Dale's shoulder. What I discover pulls me apart and puts me back together like an unraveled string weaved back into place in just one second.

My father's name.

His bank account.

Money.

All the pieces come falling into place.

Gasping, I slap my hand in front of my mouth and back away slowly, tripping over a box. I manage to catch myself on a shelf, but not before X's eye finds me.

"What are you doing?" he asks.

For a moment I'm baffled, but then I realize I have to pretend like I didn't see a thing. "I fell. I wasn't looking," I stammer.

"You sure you're okay?" he asks, raising a brow.

"Yeah, yeah … go on," I say, laughing a bit. It's totally fake, but he turns his head anyway. Guess I never forgot how to fake my way through things.

Swallowing, I look around the room. I feel naked. Vulnerable. Not here. What I saw was real, and I fight to make myself believe. I cannot let this pass. Live, Jay, live. See with your eyes, not with your heart. X has blinded you all this time.

I rush to his coat, careful not to make a sound, and rummage in the pockets. My fingers tremble as I take out his cell phone. My first instinct is to call for help, but I can't stop wanting to snoop through his messages. I don't trust him. Each time I press a button, I check to make sure X isn't looking, and then go back to scrolling. Names pile up, but those I recognize I press. I find a man named Antonio and his job for X: killing me. Pictures of me pop up under a contract that was signed with the name Al John. The same name I saw on the television. That man I recognized. The news channels said he was killed the night X came back bloody. Fuck, I was right.

Scrolling further, I find the name of the man who sold me drugs. My hands shake violently as I read the texts. There were many, even from a few years ago. X gave him the job to get me on the drugs. It's in here, over and over again. He kept asking for it, kept paying this man. These texts tell the truth.

And as I scroll further, I find more horrible truth in his lies. Hannah. He had her introduce me to the drug dealer. He had her bring me into the club. He told her to make me a whore.

And then I find a text between them that was sent the night X came to kill me, which says:

Tell him to fuck her hard until she screams for mercy.

They're talking about Billy. Hannah told me he wanted to fuck me.

But it wasn't her idea. It was X's.

Tears trickle down my cheeks. The last messages that were sent between X and all these people … were right before he burst into my motel room and killed Billy.

He set me up.

He wasn't lying when he said he followed me. He put everything into motion that got me swallowed into the abyss. X got me hooked on drugs thanks to my dealer, he got me into the whoring, and he even got Billy to rough me up.

The realization hits me like a fucking brick to the face.

"No …" I stammer.

I don't want to believe it, but it's true. It's all in here. These are no lies. This is reality. These texts speak the truth.

He planned everything.

"You ..." I say.

From the corner of my eye I see X turn toward me, his eyebrows knitting together.

"You lied to me," I utter, raising his mobile phone to show it to him.

His eyes widen.

"You ruined me. You ruined everything!" I yell. Then I turn around and run out the door as fast as I can.

It takes him a while to come after me. I guess he didn't expect me to bolt. As if I would fucking stay after reading all that. As if I would fucking forgive him for betraying me. Like he could get away with making me suffer through the years.

When I asked him if he'd had his fill of revenge I should've known it would never end. I should've known it started long ago. This was all for nothing. It was what he wanted. I was his toy and still I came to need him. How stupid of me to fall for his trap. I should've known it was all part of his plan.

***

X

"Jay, wait!" I say, running after her. "Stop."

"No fucking way!"

"Let me fucking explain."

"Explain what? That you fucking got me hooked on drugs? That you were the one who sent that dealer to me, the same one we shot at the diner? That you got Hannah to push me into the whoring at the club and that she was a spy for you? That you even fucking had her select Billy to rough me up?" Tears stain her cheek as she briefly glances behind her while running. "Yes, I saw all the messages, X. You can't hide it from me any longer."

Fuck.

I do the thing I must to prevent her from leaving. She can't leave me. I won't allow it. So I pull my gun and point it at her back. She freezes. Then she turns around.

"I did not want him to fucking do to you what he was going to do," I say. "Yes, I wanted Hannah to get you a fucking rough guy, one who would force you to deep throat him. I didn't want one who would just take you against your will. Why do you think I killed him when I saw you with your gun and him running off like the fuck-face he was?"

"It's the thought behind it that matters. You

wanted me to be punished."

"Yes, I did it all. I wanted revenge for what you did," he says. "I wanted you to pay for all the pain you caused me."

"You blame me for something I had no part in."

"You seduced me. You should've known."

"So fucking what? Yes, I wanted you, I was desperate. There's nothing wrong with wanting sex. You hate me for something that wasn't even my fault; I just didn't notice, and you blame me for it. You're blinded by hatred," she spits.

My eyes turn to slits, because I'm fuming. I hate that she's doing this. I wanted to explain it to her myself, but now it's too late. She's already concluded what she thinks she knows. "Yes, I am." I take a long, deep breath to calm down. "But I also fucking love you."

She snorts, adding insult to injury. "Give me a fucking break. It was all a lie to get me to be with you. To make me weak and vulnerable so I would trust you and stay with you."

"It was not. A. Lie," I hiss.

Does she honestly not see? Does she really fucking believe that I have no feelings for her?

"I want you," I say. "I always fucking wanted you. I hated you for what you caused, but I never stopped wanting you. That's what drove me to do all those things. By punishing you I gave myself the chance to hate you and made myself believe you would never,

never want a guy like me again. It gave me a way out."

"And what did it bring me? Misery," she says, making fists.

"I realize now what I wanted was not to hurt you, but to control you. To do all the things I wanted to do to you, but never could because of our history together." It's the full fucking truth. It makes me weak, but still it is the truth, and I can no longer ignore it. I need her.

I take a step closer. Then another. "I am no longer that guy that wants to see you in misery. I am the guy who wants to keep you from harm and protect you. The only guy who knows how to truly push your buttons and make you fly, little bird." I hold out my hand. "Don't leave. I will give you what you need. Love. Passion. Anything you desire."

She frowns and slams her lips shut. A big sigh comes out. Then she says, "My freedom. I want my freedom."

"You know I ca—"

"If you love me, you will give me my freedom. It is what I want the most." She swallows. "Loving someone means letting them be who they want to be, because that is what you love about them. I want to be free."

She's got me.

I'm stunned.

My chest feels constricted, sweat bursting from every pore. I've never felt this before.

She'll leave me. Her eyes say enough. She cannot see past this, no matter how much I try.

I will not lose her.

So I pull the lever on my gun and aim.

"No," I say through gritted teeth. It pains me to do this, but I must.

"Yes. I'm not coming back to you, X."

"I'll kill you if you walk any further."

Her face turns blank. Completely, utterly blank. No emotions whatsoever. It frightens me. I don't get frightened. Ever.

"No, you won't."

Slowly, she turns around. I fill my lungs with air and point the gun at the back of her head. My hands are shaking. They never shake.

Her foot moves. One step. Then another. She doesn't stop.

"Stop. I'll do it. Don't take any more steps or I will do it," I say.

She turns to face me one more time. "You won't, because you don't want your property damaged. Oh, but wait, I'm not yours anymore." She raises an eyebrow. "You love me. You can't hurt me. You have no power over me anymore."

My jaw drops. I stare at her in shock. "You made me believe you wanted me too."

A smile curves on her lips. "You made me a part of your game, so don't be so fucking surprised I decided to play."

And then she turns and keeps walking.

My finger lingers on the trigger, desperate to pull. Except, I can't. I fucking can't go through with it. I played with fire and now I must feel the burn, yet again. The game was won, but not by me. My clever little bird beat me at my own game.

I will not let this pass.

"Those who hate most fervently must have once loved deeply; those who want to deny the world must have once embraced what they now set on fire." – Kurt Tucholksy

CHAPTER 26

Jay

WEDNESDAY, SEPTEMBER 18TH, 2013. 1:45 P.M.

I'm shivering from top to bottom, but I will not cease my search. I have to think of a way to contact my father and hope he'll forgive me for everything before it's too late. X is taking his money; I have to warn him. Maybe he'll take me back.

Now that I remember everything, I realize my father is the only one I have left. Even though he did some pretty disgusting things to me, I remember he once loved me. It's because of my wildness that he rejected me. I'm different now. Maybe I can still fix things.

After all, I've been through hell and back. I think I can handle my father.

In a moment of incredible bravery, something I did not believe I had in me, I pushed X aside and ran. I did it. I succeeded in my goal. I vanished from his life. I'm free of the chains he put on me. The chains that bound my body, mind, soul ... and even my heart.

I'm free now, completely free to do as I desire. No more listening. No more doing as he pleases. No more X. No more ... nothing.

Just nothing ...

Nothing is terrifying.

It doesn't matter where I go, I can't escape this anxiety, this feeling of despair. It's like my heart has been ripped from my chest and splattered apart on the street. I could cry, but I won't. Not for him. No matter how much my heart wants to. Even though I realize our bond has grown these last few weeks, and that there's no one who feels as much for me as he does, I won't allow myself to think about it. Not now. Not ever. I can't.

Clutching myself, I walk down the streets of Atlanta, having no fucking clue where to go. I didn't have the courage to ask anyone where I need to be, even though I've been wandering around for hours. I'm too scared of what their reaction might be to what I have to say. There's so much I want to say, but I know that if I did, they'd call me insane. Who'd believe me anyway? Dressed as fancy as I am, nobody would believe I was held captive. Oh no, they'd laugh and send me away, or worse, they'd bring me to the police. No, I should definitely not go there. I've killed someone for fuck's sake. They won't take that lightly. I'm as much of a criminal as X is.

I check the phone again. Only a few dots remain on the battery. If I had my dad's phone number I would've called him by now, but sadly it's not in here. Sighing, I struggle along my path, trying to figure out where to go next.

Suddenly, the phone buzzes, and I jolt up from the sound and feeling. It's a strange sensation when you haven't used a phone in weeks. When I look at it and see the text message, my heart stops.

Jay. You are free now. His money will pay for the hit on your head, but it needs to be more, so I've taken your father hostage. I know you don't care, but I wanted you to know anyway. Rest assured I will punish him for making you forget everything that was once important to you. Let go of your fear; nobody will follow you anymore. I will kill them all.

X

***

X

WEDNESDAY, SEPTEMBER 18TH, 2013. 1:19 P.M.

A hole remains where my heart used to be. The last pieces of my soul got chipped away. There's nothing left. She took what was left of me.

After all these years of torture I realized that real torture means not having her.

And now the volcano of anger inside me is erupting.

Anger takes control of me as I walk toward the stage, looking up at her father through the crowd. She wants me gone? She wants to be free? Fine, but I won't go out without a bang.

Her father is being bombarded with questions from journalists, eager to know what happened to his recent campaign. I know what happened. Me. He cast away his daughter in the hopes of saving his political career. Instead, what he got was more humiliation than he bargained for. All his fears came to life.

And now another one will be set loose.

I walk into the alley to the side of the building and enter a door that says "NO ENTRY." There is a girl on the phone behind a desk, and when she spots me she holds up her hand to halt me. I raise my gun and fire away, killing her straight away.

Blood stains her chair as I walk past her and enter the bathroom closest to the front door. There, I position myself behind the door and wait. A few minutes ago, before the press meeting, I slipped a laxative into his drink. I check my clock. It should be no more than five minutes until he's here. The conference already ended, and he must've been jumping up and down for five minutes holding his shit together. Literally.

As the door opens, I raise my gun and point it at the back of his head. When he hears the clicking noise he stops in his tracks.

"You will come with me now," I say.

"Please, I really need to take a shit, can't this wait?" he says.

I laugh, grab his collar, and drag him out the door. Oh, he'll get to shit all right. On himself.

***

WEDNESDAY, SEPTEMBER 18TH, 2013. 2:17 P.M.

I've got him tied to a fence, his face scarred with my knife. The slashes are beautiful, as is his screaming.

Fuck, I can't believe I forgot how much I loved to hear those sounds. Killing is the opposite of sex, but both are so very, very gratifying. It sends shivers down my spine just watching him squirm against the metal. His pants are dark from him shitting himself after I cut off a piece of his ear.

I fish my new phone from my pocket and start texting.

"What are you doing?" the man in front of me mutters.

"I'm letting your daughter know where you are." He frowns, confused. "I've decided I'm going to play the Good Samaritan here and give you a chance to make up with her before you die."

His lip quivers. "You're sick."

I laugh. "Says the man who cared more for his career than his own daughter."

He spits in my face. Growling, I wipe it off before cracking my knuckles. Then I punch him straight on the nose, breaking it.

He groans, blood dripping from his nose. "Please, no more," he begs.

I laugh. "Oh, but I've only just started."

He winces. "You'll pay for this. You and all the other fucking scum on this earth."

"I think you've got that wrong," I say, drawing another line on his face with my knife. His screams make me smile. "Scum are the ones who taint the young with their evil. Disgusting people like you." I chuckle. "Do you know what I do to people like you?" I hold up my hands and show him my knuckles, sending him a message. "You belong there, along with all the other fuckers." I smack him in the face again.

"Fuck you. You'll die for this," he spits.

"How, exactly? I already got everything I wanted and nobody knows we're here."

"You won't get away with this," he snarls.

I punch him in the face, and he groans in pain. His blood feels filthy on my hands, so I wipe it on his clothes. "I already have."

Smiling, I walk to my laptop, which is lying on an old chair. Torture is not only fun, but a means to an end as well. It was easy to get what I wanted off him. A few minutes ago he gave me the password to his extra bank account in Switzerland.

This fucker will lose everything he ever loved.

There is only one thing I regret, and that is letting her go.

***

Jay

WEDNESDAY, SEPTEMBER 18ᵀᴴ, 2013. 2:51 P.M.

It's broad daylight, but I fight to keep my eyes

peeled. My legs are tired of running, but giving up is not an option. The warehouse X is keeping my father at is only one block away now. He always takes his victims there.

I run as fast as my legs can take me until I reach a red building with plenty of loading docks, but not a car in sight. At the far left of the premises I see my father tied to a fence. His suit is soaked in blood, and as I come near I notice his face is equally messed up. Scars litter his face, blood running thick.

In shock, I gasp as I approach the scene. X is leaning over a chair, typing on a laptop, too busy to notice someone coming closer. I try to make as little noise as possible as I creep through the fence. When my father turns his head, I have to warn him not to speak. He falls silent immediately, groaning loudly so X won't hear me. I'm horrified by what X has done, but I can't let myself get overrun with emotions now. I need to free my father.

But first, a weapon. I need to be able to defend myself.

I look around and find a gun on a ledge nearby, accompanied by an assortment of instruments covered in blood. These must be his 'toys.' With soft steps I tread toward them and grasp the gun before quickly darting back to my father.

"Jay," he whispers as I come close.

"Shh …" I whisper as I fumble with the ropes twisted around his wrists. He looks horrible, but I'm not sure how I'm supposed to feel about it. I'm angry at him as well as X, but neither deserves to be treated like an animal. Like they both treated me.

My fingers work meticulously to untie the ropes around his wrists. Once they're free, I bend over and start on his ankles. My father helps me, but he can barely keep himself standing.

"I wouldn't do that if I were you."

Taking a sharp breath, I get up, turn around and stare right into X's eyes.

In an instant the gun in my hands points toward him. "Stay away."

He cocks his head. "Jay … is that a way to greet me?"

"Shut up!" I flick the gun as a threat.

X holds up his hands. "Let's talk about this, shall we?"

"You lied to me," I hiss. "You used me. All you wanted was my father's money, and now you're even torturing him?"

"No, I did not use you. It sounds as if you care a lot, though." He smiles. "Can you still honestly say you never loved me at all?"

I swallow away my doubt. "I didn't."

He squints. "Liar. You don't hate me. You didn't run because of what you saw in those texts. Deep down you knew everything already. You ran because you couldn't accept the fact that you had already fallen for me."

"Stop with the bullshit!" I spit. I have no interest in mind games anymore. Not when I'm holding a gun.

"It's not bullshit," he says calmly. "I did want to see you suffer. That is in the past now. I love you, and you know that. And I also know you feel the same way." He purses his lips. "You have to believe me, I'm doing this all for you."

"Why should I believe you?" I say. "You're a manipulator. You kill people for a living. How can I ever believe what you say?"

He swallows. "You might not believe me, but you will believe him." He points at my father.

I frown. "What are you talking about?" I turn toward my father, who begins to shake vigorously.

"Ask him about the sex tape he and the media received. The tape I shot of us." He grins.

I'm mortified.

"You ruined me!" my father shouts.

"What else did you do?" I ask in shock.

"Oh, I might've killed a hooker, then told the cops where the body was and pointed to your father as the murderer. Lucky for me, that girl also had sex with him." He laughs.

My father's eyes widen. "You motherfucker …" he mutters.

"You did all that to my father?" I say. "Just because of his money?"

"No, Jay. The money goes to the organization so they'll be happy. They'll take the mark off your head, and then you'll finally be free. Just as you wished."

My fingers tremble. I can't believe it. He framed my father so he could get his hands on his money to save me? This is ... monstrous.

"Why?"

He frowns, confused. "Do you still not see it, Jay? When the client is gone, the organization has no more job to fulfill, which they won't like since they don't get paid. And that's where I come in."

"What client?"

"The one who's after your head."

"You mean your family," I retort.

His eyes narrow, and he tilts his head slightly. "No."

"Your parents wanted me dead. You and I caused them to lose their job twice. Of course they hate me."

"You're wrong," he says harshly.

"You're lying to me. Again."

He chuckles. "No, Jay. I killed my parents three years ago."

Gasping, I grab my coat, because it's the only thing I have to hold on to right now.

"I don't believe it."

"Take my phone from your pocket and check the messages. Since you obviously did a fantastic job at searching through my history, I thought you already knew. This surprises me, Jay."

"What?" I fish the phone from my pocket, and it almost tumbles to the floor because of my hastiness.

As I scroll through the messages, my father unties his last ankle. I'm trying to keep an eye on both him and X whilst using the phone too. Fucking hell, this is tough. I can't trust anyone not to stab me in the back. Especially now that X is casually twirling his gun in his hand as some kind of silent threat.

"Want to know who it is that wanted you dead?" X asks as I struggle to find the message fast enough. "Look behind you."

And then I see the text containing a picture of the contract X stole from Al John. My father's name is on it.

No. *No.* No!

My eyes fill with tears as I glance over my shoulder at my father. His expression turns from agony to fear and then to something that resembles intense madness. In a breath he grabs ahold of my arms and pins me to his chest, knocking the air out of me. In a swooping motion, he grasps my gun and pries it from my hand. Before I can blow out my breath my father has the gun pointed at my head.

"People say you don't know what you've got until it's gone. Truth is, you knew what you had, you just never thought you'd lose it." - Anonymous

CHAPTER 27

X

"What are you doing?" Jay screams. "Let me go!"

I raise my gun, aiming at her father. Voices in my head tell me to shoot and blow his brains out. I must, but I can't. Not with her in danger. I can't put her at risk. I won't.

"Don't," her father hisses. "Or she dies."

My nostrils flare as I shake my head. "You bastard."

"Dad …" she whimpers, tears staining her cheeks. "Why?"

"You're a fucking disgrace, that's why," he says. "You and your constant whoring; you ruined my campaigns with your escapades."

"Don't fucking do this," Jay says.

"Shut up," her father says. "And you." He flicks his head toward me. "You had to butt in every fucking time. I hired your family to kill, not to stuff your dick where it didn't belong."

"Shut your fucking mouth!" I yell, veins protruding from my skin as I struggle not to pull the trigger. My mind is raging with thoughts of murdering him. The son of a bitch deserves to die, but if I shoot now, she might get caught in the crossfire.

"You fucked me once, you don't fuck me twice, kiddo. I can tell you got what you deserved."

Fuck him. I'm fuming, dying to pull the trigger. How dare that motherfucker refer to my scar.

"Please ..." Jay mumbles, pleading with me with her eyes to stop this. I wish ... that I could without hurting her.

"And you ..." her father directs his attention back to Jay. "When you hit your head, I finally had a way to rid myself of you, but you couldn't help fucking up wherever you went. Even fucking states away people still heard about 'that girl,' and obviously connected you to me. Do you know what a fucking stain on my rep you are? Disgusting." He spits on the floor. "You are not my fucking daughter."

"Enough!" I yell. I've had enough of his fucking

insults.

Her father tenses. His arm clenches around Jay's waist and the gun is pushed into her flesh. She shivers. Death looms over her shoulder. I cannot let this happen. I must interfere.

"Don't you fucking make a move," her father says to me, "or she dies." He laughs when he sees my enraged gaze. "Oh, yes, I know you don't want her to get hurt. Fucking lovebirds. Disgusting."

Of course he doesn't want us to be anywhere near each other. After the accident with her mother he's been nothing but a pain in the ass to both of us. I should've killed him when I had the chance.

He grabs Jay's chin and slaps her cheek. My blood starts to boil. "I hope this slut gave you enough pleasure, because it'll be your last," her father says. "I never wanted a filthy girl anyway. Why your mother couldn't just give me a proper boy is beyond me."

"I'll fucking kill you!" I roar.

Her father chuckles. "I wouldn't try. If you take me out, I'll take her out with me. You don't want that, now, do you?" He presses the gun even further into her head.

He'll do it. I can see it in his eyes. He never cared for her. To him, she was always a nuisance. A girl instead of a boy. Someone who brought him shame. He's always hated her, even more than I ever did. Hesitance is not something he knows. If I pull this trigger, so will he. She will not survive.

There are only three options here. I kill him, he kills her, I'm left in shambles. If I surrender, he'll kill her and then me too. He wanted her dead from the beginning, so he won't hesitate to pull that trigger. If I shoot her first to get him distracted, I hurt her. None of those is a desired outcome. However, there is one last choice, which I know now I must make. When he's distracted, she can take her chance and save herself. Retribution will be in her hands. It's all I have left to give.

I look into her eyes and see them glazed with tears. For the first time, I truly see her. Witness the depths of her heart. Wrecked. Crushed. Caused by me. I am the evil that must be extinguished. The equation is clear.

"Don't …" Jay murmurs, her lip quivering.

Clenching the gun in my hand, I do the only thing I know I can to fix this.

"Goodbye, Jay."

I place the gun to my own chest and pull the trigger.

***

Jay

Screams engulf me, emanating from the depths of my soul. Unreal.

Everything X did, all the memories come together in a vortex of emotions. Devotion. Need. The struggle for power. X wanted it all. It was too much for him. His desire for revenge and his yearning to claim me clashed, and now he has paid the price.

An explosion of emotions whirls through me, filling me with adrenaline and power. My father is momentarily distracted by what X has done, so I take the opportunity to free myself. Separating my teeth, I bite down on my father's arm. He roars in pain as I push myself from his arms and grab his wrist. Twisting it, I make him drop the gun. Then I kick him in the nuts. As he drops to the floor, I pick up the gun, pull the lever, and aim.

"Wait," my father says.

"Why should I?"

"It was a game." He holds up his hands. "I wasn't actually going to kill you. I was just doing it to be able to escape."

I snort. "Yeah, right."

"I'm your father. I would never do that to my own kid. I know he would. You hate him, don't you? He's down now, so let's run."

When he tries to get up, I shoot him in the leg. His pained squeals entice me. It's the very first time I enjoy hearing someone beg for their life. It won't be the last time. Once you know what it's like to make a person bleed, that love continues forever. The thirst never ends.

"Please, don't," he says.

"I. Don't. Hate. Him," I say through gritted teeth. "I hate you."

And then I pull the trigger. One bullet, clean through his head. His eyes roll into the back of his head, his limbs spread across the asphalt. Streams of blood draw lines on the ground like a canvas drenched in maroon-colored paint.

The thought that my father's life has ended stays with me no longer than a second. I rush to X. Tucking the gun into my pocket, I slide on my knees to his side. He's gurgling; the bullet penetrated his lungs. His black suit is stained with his own blood. His fingers twitch under the weight of the gun.

I throw it away and tear off a piece of my dress, plugging the hole in his chest with it. Of course it's no use. In shambles I sit beside him, crying my eyes out. Not in a million years did I think this would happen, and now it has. X is dying and there's nothing I can do about it, even though my heart screams for him. It begs for him to stay with me. I need him. Without him this world is too dark to handle.

"Don't die," I say out loud. I can't hold it back anymore. I know in my heart that what he said was true. He was right all along, but I didn't want to admit it. We had both already lost the game. There is no winner here.

His gaze is set on me alone as he lifts his hands and cups my face. I lean into him, feeling his loving touch.

Placing my hand on top, I entwine my fingers through his. "Don't leave me, X. You can't do this. Why did you have to shoot yourself?"

He coughs up more blood. "It was the only way."

"This was not the only way! You didn't have to die!"

He smiles. "Now you are free to do as you wish, little bird."

"How can you smile right now?" I yell at him. I regret it immediately.

"Because you're still here, sitting right next to me, holding my hand."

His words bring more tears to my eyes. In the distance I can hear people screaming. It isn't a surprise that they found us, considering it's broad daylight. I look back and see a woman holding a phone to her ear. Good. I hope she's calling nine one one.

"Jay," he croaks.

"Shh ... don't talk. It'll only make it worse. Let's wait for the ambulance. Someone's calling them right now."

"No. I need to tell you this. Whatever I did, forget all of it. Please, only keep the good memories of when you and I were still kids ..." He groans. "Forget about X."

"No!" I grip his hand and bring it to my mouth, kissing it. "You were right. I ran because I was scared. I wanted freedom ... but I also wanted you, which scared me so much more. When I saw those text messages I used them as a tool to free myself." I sigh. "The things a girl does when she's cornered."

He smiles, the look in his eye softening by the minute. "I wanted you to be mine. I sacrificed everything to get you. It was all in vain. I should've just let you live your life."

"No, it was not in vain!" I lean over him and grab his face. "Look at me." His eyes are slowly closing. "You have me. I'm right here. I'm not going anywhere."

"My scars …" He groans. "That day your father found us kept replaying in my head, over and over again. I blamed you for everything. I wanted you to feel the same pain I have. But now … I just want you, over and over again."

He coughs, and more blood pours up. I struggle to keep his wound closed.

"Don't talk," I say. "I know what you mean."

He tilts his head, trying to keep his eye on me the whole time. His fingers twitch, beckoning me to come closer. I lean in and press my lips on his. In the darkness his taste is the only thing I cling to. His rugged lips are the only comfort I have now that everything fades away. I won't let go. I won't leave him. We've been through so much together. Because he loved me so much, he hated me. The deepest feelings can shift from one axis to the other in the blink of an eye. His were ever shifting, always searching for closure. His revenge gave him a goal. By falling for me, his goal had been taken away. And then his new goal became claiming and owning me.

His kisses show me the same. His tongue still dips out to meet mine, despite having little energy to do so. He's putting everything he has into kissing me. Giving me all he has. All the suffering I was put through was a mistake. I know it was. His regret seeps through every pore, his wantonness for me clearer by the day. He's always been in love with me.

Like I am in love with him.

Despite what my brain is telling me, my heart has already caved. I wasn't struck by love; I have always had it in me. He was always there, watching over me, caring for me, desiring me. I felt needed, wanted, sexy, and strong. In his arms I felt like I could handle the world.

Nobody has ever made me feel that way.

This was never about a game. It was a battle already lost. We were just two wounded people trying to find each other again.

I kiss him to take away my worries just for a little while. Salt from my tears seeps into our mouths as I can't stop craving his lips. I need to feel him, even if it is just temporary. I long for his adoration. I am a slave to his commands. His wishes are my desires. His inflicted pain is my gifted release. With him I am able to let go and be free. Free as a bird. His little bird.

"I want to fly with you," I say. "Please." I hold his hand and squeeze it tight.

I don't want to fall. Not anymore.

But when he starts gasping I know the end is near.

This wasn't supposed to happen.

He can't die. I need him.

Time stands still and the realization hits me that I was never free. My heart wasn't free to begin with. It was already devoted to him from the moment I laid my eyes on him long ago. Even after all the misery he put me through, I still need him. I want him more than anything.

And now he's slipping away.

"I love you," I whisper, and then give him another gentle kiss.

As I take my lips off him, my mind goes into survival mode. I feel like I just survived dropping down the Grand Canyon, and find myself having to climb back up a wall covered in needles. X is unmoving, his eyes closed. My heart stops.

From that moment on everything happens in a blur. The sirens of the ambulance and police cars roar as they approach the building. X barely breathes as they lift him onto the stretcher. Policemen run to me and grab my arms, pinning them behind my back. They fish the gun from my pocket and secure it before dragging me off. I ignore them and keep my eyes solely on X. I need to see him one last time. He hasn't opened his eyes since I last said the words that meant everything but came too late.

It was always too late.

"True love will never end, for it is immortal." – Clarissa Wild

CHAPTER 28

Jay

THURSDAY, SEPTEMBER 26ᵀᴴ, 2013. 4:48 P.M.

I survived.

I made the choice to live in freedom and now I must accept the consequences.

It was not without a cost.

People know me now. They know I'm the daughter of the politician who was killed by his own blood. I hear their whispers everywhere. The man whose daughter made a sex tape and sent it to the media without shame. The man who raped a hooker and beat her to death. Of course he wasn't guilty. It was X's plan all along to ruin him beyond redemption.

Knowing he succeeded makes me smile, even if it cost me my privacy. It was worth it. My father will never be able to make me suffer again.

X was taken to the hospital, and it was the last time I saw him. They won't let me visit him. They won't give me any updates. For all I know he could be dead and in the ground by now. There's no one who cares except me. It hurts. I try not to think about it, but it still crosses my mind every day.

I scrape together a bunch of leaves and focus on the task at hand. I've been sentenced to do community service for a few months as punishment for killing my father. At first they thought I murdered him, but when I told them he almost killed me and showed them the bruises, which X conveniently left, they believed it was self-defense. Of course, the bite marks on my father's body helped with that, and the fact that X shot himself. It was all to protect me.

It's a brilliant escape. I wish X was there to see me tell them we were both innocent.

I shake my head and sigh. It's strange thinking about all the things we did. All the people we killed. Nobody knows it was us. I've gotten out of this pretty easily. Too bad it didn't end so well for X.

Sometimes I wonder how he's doing. If he's still alive. Now, more than ever, do I wish it was true. It might sound selfish, but I don't want his death on my conscience. The thought that he gave his life for me is too hard to bear.

No matter what he did to me, he stole a piece of my heart and took it with him. Wherever he is, I hope he treasures it.

I sit down on a bench nearby and wipe away the sweat on my forehead. Half the work for today is already done, but I'm not looking forward to the rest. God, I can't wait until I'm done with this so I'll finally be free for real. Then I can do whatever the fuck I want. Start that bar in Hawaii and live out my life on the beaches. That'd be nice.

I snort. As if I'd ever have the money. After all this is done, I won't even have the resume to get a job. Nope, I'll probably end up in a thrift shop selling granny clothes. Well, at least it's a decent job compared to what I used to do. Without X bursting into my life I would still be in the whoring business, working for Don at Two Minnies. I'm glad I got out of there. I can start anew here.

A gentle breeze wafts my hair into my face, and as I pluck it away, something is pushed into the palm of my hand. Jolting up, I immediately check who's responsible. Turning my head, I gaze behind me, but there's no one in sight. In the distance I see a woman scurrying away.

"Hey!" I yell, but she ignores me. She doesn't even look back, but it has to have been her; she was walking way too fast. Suspicious. I wonder what she did.

I open the palm of my hand and pick up the small envelope that was stuffed inside. A P.O. Box number is scribbled on the front, but there's nothing on the back. No mention of who this came from. I gaze around, checking there's no one looking, before I open it. Inside is something heavy, so I hold it upside down and let it fall out. It's a key.

What the heck is this for?

As I shake the envelope, a tiny note drops out onto my hand. The words that are written fill me with hope and put my heart at peace.

"I will die, but not today."

My breathing comes to a halt. X is alive.

"A new beginning is the first step, and each choice is the next toward freedom." –
Clarissa Wild

EPILOGUE

Jay

THURSDAY, SEPTEMBER 26TH, 2013. 5:26 P.M.

My fingers tremble as I put the key in the P.O. box and hold my breath while I open the lock. I gaze inside. A few items lie on the bottom. A postcard, a folded paper note, a bank card, and a passport. I swallow before picking up the passport first. It seems like the least nerve-wracking option. I open it and find my own photograph inside, but not my name. It's a fake ID, specifically tailored to match my descriptions. Blinking, I try to keep my heart rate steady as I take out the bank card. That too has the fake name on it. There's a tiny note attached to the card with a code: one nine one four.

My whole body starts shaking when I reach the postcard and take it out. It's a picture of a beach and a boat, but it doesn't seem to be a professional photo. Instead, it looks like it was taken with your average phone. On the front it says, "Meet you in Galveston, Texas."

Frowning, I flip it over.

"Find me here."

Tears spring in my eyes, but I force them away as I tuck the items into my pocket and move on to the next item. The note. I think my heart sinks into my feet.

On the top it says *"Do not open until after using the bank account."*

I'm tempted to do it anyway, but then I realize there might be something important I'm missing, which is connected to the bank account. Shit. Making sure there's nothing left in the locker, I close the door and lock it again before running outside to the nearest ATM. I plug the card in and hurry to type the code. I'm amazed it works. What appears on the screen shocks me.

Millions and millions of dollars registered under this fake name to which I have the ID.

Frozen, I stare at the screen in total silence. This ... I have access to all this? This new name ... a new identity ... a bank account filled with cash. I could start my business in Hawaii and realize my dream.

It feels unreal. Swallowing, I check the screen again. The last registered transactions coming to this account were from a bank account from someone called Azazel.

Frowning, I take a few sips of breath. Who is this? What a strange name. Is this even real? All this money ... is it mine?

I look down at the note in my sweaty palms. If I open it, I might find out. My heart is going crazy, however. Just the thought of finding a message from X inside makes me nervous. I guess even after everything that happened I still have feelings for him.

I take the card out of the ATM and tuck it in my pocket. After blowing out a long, drawn-out sigh, I open the note and start reading.

Jay,

I took a lot of things from you. I did it because I thought I wanted revenge. Like you said, I was blinded by hatred. But after being with you for such a long time, I remember what it was like to feel something other than spite. I remember why I wanted you in the first place. Your desires, your recklessness, your trust, your devotion, your lust, your love. You became my pet, and then my lover, and then my partner in crime. Somewhere along the line I forgot to give you the most important thing in life. Choice.

I did not come to you, because I want you to be able to choose without further influence from me. I want your choice to be honest and truthful. Even though I would like to see you again, what I desire most is for you to be happy, regardless of whether I am too.

I cannot claim your love. I can claim your body, your mind, your soul, but I could never claim your love. The one thing I needed most from you, but could never demand unless given freely.

Which is why I free you of the burden of forgiving me.

In this locker you'll find everything you

need to start anew. Forget who you were, start fresh. Use the money as you see fit. It's all yours. I guess that's one thing you can thank your father for. I gave you more than half of what he owned and sent the rest to the organization as a means to pay off his job. They won't be coming after you anymore. Your life is safe now.

Me? At day I find myself at peace, listening to the sound of the water rippling close to me. At night I dream of your pink, flushed flesh, buried underneath me. If only I could spank that fine ass of yours one more time.

Alas, dreams are dreams. I'm enjoying my time sailing the ocean with my boat. The nurses at the hospital were quite good to me. They patched me up, and I slipped away unseen. It was an easy feat, considering no one knows who I am.

I lost one of my seven lives to that bullet. I don't intend to lose the rest. So I've decided to enjoy what time I have left. I told myself this was what I would do when I retired, so I figured why not start early?

You're welcome to join me, of course. I have to warn you, though, I am equally as driven to give you pleasure as I am to give you pain. The lust for blood will never disappear, but I know you can handle me now. The monster inside me will never disappear, but you know I love my little bird nonetheless.

Whatever you desire is yours. I wish to make you happy and will give you everything I own. If you return to me, all I have left to give to you is my heart. And a few chains and belts to be naughty with. But you're free to do as you wish now. I won't follow you. I won't hold you back. I won't tell you what to do. Make your own decision, just like I have made mine. I will wait for you. I have always waited for you."

The note trembles in my hand as I look around for

a second, trying to catch my breath. The sky is clear and full of opportunities. 'What ifs' fill my head with hope.

I encourage myself to read on before deciding, but then I realize that one line is all it takes. Everything is clear now.

"Now, little bird, make your choice."

Life has always been about choices. The path we take cannot be undone. Consequences are a given. Personality is born.

I know who I am. I remember it all.

And so the choice is simple. I knew it all along.

I take off my work outfit and throw it in the bushes, tuck the note into my back pocket, and start walking. The past is behind me, erased from my memory, flown away with the wind. My father and anything bad can no longer hurt me. This is my time. This is my future. What I want is finally in my grasp.

The last words on the note stick with me, because they are precious. It is a secret I will carry with me to the grave and beyond. I am free.

"Forget about X. He no longer exists. I am the man who waits to begin anew, hopefully with you. And now you know my name.

Signed, Azazel.

PS: It's the truth. I promise you I'm not the devil, although I do consider myself wicked ... in a good way. Now you know why I never told you. My parents had a cruel sense of humor."

Enjoyed this book? You could really help out by leaving a review on Amazon and Goodreads. Thank you!

ABOUT THE AUTHOR

Clarissa Wild is the USA Today Bestselling author of FIERCE, a college romance series. She is also a writer of erotic romance such as the Blissful Series, The Billionaire's Bet series, the Doing It Series and the Enflamed Series. She is an avid reader and writer of sexy stories about hot men and feisty women. Her other loves include her furry cat friend and learning about different cultures. In her free time she enjoys watching all sorts of movies, reading tons of books and cooking her favorite meals.

Want to be informed of new releases and special offers? Sign up for Clarissa Wild's newsletter on her website clarissawild.blogspot.com.

Visit Clarissa Wild on Amazon for current titles.

CONNECT WITH CLARISSA ONLINE!

Website: www.clarissawild.blogspot.com
Twitter: www.twitter.com/WildClarissa
Facebook: www.facebook.com/ClarissaWildAuthor
Pinterest: www.pinterest.com/clarissawild
Google+: www.plus.google.com/+ClarissaWild

Stay up to date on Clarissa Wild's new books by signing up for her mailing list: www. eepurl.com/FdY71

Printed in Great Britain
by Amazon